Stitch

Samantha Durante

ISBN: 0985804602
ISBN-13: 978-0-9858046-0-2

To my family, for always being there
every step of the way.

TABLE OF CONTENTS

STITCH

PREFACE

She woke to the sound of heavy boot steps marching down the hall and the familiar pang in her hip bones wrought from too many nights on a rigid metal cot. The back of her throat ached from the icy air that'd ravaged her lungs all night; she could almost see her breath as she let out a weary sigh, resigned to another day in this hell.

What time was it? It was always difficult to tell from within her dim windowless cell. She listened as the footsteps approached, attuned to the jangle of the keys in the guard's pocket and the soft clap of the rifle against his back. Then she heard something she hadn't noticed before – a second set of footsteps, softer than the guard's, following slightly behind.

She shot up with a quick gasp, adrenaline surging through her body and firmly shaking off the last wisps of her semi-peaceful slumber. The footsteps paused outside her door as she registered the soft whooshing of a lab coat and the gentle tapping of fingertips against a tablet. She was certain now that they had finally come to fulfill their grisly promise.

She had known this was a risk when she'd been briefed on her mission, and she had accepted it anyway. Now she cursed her own arrogance, and the sorry luck that had landed her here. She had failed in her mission, and now she was going to reap her recompense.

She was only glad that *he* wasn't close enough to hear her impending screams. One by one she had listened from within her own lonely chamber as the others cried out in agony, and she'd been unable to drown them out with nothing but her fingertips to plug her ears. After the riot they had staged early on, the guards had learned that it was necessary to separate her from him, and she hadn't seen or heard from him for weeks, maybe months, so she knew for certain that he wasn't nearby. That one small mercy almost made the ordeal ahead of her bearable. Almost.

As the heavy automatic locks on her cell door released with a tumultuous clang, she turned to face her captors. Thinking only of him, she steeled her resolve for whatever unspeakable nightmare awaited her.

1. DISTRACTION

Alessa dropped her pen and looked longingly at the clock. She had little more than twelve hours until the exam and she just could not focus on the words swimming on the page in front of her. Instead, all she could think about was the ghost.

She turned back to the diagram in her textbook, but it was no use. The only image she could see was his piercing sapphire eyes, brimming with melancholy and longing. What could he be so sad about? The little information she'd been able to dig up about the history of her sorority house contained nothing which might indicate who the soulful young man she'd been seeing was or what he could possibly be thinking of as he stared out into whatever plane of existence he was inhabiting. Alessa guessed she'd probably never know.

She let out a quiet groan of exasperation which drew withering glances from the handful of other students studying in this corner of the library. She supposed it was probably time to go. She certainly wasn't being productive, sitting here with a head filled up with fantasies about a person she didn't even know. A person who wasn't even alive, no less.

Alessa closed the lid on her laptop and slid her pen into the spiral of her notebook. She was resigned. If she didn't know the basics of physics by now, she certainly wasn't going to learn them by tomorrow.

She'd never really been the studying type and had spent her high school years relying on the knowledge she absorbed during class to get her through exams just fine. She was lucky to have the ability to learn quickly, usually only having to pay attention to a subject once or twice before she mastered it. As a result, she just didn't understand how everyone in this library had the patience to devote hours to reading and re-reading all the same material they'd been learning day in and day out all semester long. Alessa just couldn't do it.

At least the midterm was open book. She may not get the A she was used to, but she was confident that she'd be able to wring out at least a B without wasting any more time staring at a textbook page she couldn't bring herself to actually read. She slid her belongings into her backpack as quietly as she could, hoping not to provoke any more derisive looks from her neighbors.

Alessa needed to stop obsessing about the ghost. Her disdain for studying notwithstanding, her new fixation was getting in the way of her grades and her social life. Ever since she'd started seeing him a few weeks ago, he'd been all she could think about. And the unnerving recurring dreams she'd been having weren't helping either.

At first the ghost had scared her senseless – a normal enough reaction to waking to a strange man standing at the foot of her bed while she slept or appearing out of nowhere behind her in the bathroom mirror – but after three or four encounters it soon became apparent that the ghost wasn't even aware of her presence. Once she realized that, her fear was overtaken by curiosity and she took to studying the elusive figure whenever she got the opportunity, instead of sprinting from the room in terror.

What she'd learned in the latest handful of encounters hadn't amounted to much. Though she'd resolved to stick around and see what she could learn, the ghost apparently had different ideas. His apparition never lasted more than a few seconds, which wasn't a lot of time for Alessa to gain much insight. Overall she'd probably spent less than a minute in his presence in the seven or eight times she'd seen him over the first 12 weeks of the semester.

So far she'd been able to determine that he seemed about her age – maybe a little younger than her 19 years – and that, judging by his clothes, he was probably from the early twentieth century. Besides the clothes, he looked like any other athletic male teenager she'd known – tall and lean, with tousled brown hair and unbridled energy brimming just below the surface of his skin.

The only thing particularly notable about him was his eyes. Despite the transparency of his form, his blue eyes shown clearly, flecked with green and gold and shining with a subtle indigo light. They looked like the eyes of a television or movie actor, just unnaturally blue. Alessa had never seen eyes like that in real life and had always thought that those actors were digitally enhanced. Now she wondered if people really did have eyes that vivid.

Even more striking than the color of his eyes, however, was the hint of torment that they almost always conveyed. He was constantly gazing out at the distance, a wistful look upon his face. Often Alessa had seen him clench his jaw and swallow, then breathe deep and close his eyes, exhaling with an almost imperceptible shake of his head. It was as if he were fighting back a feeling, resolving himself for some struggle ahead.

Only on one occasion had Alessa seen him anything other than distraught. He'd turned rapidly, as if in response to someone calling his name, and looked directly through Alessa as his face lit up with the most beautiful smile she had ever seen, one so genuinely overflowing with love and pride and just a hint of amusement that it brought tears to her eyes. That was the way Alessa's parents used to look at her, before everything happened.

So she had no idea who the ghost was, or what he was thinking about, or why he kept appearing to her, and these questions had become the only thing she could focus on, much to the detriment of her schoolwork and the few friendships she'd begun to develop in the first weeks of the semester.

And then the nightmares had started – always the same immobilizing fear buzzing through her in that dark, dank cell – and the lack of sleep was only compounding the distraction she felt in her waking hours. Alessa knew it wasn't healthy to let a specter take over her life, but she felt powerless to resist. Who or whatever he was, she was determined to learn the truth.

2. MEMOIR

As Alessa stepped out onto the quad, she breathed deep and let the crisp fall evening wash over her. She always felt better being outside. Her head felt clearer than it had all afternoon as the cool November air lightly stung her eyes and worked its way from her lungs into her bloodstream, bringing the feeling back to her limbs. She'd been cramped at that uncomfortable library desk for six hours and had little to show for it besides a sharp pang of hunger welling up in her gut. She decided to grab a sandwich and head back to the house to see what Janie was up to.

Wandering her way across the quad, Alessa headed toward Van Husen Hall, hoping the student-run café in the basement was still open. Leaves crunched beneath her feet as Alessa made her way towards the stately brick building ahead of her. The façade was laced with ivy and decked by massive old-growth trees still clinging to their last clumps of foliage as winter threatened to descend. The facilities department had carefully placed up-lighting behind the trees, highlighting the building's grand turn-of-the-century architecture and casting dramatic shadows across the entrance. The campus was beautiful, that much she had to admit.

Alessa had not been thrilled when she'd received her acceptance to the university. She'd felt relieved she supposed, but in truth, she was more disappointed than anything. Up until her senior year of high school, her grades had been flawless and she'd racked up an impressive resume of extracurricular accomplishments. As her last year of high school had begun, she'd known she was on the right path towards achieving her dream of getting into one of the elite private universities she'd always strived for. Then everything had gone wrong.

On a Friday a couple weeks into the school year, her parents had had plans to go to a party at the nearby home of a family friend. Alessa had been invited, but she had plans to go to the big homecoming game and join some friends at another party afterward instead. That morning on her way out the door to school, Alessa had gotten in a big fight with her mom over something petty.

Her memories of that day were a blur, but it might have been the length of her shorts – the summer heat had persisted well into September, and Alessa's old-fashioned mother always had something to say about her attire. Alessa had expressed her frustration a little too vividly and her mom had grounded her for the night. Alessa had been fuming as she left for school and refused to speak to her parents when she got home, marching straight up to her room and slamming the door behind her, a move she knew would get right under her father's skin.

Despite her bratty behavior, her ever-patient parents had come up to say goodbye before they left for the party and to remind her that they'd be home by midnight. Alessa had still been furious about being grounded and refused to let them in, so they had said an exasperated, "I love you," through the door, a sentiment that Alessa had begrudgingly returned. She was immensely grateful now that she did; it was the last thing she'd ever say to them.

Alessa had fallen asleep on the couch that night watching reruns of some terrible reality show, so she hadn't noticed when midnight rolled around with no sign of her parents. It wasn't until the doorbell rang at 1:15 in the morning that she'd realized something was wrong. She'd stumbled to the door in a stupor to find a pair of grim looking police officers. "Are you Alessa Khole?" they began. And in a matter of moments, her entire world had come crashing down.

Her parents had been killed in a car accident, hit by a drunk driver who, incidentally, was coming from the same party that Alessa had planned to attend. They'd been on a dark, winding road and something, maybe a deer, had caused the young driver to swerve into the oncoming lane, smashing head on into Alessa's parents. Everyone had been killed instantly.

It was an all too familiar story, almost a cliché, and Alessa could not believe that her parents were gone. When she had woken in the morning, she'd thought that perhaps it was all a bad dream, until she'd gone downstairs to an empty kitchen.

Alessa had been on her own since then. She'd turned 18 a few days before the accident, so she was legally empowered to make her own decisions in the aftermath. She assumed control of her parents' finances and decided to stay at her house and finish out her last year at her own school, instead of moving in with her cousins who lived on the other side of the country. In retrospect, this may not have been the best decision, but at the time, Alessa just couldn't imagine losing her whole life in addition to her parents. So she'd stayed put and made do.

As might be expected, the ordeal had taken a major toll on her performance in school. She struggled to accept the reality of the situation and fell into a thick depression which left her unmotivated to do her work or devote time to her activities, or even show up to class. The fall passed by in a haze and when December had rolled around – bringing with it college application season – she was practically failing out of school.

She'd tried her best to pull together a few halfway decent applications to the list of selective schools she had been planning to apply to, and had asked the guidance counselor to include a note in her recommendation explaining what had happened in Alessa's personal life. She'd hoped that the admissions officers would have some sympathy and give her a pass for this year's academic performance, in light of the strength of her transcript from previous years. But they didn't – these schools only had room for exceptional students, young people who were ready to change the world. At this point,

Alessa could barely even change her own clothes, and it showed.

Reality had set in once the rejection letters started piling up in late March. Alessa began putting more effort into her schoolwork to salvage her GPA, and her teachers had taken pity on her and given her passing grades. When it had finally sunk in that her old dreams of collegiate glory were out of her grasp, she'd taken stock of her options and decided to apply to some less selective schools. It turned out that a few big state schools were still accepting rolling admissions, and one – Eastern State University, home of the Fighting Gophers – was willing to overlook the disaster of the last seven months.

That was how Alessa had ended up where she now stood, reaching towards the door of Van Husen Hall in search of a late dinner. Alessa caught a glimpse of herself in the glass and was surprised at how haggard she looked. Mercifully, her long, dark hair hung straight in neat layers that framed her face. That was about the only thing her hair would ever agree to do and the only reason why she looked halfway presentable, since she certainly hadn't taken any measures to tame her appearance.

Thanks to her glossy chestnut locks, if an outside observer didn't look closely, they might not notice the bags under her green eyes, or her lackluster skin, or the jeans hanging loosely from her hips after months spent absent the desire for food. Alessa realized the sandwich she was about to buy was the first thing she'd eaten all day.

She entered the hall and steered toward the large marble staircase directly ahead of her, trailing her hand on the heavy mahogany banister as she descended to the basement. Alessa was relieved to find that the café was indeed still open. She grabbed one of the premade sandwiches out of the refrigerator case and paid at the counter with a swipe of her meal card.

Heading back outside, Alessa turned onto the wide cobblestone path that led to the far side of campus where her sorority house resided.

Approaching the porch of the chapter house, Alessa took note once again of the myriad surveillance cameras flanking her from every side. A widely-publicized hazing scandal had embroiled the university in a drawn out lawsuit, a disastrous PR spectacle which could have ended months ago with proper video evidence to prove that the university's expulsions had been justified. The administration had learned from their mistake and promptly installed a state-of-the-art surveillance network across the entire ESU campus.

Though Alessa could only see two cameras on the porch – one pointing down towards the front door and one looking out towards the walkway she'd followed here – she knew there were others as well, peeking out of bushes and camouflaged behind rocks and benches.

Alessa had first noticed the hidden cameras on one of her first days on campus. She'd been sitting on a bench between classes eating a sandwich and doing some reading, and when she'd gotten up to toss her wrapper in a nearby garbage can, subtle movement in the bush across from her had caught her attention.

At first she'd thought it was a squirrel, but the glint of sunlight off glass had held her eye as the camera followed her movement. Curious, she'd approached the bush for a better look, but before she could brush the leaves aside, a burly security guard had appeared out of nowhere. "Please do not disturb the foliage, miss," he'd commanded. It was an innocent enough request, but the menacing look that had accompanied his entreaty had chilled her straight to the bone.

Alessa knew the cameras were there for her own protection, but something about their presence made her uneasy. She didn't like the feeling of being watched whenever she left her home. And worse, a lot of the students didn't even seem to notice that they were under constant surveillance. Something about the whole setup just seemed like a violation.

She eyed the camera on the porch, her lips pressed into a hard line. The relentless gaze of that cool glass lens just felt somehow insidious to her – she couldn't explain exactly why.

On the plus side, the administration's over-the-top reaction *had* enabled Alessa to score a great room in this beautiful old house, instead of one of the standard cinderblock cells usually reserved for freshmen. To discourage future hazing incidents, in addition to the camera system, the school had also done away with rush week. Instead, they decreed that any freshman who wished to join a Greek organization had only to read the descriptions of each house and check a box on their housing form.

Though Alessa had never really been interested in joining a sorority – she didn't consider herself the "sorority type" – after living alone for most of the last year, she'd thought it might be good for her to be around other people. So she had picked the house she liked the most – Zeta Epsilon Pi's big white farmhouse with a wraparound porch – checked the appropriate boxes, and hoped for the best.

By a stroke of luck, Alessa had won one of the two available rooms. The other had gone to another freshman, Janie, who had quickly become Alessa's closest friend at ESU.

The chapter house itself turned out to be a dream come true. Just as the photo on the housing application showed, it was a gorgeous old white colonial farmhouse with stark black shutters, more of a mansion than a house really. Outside it had a large wraparound porch stretching the entire front and right side of the building – which came in handy when the sorority's parties got a little too congested – and it looked out over acres upon acres of rolling green hills, what was once probably farmland.

The house had a big kitchen, dining room, and living room on the main floor which the sorority used as shared space. The upper floor had been divided into 14 bedrooms, half of which still had the elaborate original fireplace mantles.

Alessa was lucky enough to have gotten one of the fireplace rooms, though she was disappointed to find that all of the hearths had been boarded up for safety reasons. She'd been pleased to find that her room was somewhat larger than those in the solemn gray freshman dormitory, and much more homey, with thick carpeting and chair rail moldings instead of linoleum and white-washed cinderblock walls.

The bathroom renovations were the one area where the university had unfortunately gutted most of the house's charm in favor of a more functional approach. The only spot they had overlooked was a finely-crafted old clawfoot tub housed in a tiny bathroom on the attic floor. Alessa supposed it wasn't worth the university's time or expense to remove the heavy fixture, so it remained perched on the top floor overlooking a round porthole window and was rarely used, though Alessa had been surprised to learn that it was still functional.

So even though the last year had not gone at all as Alessa had planned, in the end she supposed she was grateful for where she had ended up. After all, if it wasn't for this house, she would never have met Janie. And she would never have seen the ghost.

3. OBJECTIVE

The door to Janie's room was propped open invitingly, so Alessa poked her head in. Janie was sitting at her desk, her small frame hunched over her computer as she typed furiously, short brown hair tucked behind her ears. Alessa remembered that in addition to the physics exam, Janie also had a paper due tomorrow.

"How's it going?"

Janie finished the sentence she was keying and swung around in her chair. "Well, I might bomb physics, but at least I won't show up empty-handed to psych."

Alessa dropped her bag and crossed the room to sit down on Janie's bed. Janie's usually neat chin-length bob was mussed, dark wavy layers sticking out in all directions. It looked like Janie could use some reassurance.

"I'm sure you'll be fine. You took physics in high school, right?" She began unwrapping the crinkled cellophane around her turkey club.

"Yeah. But unlike *some* people –" Janie turned her chocolate brown eyes toward Alessa and raised her eyebrows, "*I* didn't get the highest grade in the class."

Before Alessa could explain that it was chemistry she had mastered – physics was after the accident, and she had barely scraped by – Janie reached for the sandwich.

"Whatcha got there?" Sooner than Alessa could react, Janie had already stolen a bite. Despite her pixie-like proportions, Janie had a considerable appetite. She was chewing in a loud, dramatic fashion. "Mmm, dry turkey, tasteless vegetables, and soggy bread. Let me guess – Van Husen basement?"

Alessa loosed a small smile and nodded as she swallowed her own bite. "Best I could do at this hour." It may have been a poor excuse for a sandwich, but putting food in her stomach took the edge off her hunger almost immediately, which vastly improved her mood. "Got anything to wash this down with?"

Janie swung open the minifridge to her right and pulled out a can of iced tea. She placed it on the edge of the desk nearest Alessa. "Here you go."

Janie turned back to her paper while Alessa finished off the sandwich. Alessa loved that about Janie. Neither of them ever felt a need to keep the conversation going just to fill the space.

With the other girls in the house, Alessa often struggled to come up with things to talk about. They were nice enough, but Alessa often found that they were more concerned with boys and parties than Alessa had the stomach for. She had so little in common with them that it was difficult to even fill a 30 second exchange in the bathroom, and lulls in their conversation were palpably awkward. But not with Janie. Alessa was content just to sit in the same room as her, knowing that she'd be there to talk to if anything interesting occurred to her. Janie felt the same.

The only other freshman in the house, Janie had had an easier time assimilating – she had a natural charisma that helped her get along with anyone – but privately, Janie had expressed the same frustrations that Alessa felt. It was clear that she and Janie were different from the other girls in the house and they knew that they would never truly fit in. Alessa was just glad that they had found each other.

Janie was the one bright spot in an existence that Alessa had had difficulty feeling more than apathetic about lately. A spunky, sharp little bundle of energy, Janie had the same fire in her that Alessa had once had, and Alessa found that being around Janie made her forget about her troubles for a while. For some reason that Alessa couldn't fathom, Janie had been drawn to Alessa as well, and the two had become fast friends.

As Alessa drained the last few sips of iced tea, Janie tapped a few keys with a sense of finality and sat back in her chair, a satisfied smile on her face as she turned towards Alessa. "So, how are things with your phantom boyfriend?"

Alessa laughed. "I know it's ridiculous. I feel like I've spent so much time obsessing over this when I should be focusing on my grades or trying to hang out with some people we met during freshman orientation –"

"Or trying to find a *real* boyfriend," Janie interrupted. She gave Alessa a meaningful look.

"Or trying to find a real boyfriend, yes. It's just… I don't know. I guess it's the first time I've felt excited about something since my parents died."

"I just don't understand what you're hoping to get out of this. If what you're seeing really is a ghost – and I'm not entirely convinced yet that it's not just some kind of mental break –"

"Thanks."

"You know what I mean. I guess what I'm saying is, I just don't see what the end game is here. He's dead, you're not – so where is this going?"

Alessa sighed and hung her head. Janie had a point. Where was this headed? Certainly nowhere useful. "I know, I know. I'm just so curious to find out who he is, why he's hanging around here. You know?"

Janie's expression softened. "I'm just worried about you, Less. You've been so distracted lately…" Her tone changed back to goading. "And you look like shit."

Alessa tossed a throw pillow at Janie's head.

Janie deftly swatted it to the floor, feigning insult. "What! Seriously, you look like you haven't slept in days. Have you been studying that much?"

"Oh God no. I just haven't been sleeping well. I keep having these dreams…"

"What kind of dreams?"

"Like a recurring dream. It's not exactly the same every time, but I'm always in some sort of jail cell waiting for someone to come do something horrible to me, but I'm not exactly sure what."

"Sounds miserable."

"I can't even describe it. It's just this overwhelming sense of foreboding and despair, but at the same time I feel relieved."

"Why relieved?"

"Because, well, the ghost is there, and I know he won't be able to hear me being tortured or whatever."

"The ghost is there?"

"Yeah. I never actually *see* him, but somehow I know he's there with me, in the prison. I actually don't see much of anything because it's very dark and the whole thing is a bit hazy. It's weird because the feelings are really vivid – it's so disturbing that I have trouble going back to sleep after – but besides that things are pretty fuzzy."

"Weird."

"Yeah."

There was a knock at the door and Lizzie Green bounded into the room in all her blonde, buxom glory. "Hey girls! Just wanted to remind you two that dues need to be paid by the end of the month. Is that cool?"

"Sure thing," Janie replied with a grin. Alessa forced a smile and nodded in agreement. She tried not to hate Lizzie – she really did – but it was just so easy.

The sorority president had never been openly hostile towards Alessa, but at the same time, it was clear that she would never have approved Alessa's "sisterhood," as Lizzie liked to call it, if it weren't for the university's policy. And the fact that Lizzie was a walking male fantasy and obviously reveled in the fact – while simultaneously pretending that she was oblivious to her own physical gifts – inspired nothing but loathing in Alessa. Even at seven o'clock in the morning, Lizzie always managed to look perfectly put together, not even an eyelash out of place. It was nauseating. Alessa knew that she was simply feeling envious of Lizzie, but all the same, she just couldn't shake her dislike.

"Okay, great! Have a good night, girls!" Lizzie exited the room with an exaggerated swing of her long golden waves and Alessa promptly feigned a mild gag. Janie rolled her eyes at Alessa's behavior, but her smile betrayed her accord. "She's not *that* bad."

Alessa chose not to respond.

"Oh! That reminds me." Janie started digging through her desk drawer. "I came across something that I thought might be of interest." She handed Alessa a printout of an article from the school newspaper. A photo showed Lizzie and the other board members in front of the sorority house. The headline read:

ESU'S ZETA EPSILON PI CHAPTER CELEBRATES 40 YEARS

"What's this?" Alessa asked.

Janie sighed. "I figured you hadn't been reading your emails. There's a big anniversary coming up in a couple days and the board hosted a small celebration with some university officials, including a local historian who works at the library. Read the third paragraph."

Alessa scanned the page. In the middle of the article was a quote from a Mary Brighton, the librarian Janie was referring to.

Local historian and university librarian Mary Brighton took a few moments at the commemoration ceremony to share the history of Z-E-Pi's chapter house. According to Ms. Brighton, "The house which is now occupied by the Zeta Epsilon Pi sorority was one of the first properties acquired by the university during the expansion drive of the 1930s. Eastern State officials were able to purchase 200 acres of land including the home for a very reasonable sum after the passing of a wealthy family who had owned the property. From that time until the founding of the Zeta Epsilon Pi chapter, the building was used for offices and storage."

This did look promising. Alessa looked up. "Do you think this has something to do with the ghost?"

Janie shrugged. "The timeline seems about right and that Brighton lady made it sound like a whole family died."

Alessa nodded in agreement and folded the printout, tucking it into her pocket. She'd read a little about the building on the ESU website, but it didn't mention anything about the original owners. "Thanks for this. I haven't put a ton of effort into researching the house yet, but nothing I came across so far went back further than the founding of Z-E-Pi. This is the first thing I've seen which might actually be related."

"I thought maybe that librarian might know who the family was and what happened to them. Or if there are other reports of hauntings." Janie spoke the last word in a dramatic eerie hush as she widened her eyes.

"Don't mock me!" Alessa giggled at Janie's theatrics. She couldn't remember the last time she'd giggled at anything.

Janie grinned. "I'm just kidding. Seriously, though, aren't there usually multiple reports of sightings or other 'disturbances' when a place is haunted? Have you heard anyone else talk about seeing your ghastly beau?"

Alessa ignored Janie's teasing and shook her head. "No, but they'd be more likely to tell *you* about it than me. Everyone seems hesitant to send more than a quick hello and goodbye in my direction."

Sarcasm oozed from Janie's reply. "I wonder why. Couldn't be your inviting demeanor and abundant enthusiasm for life." She gave Alessa a scolding look before continuing. "But no, no one's said anything to me either, and I certainly haven't experienced anything myself. But who knows, maybe someone has and they're just afraid to say anything because everyone will think they're crazy."

"Like you think I am?"

"Exactly." Janie laughed. Alessa knew Janie believed her, even if she didn't want to admit it. "It just seems strange to me that you're the only person who's ever seen him. It doesn't seem to fit with any other ghost story I've ever heard."

"Well maybe I'm not the only one." Alessa's interest was definitely piqued. "I'll stop by the library after the physics exam tomorrow and see if I can find that Brighton woman."

4. RECORDS

"Pencils down!" The shrill voice of the proctor rang throughout the lecture hall as the sound of scratching graphite faded to the gentle shuffling of paper against paper. Quiet murmurs sprang up in every direction as Alessa looked over at Janie to see how she had fared. Janie shrugged apathetically.

Alessa was about to relay her own expectations when the proctor's voice pierced the air once more. "No talking until all exams are turned in!" Alessa swallowed back her comment and returned Janie's shrug instead. They gathered up their textbooks and calculators and headed towards the front of the class to turn in their exams.

The open book didn't turn out to be as helpful as Alessa had hoped, but nevertheless, she still felt relatively good about her answers. It turned out that Alessa remembered more of the physics she'd learned in high school than she had thought. Despite last night's failed attempt at studying, of the seven long questions on the midterm, she was confident about four, less certain about two, and had at least written *something* for the last. She guessed that – depending on the curve, of course – she would probably wring out a B, maybe better. That was going to have to be good enough. She had other things on her mind.

Alessa and Janie turned in their booklets and filed out the door, swept in amongst the stream of students. Alessa hated these big imposing lecture halls with auditorium-style seating for 400. At first it was a little exciting – so different from her high school experience – but eventually she grew to loathe the scratchy fabric seats, the dim overhead lighting, and those cramped little desks that folded out from beside the chair. It just didn't feel like a classroom.

The moment they crossed the threshold, Janie began drilling Alessa. "What'd you get for number four?"

"The ball rolling off a ramp one?"

"Yeah."

Alessa thought for a moment. "12.4 meters."

Janie swore under her breath. "Hmpf. Hopefully they'll give partial credit."

"I'm sure they will." The last thing Alessa wanted to do right now was rehash every question on the midterm. What's done was done, and there was no sense in agonizing over something they couldn't change now.

"I can't believe Professor Liu is making us go to lecture today," Janie moaned. Janie wasn't the biggest physics enthusiast and she was taking the class just to fill a science requirement. Alessa had convinced Janie to transfer in a few weeks into the semester so that they could have a class together, so she felt partially responsible for Janie's dread. It did seem unfair that the university allowed professors to schedule class on the same day as the midterm.

"I know. I'm not looking forward to it either. But at least he didn't assign any homework." As they headed out of the building, Alessa and Janie commiserated on the injustices of midterm scheduling until they reached the quad.

Alessa stopped walking and motioned toward the library. "Have time for a little paranormal research?" she asked.

Janie smiled but shook her head. "I've got to go turn in that psych paper. But good luck! Let me know how it goes."

"Will do." Alessa and Janie parted and Alessa headed up the few steps towards the library door.

When she stepped inside, the musk of old books hit her immediately. It wasn't an unpleasant smell exactly, but it was a violent contrast to the fresh fall air outside. Alessa looked up and admired the tall vaulted ceilings and heavy wood rafters. Like most of the main campus, the library had been built in the late 1800s, a time when labor was still cheap enough that buildings were treated as detailed works of art as much as construction projects. The architectural details in the library were stunning, from the intricate woodwork in the moldings to the stained glass windows to the Versailles-patterned tile floor. From the entranceway, Alessa could look up four stories straight with nothing to block her view except a grand old chandelier.

She headed to the information desk and the student behind the counter looked up with a smile. "How can I help you?"

Alessa wasn't quite sure what to ask for. "Hi. Um, I'm trying to learn more about the history of my sorority house?" She cringed. Alessa hated feeling unsure of herself. "I saw that a Mary Brighton was quoted as an expert in an article from *The Burrow*," – the university was overrun with seemingly endless references to the ridiculous school mascot, and the campus newspaper was no exception – "and I think I read that she's a librarian here?"

"Yup! Ms. Brighton has an office up on the third floor. Just take the steps and make a right. It's down past the local history section."

"Thanks," Alessa breathed with a smile. She turned towards the large staircase on her left and headed up to the third floor. Passing stacks upon stacks of books, Alessa wondered how many tomes were housed in the building. The rows seemed almost endless.

Reaching the office, Alessa noted that the door was open. Inside was a smallish older woman, gray hair pulled back in a severe bun, thick black glasses perched low on her nose, her neutral outfit neat but frumpy. Alessa almost had to laugh – Mary Brighton was like a caricature, displaying every trait one might attribute to a stereotypical librarian, right down to the over-large book she was patiently paging through.

Alessa knocked gently on the wall. The librarian pushed her glasses back to the bridge of her nose and looked up. "Hello, dear. What can I assist you with?"

"Hi. I was actually interested in learning more about the history of my sorority house, Z-E-Pi, and I saw that you were at the commemoration ceremony a few days ago?" Alessa tried not to be awkward. She didn't know what she was going to say if Ms. Brighton asked *why* she was interested. She wished she had thought this through a bit more.

"Oh, absolutely. 33 Mason Manor is one of my favorite properties on the campus. What did you want to know?"

Alessa wondered if it would be possible to avoid the subject of the ghost. She didn't want to be known as "the poor girl who was seeing things," even to an old spinster that she didn't particularly know. Alessa took a deep breath and hoped her reply was casual enough to not betray her lie. "I'm working on a project for my history class, about the lifetime of a building. I'm supposed to choose one building and write about all the notable people who lived or worked there." She looked at the librarian expectantly.

"Of course. I can help you with that. Just one moment." Mary Brighton closed the volume she'd been reading and Alessa was hit with a puff of that old book smell again. Ms. Brighton stood up. "Come with me."

A few moments later, Alessa was seated at another uncomfortable study desk, this time in the back corner of the library's third floor. Mary Brighton had known exactly where to find all the old town records, dating all the way back to the 1700s. Alessa was pretty sure that the ghost was from the late 1800s or early 1900s based on his clothes, though her limited knowledge of historical fashion was gleaned mainly from movies, and who knew how accurate they might be. There was a thick book for every decade from 1760 to 1999, after which Ms. Brighton had explained that the records were electronic. Alessa was worried she'd have to page through all 24 books to keep up the pretext for her research, but the librarian had given her a break when she mentioned that the house was built in the 1870s, knocking almost half the books off her list.

Alessa picked up the first book and paged through to get acquainted with the organization. The book was broken down by year, then the properties were listed alphabetically by address. There was an entry any time a property was built, destroyed, or changed hands, with the date and any involved parties listed alongside it. Alessa started with 1870 and skipped to the M section, scanning the page for 33 Mason Manor.

Nothing.

She tried 1871. Still nothing.

Alessa continued in this manner until she came across the first entry in 1878:

Mason Manor, No. 33. New Construction, completed October 14th on 148 acres. Owner: Albert B. Mason. Residents: Albert B. Mason & Elizabeth Mason, children Albert Mason Jr., 3, and William Mason, 1.

Now she had a start. If the young man she was seeing was from the 1890s, it could be Albert Jr. or William. She noted that the last name of the residents was the same as the address – she supposed they had named the property after the family.

Alessa continued reading. There was nothing more in the first book, nor in the second or third. It was in the fourth volume – 1900s – that Alessa had another hit:

```
Mason Manor, No. 33.  New Owner, Albert Mason
Jr., as of April 25th.  Residents: Albert Mason
Jr. & Martha Mason, children Isaac Mason, 6.
```

That entry was from 1906, adding Isaac Mason as another possibility. Alessa read for a few more moments, and found one more related record in 1908. The family had acquired another 40 acres of land adjacent to the property and there was an additional entry beside Isaac under the children, a one year old Josephine Mason.

If it was Isaac, the ghost she was seeing was probably from between 1915 and 1920. She knew from the Z-E-Pi article that the university had purchased the property in the 30s, so that left two or three volumes to go through to narrow down the possibilities.

Unfortunately, though, it would have to wait. Alessa glanced at the clock and realized she had only 20 minutes until her physics lecture, and she still needed to run home and grab her laptop, which she had forgotten in her rush to get to the midterm that morning.

Alessa jotted down the information she had found and resolved to come back the next time she had a few free moments. She stacked the volumes of records chronologically and carried them back to the shelves from which Mary Brighton had taken them. She took one last look at the clock – 17 minutes. That was just enough time to dash across campus, grab her computer, and meet Janie at the science building.

5. ENCOUNTER

Alessa climbed the steps to her house with 13 minutes to spare until the start of her lecture. She hastily bounded to the second floor and tried to remember if she had anything edible in her minifridge. She thought there might be a few string cheeses left and made a mental note to grab one as she swung around the doorway into her room.

Alessa stopped short. Standing at the window not ten feet from her was a tall solitary figure, partially cast in shadow. He was looking out the window, breathing gently, one slim lace up boot perched on the low windowsill, narrow suspenders pulled taut across a broad, flat back and fastened to the narrow waist of his trim brown slacks. Lost in his own thoughts, he gazed pensively across the expanse of the lawn, his chin perched gently upon the knuckles of his left fist, white shirtsleeves rolled up to the elbow. She could see the muscles in his forearm flex as he clenched and unclenched his hand.

Alessa stifled the urge to scream as adrenaline rushed through her body. Panic threatened to overtake her as blood throbbed through her temples, her muscles tensing for action. But she couldn't breathe, couldn't think, so she just stood still, watching.

He was contemplative, as usual, gazing through the window but not focused on anything in particular. He dropped his left arm and ruffled a hand through the short waves of his soft brown hair. His skin was pale, but not the pallid color of sickness, more the luminous porcelain of mid-winter.

Alessa's body refused to calm, her insides churning as she fought the mayhem stirring in her chest. Terror mixed with agony, her heart sinking with each beat, overwhelmed with an aching sorrow she couldn't explain. But at the same time, she felt the firm tug of a powerful longing, the depths of which she'd never experienced before. She couldn't have torn her eyes from him if she'd tried.

His image glowed faintly, the lines of the windowpane just barely visible through his semi-translucent form. For a moment, his head inclined in her direction and she could see the gleam of one sea blue eye above a strong, straight nose and thin pale rose lips.

Transfixed by his face, Alessa couldn't get a grip on her emotions. She was frightened and anxious, every impulse in her body telling her to run. But at the same time she felt strangely drawn to him, and she knew she couldn't have forced her feet to move even if she'd wanted to. She was frozen in place, powerless to act, waves of anguish washing over her, drowning. And on top of all this, that ever-present, searing longing that rooted her in place despite her best instincts towards self-preservation. How did this strange apparition invoke such turmoil in her?

Alessa knew somewhere inside that she needed to connect with the ghost, needed to break through the barrier that separated them, but she didn't know how. The only thing she could think to do was speak, but what would she say? How could she start? And did he even know she was there? How would he react to her intrusion?

Alessa was building the courage to try to communicate when the ghost began to fade. It started with the hazy glow around him, which grew strong for a moment then rapidly drew inward, erasing his presence as it went. Alessa thought she saw a small flicker and then the form was gone.

She gasped for air; she didn't realize she'd been holding her breath. The entire encounter had only lasted a few seconds, maybe ten at the most, but she was overcome with exhaustion. Her heart was still pounding and she was trembling from her fingertips to her toes.

Worse, her entire mental state was in shambles. Alessa didn't understand the tumultuous emotions that had hammered through her and she was still reeling from the experience. Seeing the ghost was thrilling, but it was also alarming and strange, and it shook her straight to her core. That was a normal enough reaction to this kind of situation, but there was something else, too, something specific to this ghost.

Her attraction to him was magnetic, and it went beyond her natural curiosity. And yes, he was an incredibly appealing guy – the kind she would have pined over in high school – but it was more than that too. It was like she *knew* him. She just couldn't explain it.

Whenever she was in his presence, she desperately wanted to reach out to him, to tell him he wasn't alone. He was forever gazing out over some landscape that Alessa was blind to, hard lines of melancholy scored into his face. But she just couldn't bring herself to interrupt his reverie, held hostage as she was by her body's impulses.

The sound of footsteps approaching from down the hall brought Alessa back to reality. She quickly closed the door behind her. The last thing she wanted to do right now was exchange pleasantries with one of her housemates.

She leaned her back against the door, spreading her palms against the cool wood. Alessa looked up at the ceiling, releasing a deep sigh. These encounters always left her shaken and emotionally drained, and she didn't have time to deal with it today. She had to get to class.

She looked slowly around the room. Everything was in its place – the oversized original fireplace mantle to her left, her twin bed and nightstand beyond it against the wall, then the double window and finally her desk and fridge across from the bed. To her right was the large sliding door sealing off the double closet. It was amazing how such a familiar place could for those few moments feel so foreign to her, like another world she didn't belong in.

She crossed the room and snapped the lid of her laptop shut, unplugging the power cord from the back of the machine as she awkwardly attempted to scoop it up with the other hand. She regretted once again that she hadn't splurged on a higher-end model constructed of lighter materials as she exchanged the heavy textbook in her backpack for the heavier computer in her hand and closed the zipper. Looking at her bedside clock, she noted that she had 10 minutes to make it back across campus.

Alessa turned towards the door and then she remembered the string cheese. The scene inside her refrigerator was dismal. The shelves were lined with half-rotted fruit and takeout leftovers from who knows when. On the door she found a few cans of diet soda. Checking the bottom drawer, she hit upon the package of string cheese with three individually wrapped sticks remaining. She grabbed one and accidentally slammed the fridge door as she headed out, the adrenaline still ringing through her body.

Springing down the stairs of the house, Alessa set a quick pace down the cobblestone path that led back to the quad. She peeled the plastic back from the string cheese as she went, anxiously swallowing bites as she strode past ambling students. Janie would throw a fit if she could see; she viewed not peeling string cheese into strings as virtually sacrilegious.

A couple frat boys were tossing a frisbee across the quad while some freshman girls stood huddled under a tree, stealing glances at the guys and giggling to each other. Alessa watched a comic looking professor in a classic tweed blazer replete with elbow patches hustle a stack of papers a foot tall towards the faculty offices. On the far side of the quad, a team of facility workers were blowing fallen leaves into a pile and raking them into bags. Taking in the ordinary college scene around her, Alessa began to feel almost normal again.

It'd been a couple weeks since she'd last seen the ghost, and she had forgotten how unsettling it was. It was as though for a few moments her whole world turned upside-down. Ghosts weren't supposed to exist. She shouldn't be wandering into her room in the middle of the day to find a strange man standing there, only to watch him disappear into thin air seconds later. It was true that much of her life in the past year didn't make sense to her, but at least it was still firmly grounded in reality, on a planet with clear laws of nature that no one could break.

This ghost thing turned all of that on its head. She was sure that what she was seeing was real, despite Janie's half-joking hints to the contrary, and that knowledge made her wonder what else she had mistakenly taken for granted.

There had been her family's stability for one. She'd always counted on her parents to be there for her, to be a guiding voice and a security blanket whenever she needed them. In spite of the constant fighting in recent years, Alessa needed her parents. And one moment in the wrong place at the wrong time had taken them from her, forever.

Then, of course, there was her own infallibility. Alessa had been so wrapped up in her dreams for the future that she had failed to prepare for reality. Yes, her parents' death was a curveball she hadn't anticipated, and her reaction – depression, withdrawal, breakdown – had been pretty understandable. But even if they had survived the accident and things had gone back to normal, Alessa had a sneaking suspicion that she might still be in the same boat.

She had thought she was invincible, but in the end she was just deluded. Yes, she was a talented student and a good leader with a strong resume, but there were thousands of others just like her. She didn't know what had ever made her think that she was entitled to admission to only the best schools in the country. She should have known that getting accepted to any of the schools on her list was a shot in the dark, and she should have put more time into evaluating other more realistic options that might actually have been a good match for her.

She'd always preferred to be a big fish in a small pond, and she could have had her pick of decent colleges, even after all the devastation of the accident. Instead, she'd squandered her opportunity and had to settle for this massive university where she was nothing but a number.

Arriving at the door to the lecture hall, Alessa felt more lost than she ever had. She didn't know what to believe in anymore. Certainly not her own judgment, certainly not her parents' permanence, and certainly not the laws of science. In the past year, if there was one thing Alessa had learned, it was not to trust herself, not even down to the most basic truths. Like that ghosts were only stories. She knew now that there was much more to this world than it had seemed.

6. DISSECTION

Janie had saved a seat for Alessa towards the back of the huge auditorium. "Cutting it a little close, aren't you?" she jibed with a mischievous smirk.

Alessa was unfailingly punctual. She knew that Janie – who was always running ten minutes behind – must take a small amount of pleasure in seeing their roles reversed for once. Usually it was a frazzled Janie plopping down into her seat, frantically pulling out her notes seconds before the beginning of class. Today it was Alessa's turn.

Alessa looked at Janie. She didn't know where to start.

Janie's expression shifted into concern. "You look like you've seen…"

"A ghost, yes," Alessa said under her breath.

Janie's eyes popped. "Just now?" she whispered urgently.

Alessa noticed that Professor Liu was stepping up to the podium. "Yes," she whispered back, "in my room."

"What happened?" Janie breathed.

The professor had started speaking, something about being pleased with the results of this morning's exam.

Alessa lowered her voice to give Janie the summary. "The same thing as always: he was just standing there and then he disappeared."

"Kind of anticlimactic."

"No kidding."

Janie thought for a moment. "Did you find anything at the library?"

Professor Liu raised his voice, "Ladies in the back, is there something you'd like to share with the class?"

Alessa flushed. She hated being reprimanded. She shrunk back into her chair and mouthed a sheepish, "Sorry."

The professor returned to his lesson plan, but as had been the case of late, Alessa just couldn't focus on what he was saying. She unfolded the little desktop from its storage space under her armrest and took out her laptop. Opening a blank document, she angled the screen toward Janie, intending to write a short note explaining what she'd learned at the library. Luckily, there was no one sitting directly behind them, so she didn't have to worry about anyone reading over their shoulders.

"I found the librarian from that article – she pointed me towards some old books of property records and I was able to find the house in there."

Feigning attention to the lecture as she scribbled in her notebook, Janie quickly shifted her eyes to Alessa and raised an eyebrow, encouraging her to continue.

Alessa cleared what she had written and started a fresh sentence. "There was a Mason family who built the house in the 1870s, and they had two sons, Albert & William. Then Albert took ownership of the house about 30 years later and had a son named Isaac. I think it might be one of those three."

Janie nodded and wrote something in her notebook. She slid it quietly towards Alessa. Alessa saw something scrawled in the margin in Janie's signature tiny capital letters. She leaned closer for a better look. "ALBERT? SEXY." Janie had underlined the last word for emphasis. It was amazing how Janie's voice rang clear in Alessa's head, even just from her writing. Alessa could hear the sarcasm dripping from those two syllables.

Alessa rolled her eyes playfully. She turned back to the keyboard and typed, "Isaac?"

"DEFINITELY BETTER."

Alessa laughed silently and shook her head at Janie's antics. Albert, William, Isaac… She didn't care what the ghost's name was, only *who* he was.

She was opening the file with her physics notes as Janie pushed her notebook in Alessa's direction once again. "SO WHAT'S THE PLAN?"

Alessa looked at Janie and shrugged. She typed, "Going to see if I can find death records for these people. Beyond that, not sure."

Janie acknowledged the response with a nod and went back to her notes. Alessa did the same.

An hour and fifteen minutes later, Professor Liu was reminding the class to check the syllabus for the reading due next session. Alessa was surprised at how much she had absorbed once she started paying attention. With what she picked up in class today she thought she should be able to skim through the reading, which might give her enough time to continue her research about the ghost between now and Thursday's class.

Janie turned to Alessa as she was packing her notebook into her messenger bag. "Did you eat lunch yet?"

Alessa was surprised to find that she actually had an appetite for once. "Nope. Did you want to grab something? I've got a half hour until my next class."

"Let's go to the cafeteria."

Alessa nodded her assent.

Janie led the way down from the back of the lecture hall, following the tide of students to the door. As they passed the front podium, Alessa was startled to hear someone other than Janie call her name.

"Ms. Khole?" Alessa and Janie stopped in their tracks and turned around. Professor Liu was looking directly at Alessa.

"Yes, Professor?"

"Yours was one of the few exams I had time to grade before class today." Alessa felt a twang of trepidation; this couldn't be good news. She braced herself.

The professor continued. "I was quite impressed with your performance."

"Oh, uh, thanks," Alessa stammered. That was not what she was expecting. She reminded herself to smile.

"I haven't finished the curve yet, but I think you can expect at least an A-minus. Keep up the good work."

Alessa perked up. "Thanks, Professor." She turned towards the door and caught a surprised look on Janie's face.

As they exited into the hallway, Janie said, "He knows your *name*?"

Alessa was just as puzzled. Besides his brief chiding in the beginning of class, Alessa had never had any direct interaction with her physics professor. "I guess so… He probably looked up my photo in the student directory or something."

"You must have really done well on that test."

Alessa thought she had done okay. She must have gotten more right on those last few questions than she expected. "I didn't think I did *that* good." After a second, she added, "Guess we have to be more careful not to get caught talking from now on."

Janie chuckled. "Guess *you* need to be more careful. He still has no idea who *I* am."

Alessa laughed. "True."

After a short walk, they arrived at the cafeteria. As it was almost 1:00, most of the lunch rush had died down and there were only a few stragglers remaining inside. This was always the best time to come. With 20,000 hungry students and only one main dining hall, the ESU cafeteria was not Alessa's preferred dining venue between noon and one o'clock. If she ate lunch, she usually grabbed something quick from one of the smaller vendors elsewhere on campus, like the Van Husen café.

The dining hall was one of the few modern buildings on campus. With that many mouths to feed every day, the original cafeteria – which was built back in the 40s to accommodate one tenth the number of students – just wasn't going to cut it. A few years ago the university had used a large grant to build the enormous structure, with a huge kitchen and serving area on the main floor and three floors of seating above.

Alessa and Janie swiped their meal cards then diverged to opposite ends of the cafeteria. Janie, as usual, went to the salad bar. Alessa scanned the hot food entrees. It was a chilly day and after her earlier incident with the ghost, she could use some comfort food.

Bingo. Macaroni and cheese, her favorite. Alessa scooped herself a modestly sized portion, then added a spoonful of steamed broccoli to her plate as well. She didn't want to hear Janie's nagging to eat her vegetables.

Sure enough, the moment they sat down across from one another, Janie eyed Alessa's plate. "You really shouldn't eat that junk." Janie's plate was piled literally eight inches high with fresh raw vegetables and nuts. For someone who was so health-conscious, she had a voracious appetite.

"I got some broccoli," Alessa offered. She watched as Janie dug a fork into her mound of produce and shoveled it towards her mouth. "I really don't know where you put all of that."

Janie swallowed. "It's low calorie and healthy fats."

"No, I mean, physically. How can you fit that much volume in your stomach?"

Through a mouthful of food, Janie replied, "Practice."

Alessa smiled and started in on her own plate. The mac and cheese was definitely hitting the spot. It reminded her of her mom's homemade recipe, creamy and buttery with a thick layer of crisp breadcrumbs across the top. Heaven. It felt like forever since she'd eaten something so rich.

Janie looked up from her tray and took a deep chug from her glass of milk. "So, how are you feeling? You look better than when you walked into class."

Alessa definitely felt better. "Yeah, I'm okay now. Thanks for asking." She took a sip of water. "I forgot how –" she searched for the right word, "– *distressing* it is to see the ghost. I mean, beyond the expected scared-out-of-my-mind reaction, for some reason he stirs up all these other emotions in me. I know I've told you that I can see that he's distraught, but it's more than just empathy. I *feel* it. It's like a whole bucket of emotions are dumped on me in the span of a few seconds, and it just leaves me feeling like a wreck."

"Is that normal for ghosts?"

"Is what normal?"

"Making you feel things, like maybe what *they're* feeling."

Alessa hadn't thought of that. She certainly couldn't explain how she felt in his presence, and at least some of it did seem to match his expression. "You know, I'm not sure. It kind of makes sense, and it would help to explain why these encounters keep affecting me like they do."

Janie thought for a moment. "Was it always like that? I don't remember you being such a mess at first."

Alessa reflected back over her history with the ghost. At first the encounters were much briefer, lasting only a second or two. In fact, she may even have had incidents that were shorter. In the beginning of the school year, sometimes she would see something out of the corner of her eye, but when she looked nothing was there. So she wasn't even sure at first that anything had happened.

Then one night, she'd woken up at three in the morning feeling that eerie sixth sense that she wasn't alone. When she'd opened her eyes, she'd seen the silhouette of a man standing at the foot of her bed, near the fireplace. She had frozen out of fear and pretended she was still asleep, squinting in the darkness to try to figure out if what she was seeing was real. She could only faintly make out his shape and thought it might have been a trick of the light coupled with her sleepy eyes, but she just had that feeling that she wasn't the only person in the room. Then all of a sudden the feeling had passed, and when she'd reached out to her nightstand to switch on the lamp, there was nothing there.

When she finally did see the ghost for certain for the first time, she'd flown from the room. She'd been alone in the bathroom one evening brushing her teeth when she looked up from the sink and saw the ghost lurking behind her in the mirror. He didn't seem to have noticed her, but Alessa hadn't stayed long enough to look closely. She'd sprinted from the bathroom toothbrush in hand and locked herself behind her own door until she'd calmed down enough to go tell Janie what had happened.

So she supposed in those early incidents it wasn't quite the same. Today, she had been transfixed. She couldn't seem to summon the will to flee, even as every instinct screamed at her to go. But those first few times, she had been able to take action.

Alessa confirmed Janie's suspicions. "You're right. It didn't used to be like this. I think the encounters are lasting longer and longer, and they're getting more intense."

"That's a little scary."

Alessa agreed. "I'll look into it when I get home tonight. I'm sure there are plenty of ghost stories on the internet – I'll see if I can find reports of anything similar."

"Good idea."

Alessa savored the last bite of her mac and cheese and put down her fork. "Okay, I think it's time for me to head to my ethics seminar."

Janie still had a sizable pile of veggies in front of her. "Okay. I'm going to stay and finish up. See you back at the house tonight?"

"Absolutely."

7. RESEARCH

Alessa was flooded with relief as she climbed the steps to Zeta Epsilon Pi's front porch. Between the exam that morning and her lunchtime rendezvous with the ghost, she was wiped. Her ethics seminar had dragged on interminably, and as she yawned and drooped in her chair, Alessa had found herself wishing she was back in one of those massive lecture halls so that she could sink into the crowd.

Instead, she had spent the entire class struggling to keep her eyes open in full view of her ethics professor, who quickly took notice given that there were only twenty or so students in the room. Alessa had spent the better part of the last hour with the professor's affronted expression boring through her and was glad to put the class behind her. It felt good to be home at last.

As Alessa opened the front door, she noticed that there was a group of seven or so sorority sisters gathered around the coffee table in the living room. They alternated between nodding furiously and looking intently at Lizzie's laptop as she spoke rapidly about something, gesticulating enthusiastically as she went. Alessa caught wind of the words "party" and "delegate" and quickly scurried up to her room before anyone noticed her presence.

Alessa switched on the light and flopped onto the bed, letting out a deep sigh. It had been a long day. At least she could expect a little respite before her next encounter with the ghost, since he didn't seem to drop in more than once every other week or so. With the way she was feeling at the moment, she thought she might need that much time to recover. She ached with exhaustion right down to her bones.

Alessa rolled over facing the wall and pulled her knees toward her chest, her long hair strewn out behind her. She rested her head on her arm and closed her eyes. She still hadn't fully processed everything that had happened earlier, the emotions that had tugged at her from seemingly every direction. She wondered if there was any validity to Janie's theory that they were actually the *ghost's* emotions being projected onto her.

She didn't want to think about it. It was bad enough that she was *seeing* the apparition. Did she really need to feel it too? She didn't like the idea of some foreign entity hijacking her emotions, making her feel like someone she wasn't. It was troubling to think how little control she had over her own faculties during those moments. And now it was hours later and she was still feeling the effects.

She needed to get to the bottom of this. With a weary sigh, Alessa rolled back over and swung her legs to the floor, pushing herself out of bed and over to the desk. Sinking into the chair, she snatched up her backpack from the floor and slid out her laptop, dropping it onto the desk with a clunk. She popped the lid open and reattached the power supply while she waited for the system to boot up. Once the familiar startup chimes sounded, she opened her browser and navigated to a search engine.

Alessa wasn't even sure where to begin. She decided to start broad and entered "ghost stories." 120 million results. Perhaps she was going to need to be more specific.

This time she tried "real ghost stories." That narrowed it down to 5 million results. She tested to see if adding "emotion" or "feeling" to her query would help, but scanning the results, she didn't see anything that looked useful. Alessa backed up to the "real ghost stories" search and randomly opened the first few results.

They were all stories from people who claimed to have experienced a ghost encounter, but the only emotions they reported feeling were the expected ones: that something was "not right," like they weren't alone, and of course terror, anxiety, panic. It sounded pretty similar to Alessa's first few experiences.

She tried entering "ghosts projecting feelings" which narrowed it down to 3 million results, but still nothing seemed quite right. One of the top results was a general information page about ghosts, so she decided to check there. Scanning the page, she noticed that the words "projecting" and "feelings" were there but nowhere near each other, which didn't really answer her question. However, there was a list of alternative hypotheses attempting to explain the existence of ghosts, so she decided to read further.

Of course there was all the usual theorizing about the existence of spirits on another dimension or plane, a soul caught between life on earth and the afterlife envisioned by most major religions. This was generally thought to be caused by "unfinished business" on the part of the deceased or a great trauma experienced at the time of death. Both scenarios seemed reasonable enough to explain her own experiences, though Alessa didn't know enough about her ghost to guess what might have been his particular hang-up. And another issue, of course, was that this entire theory hinged on the premise of being willing to accept the existence of the soul, which Alessa also wasn't sold on quite yet.

As expected, there was also plenty of scientific skepticism. Carbon monoxide poisoning, air pressure changes, and mistakes interpreting peripheral vision were all cited as rational explanations behind what one might interpret as a ghost sighting, but none of these rationalizations seemed to hit the mark in Alessa's case. Alessa remembered that she had cited many of these same arguments herself in debates with friends over the years, an irony that was not lost on her.

There was also some discussion of a phenomenon called infrasound, sound waves emanating at a low enough frequency that they're inaudible to humans but still detectable in other ways. There were experiments where people reported seeing things and feeling uneasiness and even sorrow when exposed to sound at these frequencies. However, in those experiments 20% of the tested population was affected by the presence of infrasound, which meant that if there was some sort of infrasound source affecting her house, at least a handful of her housemates should have experienced something similar. As far as Alessa knew, no one else had, so that didn't seem like the culprit.

Other theories hypothesized that ghosts were projections of the viewer's own emotions, some sort of low-level telepathy that resulted from stress. Alessa thought this theory might have some merit, especially given the recent loss of her parents and her difficulty coping with the experience. However, that didn't explain why her emotions might take the form of a guy from the early 1900s. Shouldn't it be her parents she was seeing if in fact her stress over their death was the root of all this?

Yet another set of theories considered the possibility of a time warp. In these cases, by some unknown process the fabric of time was momentarily folded in such a way that someone in the present either got a glimpse of a person from the past, or – in the case of what was called a "time slip" – was fully transported into the past for a few moments. Besides the usual lost soul hypothesis, this theory seemed probably the closest of everything Alessa had read. However, in most reported instances, the person in the past had noticed the person from the present as well, which had not been the case with Alessa's ghost. And even if this theory was correct, Alessa didn't understand *how* it was possible or *why* it was happening to her, in this house, with this ghost.

Alessa closed her laptop lid in frustration, snapping it a little harder than she'd meant to. All in all, she was disappointed with what she'd been able to turn up. There was practically nothing she came across that she didn't already know, and none of the various theories seemed to quite match her experiences. Most of the information online seemed like it was written by either lunatics or dedicated skeptics, neither of whom she trusted for a reliable opinion.

Most troubling was the fact that she wasn't able to find *anything* related to the emotional disturbance that had accompanied her recent encounters. There were occasional stories about feeling sorrow or loneliness when bumping into a spirit, but nothing to the degree of what she had experienced, and certainly no inexplicable sense of allure in addition to the sadness and pain and fear. She had truly expected to find *something* that might help explain what was going on, or at least accounts from other people who had experienced similar sensations. Instead, her search had left Alessa feeling more alone than ever.

Glancing at the pile of textbooks on her desk, Alessa remembered the slowly accumulating mountain of reading that she had yet to tackle. She didn't even want to try to calculate the number of pages she had due in the next week. Alessa weighed the possibility of powering through some text tonight, but the thought of delving into economics or physics or history was just more than she could bear at the moment. The reading would have to wait.

Alessa grabbed a hair tie off the desk and pulled her locks into a low ponytail. She slid open her closet and dug into a dresser drawer, fishing out a comfortable pair of old sweatpants and a cozy long sleeve tee. Changing out of her jeans and sweater, she tossed the discarded clothes in the laundry bag then headed for the bathroom.

In the hallway she passed by a sophomore housemate that she'd barely traded ten words with all year. Sara, was it? Alessa wasn't positive. She forced a quiet smile, a gesture that maybe-Sara returned with a quick wave. She seemed relieved not to have to make conversation, so Alessa continued on without breaking her stride.

Reaching the bathroom, Alessa was grateful to find that it was empty. She washed her face in the second of the triple sinks, splashing cool water over her skin until it flushed with pink. As the water dripped off her chin, she looked up at the mirror, locking sight with her own green and gold eyes. Janie was right – she looked like shit. She was glad she'd decided to get some rest tonight instead of trying to force the reading, which would surely have been an exercise in futility.

Alessa dried her face and hands on the fluffy towel she kept hung on a hook by the door and returned to the sink. As she reached for her toothbrush, she heard footsteps approaching. She considered forsaking dental hygiene for one night if it would allow her to avoid another awkward exchange with one of her sorority sisters.

It was Janie. “Hey, Less.”

Alessa breathed a sigh of relief. “Hey.”

Janie was wrapped in a towel and headed towards one of the shower stalls. She closed the curtain behind her and flung her towel over the top of the stall as Alessa began brushing her teeth. A moment after the shower started pattering against the floor, Janie let out a yelp.

Alessa spat a mouthful of foam into the sink basin. “You okay in there?” she asked, glancing in the mirror toward the shower.

“I always forget how cold it is when you first turn it on.”

Alessa knew the feeling. She finished brushing her teeth and rinsed her toothbrush.

After a short pause, Janie continued. “So did you get a chance yet to look into my projection theory?”

Putting her toothbrush back in its holder, Alessa turned to face the shower curtain. “I did actually. It wasn’t very successful.” Just thinking about her failed research attempt caused the frustration to well up in her stomach again. “None of the stories I found involved anything as intense as what I’ve been experiencing.”

“No?” Janie prompted.

“Nah. There were some people who said they would be overcome with feelings of loneliness or grief, but there was no mention of anyone simultaneously feeling…” Alessa hesitated. She knew Janie was going to goad her for this. “… attracted.”

Janie snorted. “Figures.” She thought for a moment. “I don’t know what to tell you, Less.” Alessa could hear the concern in her friend's voice. More playfully Janie added, "Well, maybe your *loins* know something you don't. Maybe this ghost was your lover in a past life or something, and just like muscle memory you're *longing* for him with every cell in your body. Except the ones in your brain, of course."

Alessa shook her head and laughed, out of frustration as much as amusement. Now that she was seeing ghosts, how could she just dismiss other possibilities? Even reincarnation wasn't out of the question. "You know what, Janie? At this point, I'm not ruling anything out."

8. EXPECTATION

Alessa had expected to be up half the night reliving her most recent encounter and mulling over the assortment of potential explanations. But she surprised herself by slipping into the cool dark peace of slumber almost the instant her face struck the pillow.

Unfortunately, her peaceful repose did not last for long. Halfway through the night she awoke in a cloud of anxiety, a pervasive sense of unease coloring the air around her. She'd had another nightmare.

This time, instead of a dim prison cell she'd been outside on a brilliant winter morning, the chill air bracing against the cool sweat that dripped from her brow. She was digging a hole, struggling to pierce the frozen ground as the harsh winter sun glared down on her back. She felt weak and exhausted, her body fighting her every movement. And hungry, so hungry.

"Need some help with that?"

She looked up to find a handsome young man, tall, strapping, with short chocolate hair and striking blue eyes. He looked familiar, like someone she should know, but she couldn't seem to place his face. And he was breathtaking; though he approached her with affection and ease, Alessa's heart pounded at the sight of him.

He took the shovel from her hands and plowed it into the ground, easily loosening the section of dirt that Alessa had been battling with. Leaning over the shovel, he turned his back to the others working in the courtyard and dropped his voice low enough that only Alessa could hear.

"I have an assignment today."

She felt her body react with alarm. She didn't understand why, but something about his statement rang of danger.

"What kind of assignment?"

"We're stealing rations. Everyone is hungry," he glanced with concern over Alessa's angular frame, "and we need to keep up our strength. So we're going this afternoon."

Alessa didn't like the sound of this. She wished – not for the first time – that he hadn't gotten involved with these people, regardless of how righteous their mission may be.

"Who's we?" she asked, wondering who would be accompanying him during this harebrained scheme.

He motioned over his shoulder at another young man. This one she recognized – it was her ghost.

"*Him?*"

"Yeah, why not? He's perfectly capable, and he's been dying to get more involved."

"But you're supposed to be looking out for him!" she heard herself say. "How can you put him in this kind of danger?"

He shot her a warning look. Alessa lowered her voice before continuing.

"Has he done *anything* remotely this challenging before?"

Alessa could see the flash of doubt in his eyes, but only for a moment before he set his jaw. "Listen, he needs to learn sometime. I can't hold him off anymore – he wants a part in this, and I can't protect him forever. Not to mention, I think it will make him feel better."

"Better about what?" she hissed. She still couldn't believe he was going to go through with this.

He hesitated for a moment. "I don't know how to explain this to you. He feels... responsible, for what happened. For everything. He thinks it's his fault, what happened to our family."

"What? How does that make any sense?"

"It doesn't, but nothing I can say will change his mind – trust me, I've tried. He feels like he needs to prove himself, like he needs to make up for it somehow. So I'm giving him the opportunity."

Alessa's head thrummed with apprehension – she had a very bad feeling about this – but she knew she couldn't change his mind. She stepped forward and grabbed hold of his shovel, locking her eyes with his. "Just be careful."

He smiled brightly, suddenly cocksure. "You know I've got this. Don't even worry about it."

His grin was meant to be reassuring, but Alessa knew better. If there was one thing she'd learned here, it was that nothing was ever as it seemed – and there were no sure bets.

"Be careful," she reiterated, the undercurrent of fear sharpening her voice.

"I'll see you tonight," he replied, intrepid as ever. "Bring your appetite."

Despite the sense of foreboding that had draped itself about her after that strange dream, Alessa had been able to fall back asleep, and the next morning she woke feeling rested and refreshed. The prior day's excitement – and the emotional toll it'd taken on her – seemed almost surreal.

After a solid night of sleep, Alessa's muscles were eager for a little movement. She indulged in a long feline stretch, finishing with a gratifying shiver as she rolled over to face the window. Sunlight streamed through the windowpanes, catching on the countless little flecks of dust floating lazily through the air. Alessa watched absently for a few moments, breathing deeply and enjoying the unseasonal brilliance of the sun.

She tossed the covers to the side and sat up, swinging her feet to the floor. Sliding into her desk chair, she gave her email inbox a cursory glance, scanning the subject lines for anything that might be important. As was usually the case, there wasn't much there besides a lot of insubstantial chit-chat on her sorority's discussion alias. As she finished skimming the list of messages, a new one popped to the top of her inbox:

[Z-E-PI ACTION REQUIRED] PARTY PREP ASSIGNMENTS!

Alessa groaned. On her way into the house last night she'd thought she'd overheard Lizzie and Co. discussing a party, but she had been hoping she was wrong. Now her suspicions were confirmed.

The last party Z-E-Pi threw over Halloween weekend had attracted a crowd of 300. The house had been overrun with a rowdy jumble of drunken coeds decked out as everything from a bloody vampire to a sexy bumblebee. By the end of the night, the acrid smell of vomit had wafted under the door of Alessa's room all the way from the bathroom down the hall. On that occasion Alessa had been stuck on cleanup duty. The smell of stale beer still gave her flashbacks.

She made a quick decision to ignore the email and continue on with her day, rationalizing that she couldn't possibly feel guilty for neglecting her "sisterly duties" if she didn't know what they were. If anyone asked, she'd just pretend she hadn't seen the email yet. Hopefully no one would ask.

The rest of Alessa's day was unremarkable, as was the next. She went to class and did her best to pay attention. She chipped away at the bulk of the reading she'd amassed. She checked in to see what Janie was up to every so often. And whenever she found her mind unoccupied, her thoughts unfailingly drifted back to the ghost.

Her last encounter had been nothing short of disturbing, but after a couple of days, the unpleasantness had faded and she found herself anticipating her next opportunity to see the ghost. Alessa knew that looking forward to that sort of harrowing emotional experience probably wasn't healthy, but she couldn't help herself. If the encounters continued getting more and more intense, she couldn't imagine the toll it might take on her, but it was no use trying to resist. Alessa's curiosity had overtaken her sense of self-preservation.

She'd been meaning to make it back to the library to finish the search for the house's previous inhabitants, but had yet to find the time. William, Isaac, Albert… Alessa rolled their names on her tongue, wondering if her ghost was one of them. At this point, all she really had to go on to narrow down the time period was the style of his clothes, and it seemed to her like any of them could be a fit. Albert was probably a stretch given that the records showed he'd survived well past his teenage years, but she was still hesitant to cross anyone off her list just yet. And then there were the remaining volumes of records to consider. Who knew how many other potential names she might uncover?

Once she had compiled a list of possibilities, she planned to research each one to see if she could discover the manner of each person's death or any other major events in their lives. If there was anything traumatic, she hoped the library might have some old local newspapers documenting what had happened. It was probably a longshot, though. In all likelihood, she would leave this experience knowing exactly as much as she did coming in, which was nothing. Alessa couldn't imagine anything more demoralizing.

After a busy Thursday attending physics and ethics class and cramming reading for world history and econ in between, Alessa was back in her room preparing for bed. She heard a quick knock on her door and a bright voice asking, "Alessa? Are you there?"

Alessa sighed. It was Lizzie Green. Her time on the lam had come to an end. "Yeah, come on in," Alessa called out.

"Hey Alessa!"

"Hey Lizzie." Alessa was already dreading the next part of the conversation.

"So, you haven't stopped by yet to pick up your flyers for the party…"

Alessa put on her best befuddled face. "My what for the what?"

Lizzie hardened. She didn't look amused. "Your flyers? For the big anniversary party on Saturday? Didn't you see the email that went out yesterday morning?"

"Oh…" Alessa paused and pretended to think for a moment. "I guess not? Sorry."

Lizzie's expression softened, though she was still grimacing. It was clear that she was making an effort to be nice. Alessa assumed that for someone who was used to being listened to, it must be difficult to feel ignored. She decided to be more compliant. She didn't really have a choice, anyway.

Lizzie continued. "Okay, well, you must have missed it, no worries… You were assigned to marketing duty this time, so there's a bunch of flyers that we need you to hand out and hang up around campus. Preferably tomorrow," she added. She extended a stack of brightly colored paper towards Alessa.

HELP THE GIRLS OF Z-E-PI RING IN 40 FABULOUS YEARS!

PARTY AT THE CHAPTER HOUSE SATURDAY @ 10 PM

Alessa looked up from the flyers and smiled at Lizzie. "Okay, no problem. I should be able to take care of it in between class tomorrow – I have a light schedule, just a lab and a lecture." She would have preferred to go back to the library and continue her research, but decided to keep her reservations to herself.

"Ok great! Thanks for your help." Lizzie beamed her million dollar smile and headed for the door. She paused before exiting. "Oh, and Alessa? Remember to recruit lots of boys. *Cute* boys."

"Sure." Alessa breathed a sigh of relief as Lizzie closed the door. That wasn't nearly as painful as she'd expected. On the spectrum of party prep assignments, flyer duty was about as good as it could get. Nothing heavy to lug, no money to spend, and no chunks of puke to pick out of the carpet and couch cushions. Given Alessa's surly temperament towards most of the girls in the house, she had expected to get sallied with something on the lower end of the spectrum, if not clean-up again, at least something cumbersome like transporting the keg. Flyers she could handle.

Alessa put the stack of paper in her backpack along with a stapler and some tape, then promptly crawled into bed and drifted off to sleep.

Alessa woke with a start. Frantic, she gasped for air as her eyes struggled to focus in the dark. What is this place? Alessa searched her mind, the strange surroundings taking their time to resolve. The mantle, the desk, the bedspread… she was in her room at school. She glanced at the clock – 3:47 AM. It was only a dream.

She was in a cold sweat, breathing heavily, her heart still pounding against her chest. She wiped the tears from her face and tried to get a grip on her emotions as fear and panic continued to surge through her body. She felt vigilant, ready to jump at a moment's notice. What had she been so afraid of?

Alessa could feel the tendrils of the dream slipping back into her subconscious, even as she strained to weave them together into a cohesive whole once more. She felt like she was looking through a fog. She remembered being crouched in some small dark place, hiding, the feel of cold metal seeping through the thin leg of her pants. She wasn't alone. She was holding someone's hand, clutching it, not daring to breath. She knew they were being stalked.

Who was hunting them? She couldn't remember. Boot steps… She remembered the sound of boot steps approaching their hiding place. She remembered panic welling up in her chest, tingling in her fingertips, her muscles taut and ready to spring. She remembered regret, thinking of the sturdy knife stored inaccessibly in her knapsack, the hopelessness of fighting. Most of all she remembered dread. She knew that if she was caught, it would be the end.

Finally she recalled the light, a bright dazzling light suddenly filling the alcove, blinding her. She remembered a dark gloved hand emerging through the light, snatching at her, at him. Him… The ghost! But not a ghost – he was alive, next to her, grasping her hand in the same grip of terror as the gloved arm reached for them.

What happened next? The dream was slipping… The images frosted over in her mind and she could feel them sliding from her grasp. They had grabbed him, yanked him from her side. She knew it was over. She couldn't face what came next. A crushing sorrow descended on her, the tears streaming down her face. And then she had woken up.

What had woken her? A scream. Her own scream. One word cutting through the blinding light and ringing clearly into the night. One word filled with all the pain, all the loss, all the hurt that one person could bear. Her own ravaged voice, desperate to bring back the one thing that meant everything to her, the one thing that would enable her to survive.

"Isaac!"

9. PREPARATION

By the time she got out of her physics lab, the last thing Alessa wanted to do was hang up flyers for the party. She had slept fitfully after that terrifying dream, unable to shake her anxiety until the first rays of dawn peeked through her bedroom window. When she'd finally fallen back asleep, there had only been a couple hours until morning, and though she couldn't remember any other dreams, she suspected that those feelings of panic and dread had chased her through the remainder of the night.

The worst part was that she hadn't even been able to talk to anyone about it. Janie unfortunately was assigned to a different lab session, so Alessa was forced to work with a stranger to complete the day's experiment. Mercifully, her partner took charge of manning the motion sensor and calculating the coefficient of restitution while Alessa stood on her stool and mindlessly bounced the basketball, leaving her alone with her thoughts.

She spent most of the lab mulling over what the dream might mean and why it had affected her so deeply. By that point she had already lost most of the details, so she focused on piecing the major elements together. Trapped, with the ghost, terror, sorrow, Isaac. It did sort of make sense when she broke it down.

Feeling trapped seemed to be one of the overriding themes of her life right now, in a variety of ways. Trapped at this school, trapped into participating in the sorority's nonsense, trapped in this world without her parents to guide her. She was even almost physically trapped whenever she saw the ghost lately, unable to move her feet. Yes, trapped was a feeling she was familiar with, and it was only logical that her subconscious might surface this feeling as literally being trapped in some kind of small recess.

The ghost had obviously also been a major player in her life lately. She'd been devoting most of her mental resources towards thinking about him – who he is, what he's feeling, why he's here – or trying to recover after he ransacked her emotional state. And there was always that strange yearning she felt to be close to him. That might have emerged in the dream as their physical closeness, being squeezed in that small place together, holding hands even.

The feelings of fear and despair also made sense. After all, she had just experienced these emotions both very acutely during her last encounter with the ghost, which was only a few days ago. And unfortunately those feelings were applicable to other parts of her life as well – the death of her parents, for example.

And the Isaac thing wasn't exactly inexplicable either. She had three names – Isaac, Albert, William – who were possibilities, so her mind just must have chosen one. Maybe she had latched onto Isaac since Janie had commented on it being an attractive name.

When she considered all this together, it also explained why she felt so unnerved by the dream. There were a lot of unexpected things going on in her life and a lot of emotional turmoil surrounding them. The dream had taken all those messy feelings and boxed them up into a neat little narrative, forcing Alessa to face all the negative emotions she'd been trying to suppress. Of course she would feel disturbed after having to face that head on, without any warning, in a dead sleep no less.

Alessa felt better after giving the dream some thought, but that didn't change the fact that she had lost hours of rest to its aftermath, and now she was tired. When her lab was over all she wanted to do was go home and take a nap, but instead she was obligated to deal with the flyers.

She trudged from the science building to Van Husen Hall, flyers in hand, half-heartedly thrusting one toward whomever she happened to pass. Inside Van Husen, she tacked a flyer to the bulletin board on the main floor and also the one in the basement café. She asked the student behind the register if it was okay to leave a stack of flyers on the counter, a request he cheerfully obliged while also pocketing a flyer himself. Having distributed half of her stack, Alessa decided that it was a good time for a break.

It was nearing lunchtime and Alessa of course had not eaten breakfast, so she decided to pick up a cup of soup from the vat in the corner of the café. Remembering the pathetic contents of her fridge, she also grabbed a handful of items to restock it – apples, individually wrapped cheeses, a pint of milk, and a box of cereal. Now at least she wouldn't have an excuse for not eating.

She paid for the items and took a seat at one of the small round tables to eat her soup. It was a thick, almost gelatinous chicken noodle that was lacking in vegetables and – she knew from prior experience – heavily salted and far too hot. She stirred to release some heat, then crushed a packet of complimentary crackers into the soup and sampled a spoonful, lightly burning the back of her throat as she swallowed. The bland crackers had done what she'd hoped and absorbed at least some of the salt flavor. It was passable. What more could she expect from Van Husen?

After finishing her pitiable lunch, Alessa decided to take a lap around the quad to distribute her remaining flyers. There were a few covered bulletin boards staked at odd intervals around the green along with a plethora of lampposts and, of course, mounting poles for the university's ubiquitous security cameras. Even if Alessa didn't pass a single soul as she lapped the quad, she should still be able to finish off her stack. It was technically prohibited to post flyers anywhere except on university-approved spaces like the bulletin boards, but in practice it was done all the time. Alessa was eager to get rid of her flyers and get home for a quick rest before her afternoon history lecture, so she decided to risk it. Anyway, she didn't see anyone in the immediate vicinity who looked official enough to reprimand her.

She headed for the bulletin board on the south end of the quad near the library. On her way she passed a group of three female students and handed them each a flyer with a perfunctory, "Party Saturday." She remembered Lizzie's admonition to invite "...lots of boys. *Cute* boys," and felt a small pang of guilt. Oh well. Was it her fault that all of the cute boys were apparently in class during her only flyering opportunity?

Reaching the bulletin board, she dropped the strap of her backpack from one shoulder and swung the bag forward to where she could reach the front pockets, withdrawing the stapler and tape from the larger compartment. She righted her backpack and held a flyer against the bulletin board, securing it in place with the stapler. Taking a quick glance around to make sure no one was looking, Alessa reshuffled some of the other printouts on the board to slightly obscure the flyer she'd just posted. The fewer people who showed up to this party the better.

Alessa headed toward a lamppost about ten yards past the bulletin board. She taped a flyer at eye level, then crossed the cobblestone path toward a camera pole another ten yards away. Alessa worked her way in a loop around the quad, crisscrossing the path as she encountered any surface she could stick a flyer to. There were only a handful of other students out and she made sure to give flyers to them as well.

At last Alessa was down to one final printout. She surveyed the quad and was satisfied with the job she'd done. A little too satisfied, in fact – her subtle attempts at sabotage stood no chance against the barrage of colorful papers waving in the brisk fall breeze as far as the eye could see. It actually looked rather festive with all that pink, yellow, and blue.

Alessa turned to the mounted camera beside her, staring quizzically into the lens as she approached the base. She wondered if anyone was actually watching. There had to be thousands of hours of footage logged across the absurd number of cameras on campus – too much to actually review in its entirety. She decided the university was probably just storing all the recordings in a vault somewhere in case one was ever needed for another lawsuit. Once again, Alessa mused that the whole practice really seemed unnecessary. Unnecessary and unnerving.

Reaching the camera mount, Alessa tore off an inch of tape and held her only remaining flyer against the pole. She pressed the tape down and was about to release a satisfied sigh when she heard a deep male voice behind her.

"Excuse me, miss. This is a violation of university policy. I'm going to have to ask you to remove that."

Alessa swore under her breath. She'd never heard of anyone actually getting in trouble for flyering. Of course she had to be the first. She prepared her best perplexed face – she had decided her best option was to feign ignorance – and turned around to face her accuser.

She was surprised to find not the burly university official she was expecting, but a student. In fact, he was what Lizzie Green would have called, "a cute boy," which Alessa thought was probably an understatement. He was tall and dark and – oh, she hated to say it – handsome, with neat black hair and deep brown eyes. He flashed a mischievous white smile which glowed against his tan skin.

He introduced himself in a slightly higher octave than before. "Nikhil. Sorry to scare you. I couldn't help myself." He gestured at the expanse of the quad, the multicolored papers seemingly adorning every available surface. "Is this all your handiwork?"

Alessa laughed sheepishly. Was this attractive guy really flirting with her? It'd been a while since that had happened – she flushed as she tried to think of something clever to say in response. "Yeah, that was all me." Fantastic.

Nikhil smiled nonetheless. "So, will you be at this party –" he paused expectantly, motioning towards her with his hand.

Alessa picked up on his meaning. "Alessa. And yes, I will absolutely be there." Ugh, so boring! She tried to make up for her inadequate banter with a smile, a real one for once.

"All right then, I'll have to look for you." He flashed that smile again and Alessa's grin brightened. "So do you have any more of those left?" He indicated the pink flyer she'd just hung.

Alessa quickly peeled it off the pole and held it out to him. "Why don't you take this one? You'll save me from adding yet another infraction to my colorful record." He laughed. *Finally* she'd come up with something worthwhile.

Nikhil folded up the paper and slipped it into his pocket. With a coy smile he turned to go, locking eyes with her one last time. "See you tomorrow, Alessa."

"Bye," she replied, unable to wipe the goofy grin from her face as he sauntered down the path away from her. Perhaps this party wouldn't be so bad after all.

10. PREENING

The next evening, Alessa found herself staring critically at her own reflection in the full-length mirror that was affixed to her closet door. It'd been over a year since she'd last devoted more than minimal effort to her appearance, and unfortunately one enthusiastic hour of preening could not quite make up for all that neglect.

She stepped closer to the mirror, squeezing gently at her skin with her fingertips. One by one the little bits of goo popped to the surface and she wiped them away with a tissue. Satisfied with her efforts, she stood back to observe the results. She was mildly horrified by the splotchy mess she'd made of her face, but she figured the redness would subside in the hour before people started arriving for the party. Hopefully.

Alessa had spent the last 24 hours anticipating the upcoming party in a way that she hadn't felt about anything lately. She supposed it was due to Nikhil and his promise to seek her out that evening. She thought about his dark almond-shaped eyes and warm smile, his broad shoulders and unmistakable air of confidence. For the first time in months, she felt slightly giddy.

She had spent much of the day replaying her short conversation with Nikhil over and over in her mind, grimacing at her lack of charisma. She thought about how she could have responded better – should she have been more coy? More witty? More playful? She knew she was probably overthinking it, but she was determined to be mentally prepared to turn on the charm the next time she got the opportunity.

She wanted to feel confident tonight, but her recent lack of practice conversing with the opposite sex made her wary. Even before everything had happened with her parents, she'd always found herself clamming up around guys, remaining quiet when she was usually outspoken. As someone who usually felt relatively self-assured and in control, she found her inability to act normally around guys extremely frustrating. And in the past year, it'd only gotten worse. She'd hoped she would feel better tonight if she *looked* better, so she had spent the last hour conducting a mini-makeover to boost her spirits.

Overall, her plan had somewhat succeeded. Alessa at least had to admit that she could be much worse off. Her skin had always been less prone to blemishes than that of most teenagers, so her complexion was still relatively clear even after months of neglect. She could have used a little more exfoliation in all that time, but she'd done her best to make up for it with a vigorous scrubbing earlier that evening and her skin glowed faintly as a result.

Being out of practice with makeup, she'd kept her beauty routine minimal – just a heavy coat of mascara, a thin stroke of eyeliner, and a swipe of shimmer eye shadow in a neutral beige tone. Though the technique was simple, the result was actually rather striking. Her bright green eyes smoldered and were the obvious focal point of her face.

Which was fortunate, since she was in desperate need of a haircut. Regrettably she hadn't thought of it until well after the nearest salon had closed, so instead she'd taken extra care in blow drying her long layers into smooth, shiny tresses. The blowout helped to hide most of her split ends and she was reasonably certain that no one else would notice the damage. From a distance, her hair actually looked glossier than she remembered it ever being. Perhaps all those months away from heated styling tools had done some good.

Alessa curled her fingertips and held them up to her face for a closer look. Her nails, as usual, were bitten down to nothing and her cuticles were peeling from dryness. She certainly didn't have the time – or the patience – to polish them this close to the start of the party, so she turned instead to the fireplace mantle where she had stashed a bottle of lotion next to her hairbrush and makeup bag. Squeezing some into her hands, she massaged it into her fingertips. Better already.

Alessa turned back to her closet and groaned. Clothes were going to be the most difficult part. She hadn't bought anything new since before her parents died, even though she'd dropped a good 15 pounds in the interim. She unfolded a pair of dark-wash skinny jeans and slipped into them. They bunched unflatteringly in the back and hung lower on her hips than intended. At one time, Alessa had been thin but curvy, a tall well-muscled athlete with a strong yet feminine physique. Now she was more angular than anything, and she found herself missing the rounded behind she'd once cursed.

She tried another pair of jeans, old ones that she had not worn much after accidentally shrinking them in the dryer a few years ago. They fit a bit more snugly than the last pair and were definitely more flattering in the rear. She decided to stick with these, as she didn't have many more options in the denim department.

Alessa wasn't sure what kind of top to wear. She'd normally put on a light sweater at this time of year, but with hundreds of people crowding into the house, it was bound to be warmer than she was used to. She pulled out a sleeveless printed blouse that was fitted around the waist and slipped it over her head. It hung loosely from her shoulders like a sack, the cinched waist doing nothing to improve the appearance. No good. Alessa stripped it off and tossed it on the bed.

Working her way through half the tops in her closet, Alessa found fault with each one in turn. Too boring, too loose, too old, too frumpy. The pile of discarded shirts on the bed grew. She let out an exasperated sigh as the rhythmic bass from the stereo system downstairs started to bump through the floor. Guests would be arriving any minute.

There was a knock at the door and Janie poked her head in.

"Hey, are you almost –" she paused midsentence as she took in the mound of clothes on the bed, "…ready…" she trailed off. Janie sniffed the air with a small twitch of her nose and considered for a moment.

Suddenly her face lit up as it dawned on her what Alessa had been up to. "Perfume… makeup… clothes… Oh my God, you met a guy!"

Alessa smiled abashedly. "Guilty."

"Ooooh!" Janie squealed. "What's his name? Where did you meet him? When did this happen? And why haven't you told me about this yet?!" Janie was spewing questions faster than Alessa could take them in.

Alessa laughed. "Okay, okay… slow down! His name is Nikhil and I met him yesterday while flyering on the quad."

Janie clapped with excitement. "And is he cute?" She drew out the last word for emphasis.

"Very."

Janie laughed and clapped her hands some more. Alessa blushed. Practically skipping to Alessa's side, Janie crossed the room and stood facing the mirror alongside her. "So what are you going to wear? I hope not that…" She scowled with disdain at the cheap sequined tank top Alessa had on at the moment. "It's skank-a-licious."

Alessa laughed and shook her head. "I honestly don't know *what* to wear. I have nothing!" She motioned at the pile on her bed.

Janie held up the first few shirts off the top of the heap and eyed them critically. "I see what you mean." Tossing the shirts back into the pile, she blurted, "Hold on a minute," and dashed from the room.

A moment later, Janie returned carrying an emerald green v-neck tee in a smooth thin cotton. "I know it's just a t-shirt, but the fit is really nice and since we have similar coloring, I think it would work on you. Actually, with your eyes, the color might just be perfect. Try it on." She tossed the shirt in Alessa's direction.

Alessa caught it and peeled off the sequined number. Once she slipped the t-shirt over her head, she knew at once that Janie, as usual, had been right. The shirt's slinky knit clung to her body in all the right places and the color more than complemented her eyes, which were glowing like gems. Alessa was pleased with the overall effect – even though she'd put quite a bit of time into getting ready this evening, with such understated clothes and simple makeup she looked effortlessly beautiful. This must be how Lizzie Green felt all the time.

"Hot." Janie, apparently, was pleased too. "This Nikhil doesn't know what he has coming."

Alessa laughed as she slipped on a supple pair of flat knee-high boots, one of the few pre-college splurges she'd indulged in with her parents' inheritance. She could smell the rich brown leather as she slid the zipper closed. "Definitely not. You can imagine what I looked like when we met yesterday afternoon. It's a miracle he even wanted to talk to me."

"Nah, you don't give yourself enough credit," Janie replied. In a mock announcer voice, she continued. "Alessa Khole, breaking hearts from this life to the next!" Janie laughed heartily at her own joke.

Alessa's amusement faded as she was stung by a sudden pang of guilt deep in her gut. She hadn't thought about the ghost even once since meeting Nikhil.

Janie noticed the change in Alessa's expression and suppressed her mirth. "What's wrong?" she asked, inquisitive.

Alessa didn't really know what was wrong. She certainly had no obligations to this ghost but, strangely, for some reason Alessa felt like she was betraying him. It didn't make any sense.

Alessa tried to put on a smile for Janie. "It's nothing. I just… realized I forgot to put on deodorant." She crossed the room to grab the stick of antiperspirant on the mantle, eager to shield her face from Janie's inquiring eyes.

Alessa knew Janie wasn't fooled, but Janie let the topic drop nonetheless. Alessa was relieved. She had a hard enough time rationalizing her ridiculous thoughts about the ghost to herself, let alone trying to explain them to someone else.

Alessa had a nagging feeling that she was doing something wrong by seeing Nikhil, and the feeling had washed away all of the excitement that she'd been reveling in all afternoon. Now she just felt resentful. Why couldn't the ghost just let her be?

She swiped the stick under her arms – for the second time that evening – and put it back on the mantle. Alessa swallowed her frustration and tried to compose herself before she turned around to face Janie again. She was going to put the ghost out of her mind and enjoy herself. There was no reason she couldn't go to a party, have a couple beers, and flirt with an attractive guy like any normal college freshman, at least for one night. She owed it to herself to try.

A shriek of glee pierced the air from downstairs and Alessa took the opportunity to change the subject. "Sounds like the drinking games have begun."

Janie picked up on her cue and obliged, smiling good-humoredly. "Ready for a little action?"

"You bet." Alessa took one last look in the mirror and headed out the door towards the party.

11. REVELRY

Alessa and Janie descended the stairs into the main foyer and took in the scene. The front door was propped open invitingly, cool air streaming over the threshold and regulating the temperature inside. Alessa observed that the house was already starting to feel sweaty and humid in a gross sort of way; she was glad she'd opted for the t-shirt over a sweater.

To the right of the steps in the living room, the couches were pushed back against the walls and the DJ – who Alessa recognized as a fraternity brother from one of the other houses on campus – had set up a pair of massive speakers with thick cords running to his laptop. He was playing dance music so loudly that Alessa could practically see the speakers vibrating. There was a large hand-painted sign hung on the wall that read, "Happy 40th Zeta Epsilon Pi!" Nearby a group of sisters and a few male guests stood chatting and swigging back gulps of what Alessa could only assume was the cheap, flavorless beer that always seemed to be served at student-funded events.

To the left, there was a rowdy game of beer pong underway on the dining room table. Two of Alessa's housemates – maybe-Sara and another sophomore who lived down the hall – had two very dumbfounded guys down to their very last cup, with only two cups missing from their own side. Alessa looked on with amusement as maybe-Sara sunk the ball in the last cup – the guys had probably thought the two sorority girls would be an easy win, but no such luck at Z-E-Pi. Alessa felt a small swell of pride, which surprised her immensely.

There were two kegs stashed to the side of the dining room table, a giant bag of red cups balancing between them. Alessa guessed someone had made a trip to the bulk discount store earlier that day to stock up.

Janie saw Alessa eyeing the beer. "Shall we?"

"We shall." As the beer pong teams set up for another match, Alessa and Janie made their way past the table to the kegs and each grabbed a cup off the top of the stack. The light yellow beer streamed from the tap, foaming up the moment it touched the white interior of the plastic cup. Alessa's foam nearly overflowed and she took a quick sip to prevent the spill. As expected, it was bland and flavorless except for an unpleasant hint of sour. Ugh, she could already imagine the stale taste that would pervade her tongue tomorrow morning.

Janie took a sip of her own beer, her face contorting into the same grimace as Alessa's. "Nothing but the best for Z-E-Pi," she joked.

Alessa smiled and shook her head, choking down another frothy sip. At least the beer was cold. For now. "Come on, let's go find somewhere to sit."

Janie gave Alessa a disapproving look. Alessa knew that sitting alone in a corner was not Janie's idea of a party, but she followed Alessa into the living room nonetheless. Alessa plopped onto the couch as far from the speakers as possible and Janie perched on the arm cushion next to her.

For the next hour or so, Janie and Alessa sat devotedly sipping their beers, making occasional small talk with the few sisters who stopped by to say hello. They finished their first beers and each started a second. The house started to fill up, another group of students pouring through the door every few moments and heading straight for the kegs. Before long the party was in full swing.

Her field of vision now entirely obscured by bodies, Alessa decided to stand up and get a better view. There were students packed in every direction, mingling and laughing and guzzling their cups. Shrieks of triumph sounded from another raucous game of beer pong, the talented Z-E-Pi team reigning over their next victim no doubt. The air buzzed with the din of voices shouting over the aggressively bumping music, the crowd's bodies swaying almost involuntarily to the beat. Alessa could see a few small groups slipping into a full-out gyrate, which was slowly starting to spread to neighboring circles.

The atmosphere had ripened with the musky human smell of sweat. An already intoxicated male guest leapt onto the couch and thrust his red cup skyward, splashing beer in every direction as he bellowed a hearty, "Z-E-Pi!" at the top of his lungs. Most of the guests cheered in response, then resumed their carousing. Yes, it appeared the party had begun.

Janie poured the last drops of beer number two down her throat and turned to Alessa. "Ready for round three?"

Alessa threw back the remainder of her own beer with a grimace. She was going to need to choke down a lot more of these to make this chaos enjoyable. "Let's do it."

Janie led the way towards the dining room, weaving her way in between pockets of dancing students. Alessa followed in her wake, apologizing to everyone she bumped into as if they could hear her over the noise. As they crossed through the foyer, Alessa paused at the threshold of the door to take in some fresh air, and at that exact moment, Nikhil came striding up the steps onto the porch.

"Alessa!" He spotted her inside the doorway immediately and started heading her way.

"Nikhil. Hey. You came." Great opening. She took a deep breath and tried to swallow her awkwardness, taking a step in Nikhil's direction. Then she remembered Janie heading for the beers. "One sec," she said to Nikhil. She turned around and shouted Janie's name. Janie was almost to the dining room but she heard Alessa and stopped, swinging around in the direction of Alessa's voice. Alessa waved for Janie to come over.

Janie's face lit up when she saw Nikhil. "Nice work," she murmured to Alessa under her breath.

Alessa suppressed a laugh and turned back to Nikhil. "Nikhil, this is Janie. Janie, Nikhil." They shook hands.

"Nice to meet you, Janie."

"Likewise."

Another tall, handsome male loped up the steps behind Nikhil, playfully punching him in the shoulder with a sarcastic, "Thanks for waiting for me, bro."

Nikhil turned to his friend and laughed, and Alessa found herself blatantly staring at the two of them. They looked like they'd stepped out of some sort of preppy catalog that catered to the wealthy and privileged – twin Adonises, one dark and one fair. She normally found the popped collar look a little over-the-top, but somehow these two managed to pull it off with ease. They were quite possibly the most attractive men Alessa had ever been within touching distance of.

Nikhil turned back to Alessa and Janie, completely oblivious to the effect he and his friend were having on them. Janie was practically drooling. "This is Josh, from my water polo team." Water polo. That explained it. Josh extended a hand in their direction and Alessa and Janie introduced themselves in turn.

Alessa was fumbling with how to proceed when Janie stepped in to save her. "So, we were just about to get a beer. Would you gentlemen like to join us?"

"Sounds great," Nikhil replied.

"Follow me." Janie led the way with Alessa, Nikhil, and Josh in tow.

Reaching the dining room, Alessa saw that the beer pong tournament had deteriorated and Lizzie Green was attempting to organize a battle-of-the-sexes game of flip cup. She was clearly tipsy, which only brought out her good-natured bubbliness. She spotted Janie and Alessa and waved them over. "Janie! Alessa! Come play with us! And bring your –" her eyes widened when she saw Nikhil and Josh, "– friends…" Fantastic. Just what Alessa needed – Lizzie Green as competition.

Janie, however, didn't seem concerned. She turned to Alessa and the guys with an enthusiastic, "Let's play!" Her competitive side sometimes overshadowed her better judgment, in Alessa's opinion at least.

Alessa begrudgingly followed Janie to the female side of the table, hiding her displeasure as best she could. Janie grabbed two more cups for Nikhil and Josh and filled them each a quarter of the way with the now-warm beer while Alessa did the same with the girls' cups. Lizzie turned to the new players. "I assume you all know how to play? When it's your turn, chug your beer, set the cup down on the table, and tap it from the bottom to flip it upside down."

"We got it," Alessa replied, gritting out a smile.

As the game initiated, the eight players on each team held their cups aloft, tapping them together with their opponents across the table. Janie stood across from Josh, beaming, and Alessa lined up with Nikhil. She noted with satisfaction that Nikhil was looking only in her direction.

Everyone placed their cups on the table in front of them, goading the other side with cheerful trash talk and spirited promises of defeat. Lizzie, who was to start them off, viciously stared down the guy across from her until he looked visibly shaken – apparently the combination of so much beauty and so much ferocity being flung at him at once was a little too much to handle. She raised her glass to his to signal the start of the game, her opponent wavering for a moment before he realized what was happening. It was all Lizzie needed. She threw back her beer without pause, slammed her cup to the table, and deftly used her fingertip to flip it on its head in one graceful swipe. Perfect, as usual.

The game continued down the line, each side cheering on their own players as they downed their beers and flipped their cups with varying degrees of success. When the game reached Alessa, the girls had a small lead and she was determined not to jeopardize it. She chugged her beer in one swift motion and placed her cup on the table, the lip overhanging the edge of the wood. Alessa tapped it gently with her finger, but the cup just fell over and rolled on its side. In a moment of panic she glanced across the table at Nikhil; he was only now starting to guzzle his beer. She quickly reset her cup and hit it with a little more force. Success!

Janie finished off the game with a win for the women's team, to much applause and uproar. The men immediately demanded a rematch. After another close round the men proved victorious, necessitating a tie breaker. When the men won once again, they suggested mixing up the teams and everyone happily obliged.

After four rounds of flip cup – bringing Alessa's tally for the night to somewhere around three beers – the room started to spin, in a pleasant way. The excitement of the game had brought out a zeal in her that she hadn't felt in very long time, and the adoring looks that Nikhil was sending in her direction didn't hurt either. Alessa felt deliriously happy for the first time in over a year. Damn the ghost. Tonight she was having fun.

There was a break in the action as the first keg tapped out and a couple of the guys volunteered to set up the second one. Janie took the opportunity to suggest that the four of them go dance, which sounded like a fabulous idea to Alessa. Alessa looked inquisitively at Nikhil and he consented with an affable shrug. Janie didn't even give Josh a choice. She grabbed his wrist and dragged him behind her, and he acquiesced with an amused smile. Alessa and Nikhil followed.

Finding a clearing in the living room, Alessa noticed that the pounding music no longer felt oppressive, but freeing. She could feel the beat pulse through her body and she let it move her as it pleased. She danced with abandon, completely unselfconsciously, and it felt good. She felt sexy, alive.

Nikhil and Alessa were pressed together ever closer by the crowd, their bodies moving as one in time with the music. Alessa could feel the hair sticking to the back of her neck as her skin started to glisten, but she didn't care. She threw her arms up and tossed her head with the beat, reveling in the moment.

Nikhil gently placed his hands around Alessa's hips, seemingly mesmerized. The crowd swelled and they were pressed together once more, his arms wrapped around her waist, her hands on his taut swimmer's chest and shoulders. He leaned over, nudging his face so close to hers that she could feel the heat rising off his skin. Alessa parted her lips and looked up at Nikhil, preparing to surrender to her body's impulses.

But instead of the dark brown eyes she expected, she saw only blue. Unfathomable, sparkling blue, glittering with facets of ocean and sky, boring deep into her soul and clutching at her heart. Once again, a single word rose in the back of her throat – Isaac – and she knew this night was over.

12. RESOLUTION

Alessa pushed Nikhil away with a start. She wasn't sure if what she'd just seen was the ghost himself or just a figment of her guilty imagination, but either way, she couldn't go through with the kiss.

Nikhil looked at Alessa, bewildered. Fortunately, Alessa was too tipsy to feel more than a tinge of embarrassment at her own behavior, but she did feel sorry for the hurt she saw in Nikhil's eyes, which were brown once again.

"I'm sorry, I can't," was all she said, and she pushed past him, heading for the stairs. Janie noticed Alessa's abrupt departure and made to follow, but Alessa waved her off. She needed to be alone.

Bounding up the stairs, Alessa stumbled and caught herself against the rail. The room was spinning, but not so pleasantly anymore. She staggered into her bedroom and closed the door behind her, sliding down to the floor with her back against the wood until she sat on the carpet, her knees pressed against her chest.

What was going on in her head? She was having an amazing time – the best she could remember having since her parents died – flirting and dancing with a nice, incredibly good-looking guy who was clearly interested in her, and instead of just *enjoying* it, for some reason she was fixated on some stupid phantasm that probably didn't even *exist.*

She cursed her own idiocy and hung her head in her hands. She'd definitely blown things with Nikhil. She couldn't imagine how she would face him tomorrow, or whenever she happened to see him next, if he even wanted to see her again. What must he be thinking right now? She couldn't bear to guess.

It was all the ghost's fault. Stupid Isaac. And there was that word again. When had she become so convinced of his name? And *why* couldn't she put him out of her head for *one night*? The whole situation frustrated her beyond belief.

Alessa felt nauseous. She crawled over to her fridge and pulled out a bottle of water, chugging half of it in one long gulp. Her stomach rumbled and she felt immediately worse. She needed food.

Still sitting on the floor, she reached up and grabbed the box of cereal on top of the minifridge, scooping a handful of dry flakes to her mouth. She chewed and swallowed, repeating the process until she no longer felt the urge to spew.

Alessa sat on the floor with her legs splayed out in front of her, her back slouched against the side of the fridge. She put the cereal box down. This was pathetic. She couldn't believe she'd allowed a *ghost* to drive her to this sorry state.

Alessa realized in that moment that the only way she was ever going to get past this obsession was to get to the bottom of the mystery. She needed some clue as to what might be driving him to haunt her, to know who the ghost was and how he had died. Only then would she be able to make some sense of this strange situation and finally move on with her life.

She looked at the clock. Almost 1 AM. It dawned on Alessa that the library was open 24 hours, and she already knew where the records she needed were located. She resolved to put an end to this charade this very night if she could.

Alessa pulled a warm sweatshirt over her head and tossed her laptop into her backpack along with the half-empty bottle of water. She was dreading having to sneak out through the party when she remembered the rarely-used narrow second staircase that led directly to the kitchen. She headed that direction and was able to escape out the back door having only encountered a handful people who were raiding the sorority's pantry for late-night snacks.

It was frostier out than Alessa had expected, but between her strong buzz and heavy sweatshirt, she felt mostly impervious to the cold. The back of the house was dark, which suited Alessa just fine. She stuck to the shadows as she skirted her way around to the front of the house, towards the path that led to the quad.

As she rounded the corner of the front porch, she heard rustling and voices a few yards off to the side, in the darkness near a large tree. She caught a glimpse of a couple of campus security guards hustling a tall student away from the house. Alessa gasped as she realized the student was Nikhil.

His nose was bleeding and he looked defiant, but scared. Had he gotten into a fight after she'd deserted him? She didn't know him very well, but it still seemed out of character for him. She supposed people were known to do strange things when they were drunk and upset. She wanted to help, but her presence would probably only make things worse. She put it out of her mind and continued on.

Alessa cut across the unlit lawn and leapt a low hedge to join the path, far enough from the house that she was sure no one would see her. The last thing she needed was to try to explain to one of her sorority sisters why she was trekking to the library in the middle of the night.

Alessa reached the library in a few minutes time. As she expected, it was mostly deserted except for a handful of hardcore studiers dispersed at different tables throughout the building. She felt slightly delinquent as she dizzily made her way towards the local history section on the third floor, where she knew the old record books were stored. It seemed somehow inappropriate to be intoxicated in this somber old place. Alessa hoped the other students were too engrossed in their studies to notice her.

On her previous visit, the last entry Alessa had read was the one from 1908, where she'd learned of Isaac Mason's sister, Josephine. Knowing that the university had purchased the house sometime in the 1930s, she decided to grab the four volumes documenting 1900 to 1939 to see if she could learn anything more of the house's history between the time of Isaac's arrival and the university's acquisition.

Alessa opened the first book to 1909, scanning the page for the right address as the words swam lazily across her vision. Trying to shake off her stupor, she flipped hastily through the remainder of the book, but found no mention of 33 Mason Manor that year. She moved on to the next volume.

The first half of this book was useless as well, and staring at the tiny letters was starting to give Alessa a headache. She was beginning to think she wouldn't find anything that decade when she came across an entry in 1917:

Mason Manor, No. 33. New Owner, William Mason, as of May 3rd. Residents: None.

So in 1917 when – according to her previous notes – Isaac Mason would have been 17 years old, his family vacated their home and transferred ownership of the property to Isaac's uncle, William, who appeared to have declined to move in or rent it out given the lack of residents recorded in the entry. Alessa noted this information on her laptop and continued reading. She pressed through the rest of that volume and onto the next, not finding any additional entries until 1933:

Mason Manor, No. 33. New Owner, Eastern State University, as of September 4th. Residence converted for office use.

Alessa noted that there were entries for other properties recording when they were converted to residential rentals or office space, and there was no such log for 33 Mason Manor prior to this one in 1933. From what she could tell, it sounded like the house had stood empty from 1917 until the university acquired it in 1933.

Alessa tried to list the plausible explanations for this series of events in her head. She thought perhaps it was possible that the family had just moved away and sold the property to William. That didn't explain why he had chosen not to live there or at least to rent it out to another family, though she supposed that perhaps he was wealthy enough that an empty second home wasn't a concern.

Inspecting her notes, Alessa remembered something vague that the librarian said in the article that Janie had clipped, something about "the passing of a wealthy family." If Isaac's family had died, that could provide a sound rationale for why William didn't live there. Maybe the house was still damaged from whatever tragedy had struck them, or maybe William just couldn't bring himself to do it. It might have been too painful to be in the house where he'd lost his brother's entire family. And it would also explain why he eventually relinquished his family's farm to the university, since it wasn't going to do him much good sitting there abandoned.

Of course, with this little information to go on, it was impossible to know which of these theories might be correct, or if there was another explanation entirely. But Alessa had a hunch.

She felt fairly certain now that Isaac was indeed the ghost. He seemed to be the only possibility given that William had apparently lived well past his teenage years, and Albert, having fathered two children, presumably had as well. It also seemed like an uncanny coincidence that all record of Isaac's family mysteriously vanished at the same time when Isaac would be the right age to fit the description of the ghost she was seeing. The simplest explanation was that they had tragically died, leaving the property to William, who was too haunted by their memory to make use of the house. And the simplest explanation was usually right.

It was two in the morning and Alessa's buzz was slowly twisting into a dull throb in her temples. She'd probably learned as much about the ghost – about Isaac – as she could on this particular night. She decided to return home and sleep off her impending headache.

As she packed up her belongings, Alessa hoped that this new knowledge would be enough to lay her recent preoccupation with the ghost to rest. For the sake of her sanity, she at least had to try. If she hadn't known it before, the evening's events had made it abundantly clear that her fixation was getting in the way of her life, and it wasn't healthy.

There was nothing she could do for Isaac. His life was in the past, and she would have to let him go. Now it was time for Alessa to take care of herself.

13. CONNECTION

Laying on her stomach with her face pressed into the pillow, Alessa squeezed her eyelids together, but to no avail. The relentless drumming in her head had kept her awake the better part of the morning, and the bright light creeping in her bedroom window was only magnifying the sharp pains surging through her skull. All she was asking was for a couple more hours of sleep. She knew she was just delaying the inevitable; eventually she would have to face the debacle of the night before. But maybe not quite yet.

She closed her eyes for a few more minutes, but it was no use. Until she got some water and food in her system, Alessa would never get comfortable enough to fall back asleep. Covering her head with a blanket to block out the sun, Alessa blindly reached out from her bed, groping the floor for her backpack. She withdrew the half-empty bottle of water from the night before and tossed the covers from her face with a groan.

She sat up and took a tentative sip. Her mouth had been seized by a dry, sour rot, a taste which mingled unpleasantly on her tongue with the plasticky lukewarm water. After downing the remainder of the bottle, Alessa lay back in bed and draped an arm across her eyes. She'd known last night that she was going to regret all that beer, and she'd been right.

Alessa cringed as her memory of running out on Nikhil surfaced, the flush returning to her cheeks as she recalled his dismayed expression. How could she ever explain her behavior in a way that didn't seem absurd or ridiculous? He would never understand.

She was glad, though, that she'd decided to go to the library last night. Knowing that the ghost was Isaac Mason had at least answered some of Alessa's questions, and she no longer felt the same compulsion that she once had. If Isaac had lost his entire family in some tragedy, it certainly explained why he hadn't moved on, and as long as Alessa understood where he was coming from, she thought she would eventually be able to peacefully coexist. She just needed to figure out how to block out the feelings he incited in her, and then she'd be able to ignore Isaac during their little encounters the same way that he always ignored her.

Alessa fetched the box of cereal from on top of the fridge and tumbled back into bed. She would have preferred something hot and greasy, but unfortunately dry corn flakes were the best she could do without slogging to the cafeteria. She munched away, breathing slowly, staying as still as possible to avoid jolting her aching head.

She lay back down after consuming a satisfying amount of cereal and felt immediately relieved. She was able to take a 20 minute nap and felt significantly better when she woke up again. Not back to normal yet, but better.

Being a Sunday, Alessa could at least stave off any possible encounter with Nikhil by staying in her house for the day. She was sure Janie wouldn't mind bringing back some real food from the cafeteria whenever she ventured over that way, so Alessa decided to stay put and focus on getting some work done, namely an upcoming term paper for her ethics class. Despite the sustenance and rest, though, she still felt gross. She needed to brush her teeth and shower before she could even think about being productive.

Alessa felt disoriented when she finally got out of bed and headed to the bathroom. Her equilibrium was off, and she felt like she was wandering in a daze. This hangover couldn't wear off soon enough.

When she got to the bathroom, she found that both showers were occupied, and neither of them had freed up by the time she'd finished brushing her teeth. She decided to swing by Janie's room to wait.

Janie was awake, barely. She had been half-dozing, watching an old movie on her laptop in bed when Alessa entered. She scooted over to make room for Alessa to sit adjacent to her. "Morning, sunshine. You look almost as good as I do." Even with a hangover, her sarcasm was unrelenting.

Alessa just moaned in response and rested her head on Janie's shoulder.

"I know, I know." Janie patted Alessa's leg sympathetically. "Do you want to talk about what happened with you last night?"

Alessa moaned again.

"It seemed like things were going well with Nikhil..." Janie prodded. "Why did you freak out?"

Rousing her head from Janie's shoulder, Alessa released a long sigh. "I don't know... We were about to kiss, and then I looked up and all I saw were Isaac's eyes, and I just couldn't go through with it."

"Isaac? The ghost?"

"Yeah, I went to the library last night and confirmed that it's him. Isaac Mason, 17 years old when his family died in 1917." Alessa dropped her hands in her lap definitively. Looking at Janie, she qualified, "At least I think. The records aren't exactly exhaustive."

"That must have been a sight. I'm sure the library staff appreciates having inebriated students stumbling through the stacks in the middle of the night."

Alessa laughed in agreement, then remembered that she'd wanted to ask Janie about what had happened to Nikhil after she left the party. "Oh, I wanted to tell you, on my way to the library I saw Nikhil in trouble with campus security. His nose was bleeding like he'd gotten in a fight or something. Did that happen here?"

Janie looked surprised. She thought for a moment. "I don't think I saw anything. After you left, Nikhil stormed out and

Josh went to follow him. I don't think I saw either of them again after that."

"Sorry." Alessa couldn't believe she'd managed to ruin Janie's night as well.

Janie shrugged. "Eh, it was fun while it lasted." After a moment, Janie closed the lid on her laptop and set it down on the bed. "I *really* don't feel like doing work today."

"Me either," Alessa agreed. Too bad she had that paper to tackle.

"What are your plans for the rest of the day?" Janie asked.

"I was going to shower and then attempt to get started on my ethics paper, but the showers are all full."

"Well, there's always the bathtub upstairs." Alessa knew Janie was half-joking – with only a tub, the attic bathroom was rarely used – but Alessa considered for a moment. A bath might be just what she needed.

"Hmm… I might actually go do that," Alessa replied.

"I was kidding."

"I know. But I could use a little detox, plus it will give me an excuse to put off work for another hour."

Janie reflected, and nodded her head. "Good point. Maybe I'll take one after you."

Alessa smiled. "I'll let you know how it is." With that, Alessa rose from Janie's bed and headed for the attic. She swung by the bathroom on her own floor to grab her towel and toiletries then climbed the small staircase to the attic level.

There wasn't much on this floor besides a locked storage space and the small bathroom. Stepping inside the tiny room felt like going back in time, as it was the only lavatory in the house that the university had decided not to modernize. The bathroom was very simply furnished with just the big white clawfoot tub in the center of the room, leaving only a few feet of space to maneuver on each side of the basin. A matching pedestal sink was positioned across from the foot of the tub, the same height as the brown chair rail molding. One glass and bronze wall sconce affixed to the ivory wall above the sink provided a dim light, but on the outer wall running alongside the bath, a high round porthole window set in a dormer shed plenty of sun across the black and white mosaic tile floor.

Alessa draped her towel over the side of the tub and opened the faucet. At first the water ran a little brown – sediment accumulated from disuse – but after a few moments, it was streaming in clear and hot. She plugged the drain and prepared to wait. As the bath filled, Alessa stepped around to the other side of the tub to peer out the window, her foot nudging something as she did so. She looked down and found a half-empty box of bubble bath. Well, apparently she wasn't the only one who used this bathroom.

She shook some of the bubble bath powder under the running water. The scent of lavender filled the room and a fluffy white foam floated to the surface of the water. The window began to fog from the heat flowing from the tap. When the water reached the halfway point, Alessa closed the faucet and stripped off her clothes, tossing them in a heap in the corner.

She touched one tentative toe to the water and immediately withdrew. It was *hot.* Steeling herself, she plunged the full foot into the water. It seared initially, but after a moment her skin adjusted. She stepped her other foot in and slowly lowered herself into the water, exhaling as she went. Again, the pain only lasted a few seconds before bliss overcame her.

Alessa sighed deeply and leaned back against the tub, sinking lower in the water until only her face rose above the bubbles. She closed her eyes, listening to the muffled underwater sounds that filled her submerged ears. It'd been years since she'd last taken a bath and she couldn't in that moment remember why – showering was a poor substitute indeed.

Alessa's body relaxed completely, the warm water loosening every ounce of tension from her muscles. Her headache subsided into the background as she breathed deeply and luxuriated in the soothing aroma of the froth hovering below her nose.

After a while the bath started to cool slightly. Alessa slowly peeled open her eyes, thinking of adding a little more hot water to prolong the experience. As her eyes adjusted, she thought she saw something out of place at the foot of the tub.

It was a hand, ever so faint, draped over the edge of the basin. Alessa stared, disbelieving, as the hand slowly materialized, stretching into a strong muscled forearm, a rolled-up white shirtsleeve, an elbow, a shoulder, a long narrow torso. Within a matter of seconds, there was Isaac in full form, sitting on the edge of the tub in his usual brown trousers and boots. He was facing away from Alessa, his fingers dabbling in the water behind him without disturbing even a single ripple on the surface.

Alessa felt the familiar mix of emotions – panic, sorrow, and that ever-present magnetic pull that she just couldn't seem to shake. She sat transfixed, staring at his apparition. He glanced towards the doorway every so often as if he were waiting for someone, his bright blue eyes lazily wandering across the wall in front of him to pass the time, lingering occasionally in the direction of the door. Alessa held still, waiting patiently for the image to fade, as she knew it soon would. She felt more in control than she had the last time, less unnerved, merely curious instead of overpowered. She was overcome with sympathy for this boy who had lost everything.

Isaac inclined his head toward the water, a few light brown locks of hair falling forward to obscure the blue of his eyes. He drew his fingertips from the water and extended his arm in the direction of the faucet, his head following the trajectory of his reach. As his view scanned across the head of the bathtub, he did a quick double-take. Alessa wondered what might have caught his attention.

She watched as his eyes widened and his mouth gaped, the same mixture of astonishment and apprehension flooding his expression that Alessa had felt so many times before. It was only then that she realized what he had seen. It was unmistakable – he was looking directly at Alessa.

As Alessa locked eyes with Isaac, all the old emotions came raging back, more powerful than ever before. She felt a crushing desperation to reach out to him, to clutch his hand as tightly as she had in that horrible dream and never let him go. She sat up slowly, never dropping her eyes from his, mustering all of the courage she possessed to inch her arm through the foam in his direction.

She could see him start to recoil as he understood what she was doing, but then something stopped him. He sat motionless, waiting, staring at her with anticipation, his chest rising and falling with each rapid breath. Alessa's fingertips closed the gap between them, now only a hairsbreadth away.

And then, suddenly, he was gone.

14. REVERSAL

Isaac sat down on the edge of the tub listening to the splash of the water as it spilled from the faucet into the basin. Steam warmed the chilly room as it rose from the bath and he breathed deeply, enjoying the respite from the long, cold winter they'd been enduring.

Isaac glanced at the door wondering when his sister, Josephine, would come upstairs. She had made a muddy mess of herself helping him in the stable with the horses. By the time they'd finished, she was shivering violently from head to toe and Isaac had offered to run her a bath to help her warm up and clean off. At almost ten years old she was more than capable of doing it herself, but Isaac liked to coddle his little sister in the few ways she would allow.

Jo was a bit of a tomboy, more interested in riding horses and playing outdoors than pampering herself. She was Isaac's constant companion, following him wherever he went and always wanting to be part of the action, even when she was too small to keep up. No one could blame Isaac if he'd been annoyed by her insistence on tagging along, but instead he found her enthusiasm endearing. She was almost like the brother he'd never had, but with a genuine sweetness that no boy could ever hope to match. There was no one in the world he loved more, and so he'd been glad to have this small opportunity to care for her by drawing a warm bath to ward off the winter's chill.

He unbuttoned his sleeve and rolled it up to the elbow, dangling his fingertips in the water behind him. While he waited for the tub to fill, he studied the image in the large mirror in front of him reflecting the round window on the opposite wall and the expanse of dry midwinter fields beyond. In a matter of weeks, it would be time for the farmhands to plow the long rows and sow this year's crops, a prospect that Isaac was dreading.

He'd lived in this same house on this same farm for almost as long as he could remember, and yet he'd never quite felt at home here. As much as he loved his family and appreciated the successful business his father was prepared to leave to him, something about staying here just didn't feel right to Isaac. Not to mention, he couldn't imagine anything more dull than another year of farming.

Isaac thought perhaps moving to the city might soothe his restlessness. There was so much going on there these days, so much progress passing them by at Mason Manor – new technology cropping up seemingly every week, revolutionizing the way people live. Isaac felt that if he could be a part of improving other people's lives, maybe it might ease the guilt he felt over abandoning his family, as he knew he one day surely would.

But for the moment at least, he was stuck here, watching plants grow. His only respite was the occasional mischief stirred up by Jo, and more recently, the mysterious manifestation he'd been seeing around the house.

Her appearances had started a couple months ago and never lasted more than a few moments. He would get a glimpse of a striking dark haired woman who always seemed to disappear around a corner before he could reach her. He'd called out to her, but to no avail – she didn't seem to hear him.

At first he thought that perhaps she was a new servant, but when he asked his mother if she'd hired anyone recently, she replied that she hadn't. In any case, the woman certainly didn't dress like any servant – or any*one* – that he'd ever seen. Isaac still wasn't quite sure if he was just stir-crazy and imagining the whole thing, but regardless, the presence had made the long winter much more interesting than in previous years and he was grateful at least for that.

Isaac glanced at the door once more and wondered what Josephine had gotten into now. The bath was nearly full and if she didn't come soon, the water would cool. Isaac thought perhaps it would be best to finish filling the tub once Jo was ready to get in so that it would still be hot when she did. He decided to close the tap while he waited for her to arrive.

Withdrawing his fingers from the water, Isaac reached back for the faucet handle, his long arm stretching across the tub.

As he swung his head around toward the tap, he thought he saw something out of the corner of his eye by the head of the bathtub. He looked back and – registering what he'd seen – immediately froze in place.

It was the woman, closer than she'd ever been before, and she was staring directly at him with shapely eyes that were greener than the richest of jewels. She sat in the tub, her head cocked curiously to one side, regarding him with narrowed eyes. Her expression conveyed a cross of marvel and what looked like concern.

Isaac's heartbeat quickened and he fought the urge to run. He stared back at the presence with wide eyes, his chest pounding as he gripped the rim of the tub ever harder. She was quite possibly the most beautiful creature he'd ever seen, but at the same time, the strangeness of the situation was more unsettling than anything.

Suddenly her expression changed. Her emerald eyes widened to match his and she locked her gaze directly onto Isaac's. She sat forward and he could see her hand reaching from below the water towards his own. For a moment he cowered, dismayed at the prospect of those translucent fingertips mingling with his own. But then he noticed the anguish stamped across her face, and he knew he couldn't leave.

Slowly the ghostly fingers inched nearer and nearer, her eyes never dropping his gaze. Thoughts raced through Isaac's head faster than he could process them – he'd never experienced anything so thrilling. He sat motionless but inside he was churning, his emotions a whirling eddy in a ferocious gale of anticipation, awaiting the crescendo when their fingertips would meet. She stretched toward him, nearly touching…

And then she was gone.

The apparition faded in an instant and Isaac let out a heavy gasp. He didn't realize he'd been holding his breath. His heart was still pounding as he slowly pried his fingertips from the edge of the tub. What had just happened? He could barely think – he felt almost dizzy.

He was certain now that he was not imagining the presence, or if he was, that his mind was well beyond the hope of repair. He honestly didn't know what to think anymore. Isaac was impatient to learn more about this ghost – or whatever she was – but he had no idea where to even start.

Before today he'd never even been able to capture her attention, and then once he finally had it, he'd missed his chance. Why hadn't he said something? With her startling green eyes locked on his face, he'd forgotten he had the ability to speak. He lamented his own inaction; in all likelihood, he'd never get another chance like that.

Isaac heard Josephine's ungraceful clomping up the attic stairs and tried to compose himself. He hadn't said anything to Jo about the presence for fear of frightening her. She rounded the corner into the tiny bathroom with an energetic leap and nearly knocked Isaac into the tub. He leapt up to regain his balance. "Whoa there! Since when are you so eager for a bath?"

Josephine beamed up at Isaac with big brown eyes and an eager grin. "Ma said I could bring the cat inside to play after I'm done."

Isaac couldn't help returning her innocent smile. The anxiety he'd been feeling a moment ago melted away. "All right, I'll leave you to it then. You should run the hot water a bit longer before you get in to warm it up." He headed for the door and mussed her tangled blonde hair on the way out.

Isaac made his way down the narrow attic stairs to his study on the second floor. He sat in the plush burgundy armchair by the fireplace, the only warm spot in the room. He ran one hand briskly through his hair then rested his elbow on the armrest, pondering his recent encounter.

He wasn't sure what to make of the presence. He supposed it might have been some sort of ghost but he didn't know how he might go about confirming that theory. He scanned the heavy bookshelves lining the wall for ideas.

Most of his collection was composed of thick leather-bound volumes on science and engineering, along with the requisite books about history and philosophy. He had only one work pertaining to ghost stories, but it was clearly a work of fiction; he didn't suppose it would be much use in unraveling the mystery of the presence. His eyes skimmed a row of science fiction novels, and one spine imprinted with the words "time machine" caught his attention. Perhaps she was a traveler from a distant future?

Sighing, Isaac realized that his speculation was hopeless. Until he could find a way to communicate with the woman, he'd never understand how she came to be. He stood and paced back and forth in front of the hearth.

This situation with the apparition was just one more brick of frustration to add to the growing wall that stood in the way of his starting his life. Even from his earliest childhood, Isaac had never been able to shake the feeling that he just didn't belong here, that something important was missing from his life and it was somehow his own fault. He'd always been obedient – studious, hardworking, kind – but yet he never felt like it was enough, never felt like anything he did could truly justify his own existence.

Isaac had never understood where these feelings of inadequacy had come from – his parents had never been anything less than loving and proud as far back as he could remember – but he'd harbored this discontentment with himself as long as he could remember. And now he was nearly a grown man, and every passing day saw him more and more eager to break free of the family farm and prove himself out in the world.

But at the same time, the thought of leaving his loved ones behind left his resolve wavering. And now this presence – and his ardent desire to learn who she was – was just one more thing tying him to Mason Manor. He didn't know how he'd ever disentangle himself from his current life enough to pursue what he knew he needed to do.

Isaac paced to the window, the frosty bite of winter pressing against him through the glass. His breath fogged in a small circle on the windowpane as he looked eastward out over the property, in the direction of the city. This many miles away he couldn't see the dense array of golden lights emanating from apartments and restaurants and offices, but he knew they were there, twinkling in the evening light. Isaac wondered what else he might be doing now if he were there, instead of in this solitary house on his family's vast estate.

The floor creaked in the hallway as Josephine descended from the attic and headed to the first floor. Isaac dismissed his wandering thoughts and turned his attention back to the presence. He wasn't sure how to proceed in uncovering more about her, but he was fairly certain that he wasn't going to trigger any epiphanies sitting in his study.

Isaac wondered if perhaps Jo had seen the presence as well. It was said that children were often more attuned to supernatural experiences. Maybe she had seen the woman but neglected to say anything, figuring that she'd just be scolded for making up fanciful stories. Isaac turned towards the door, intending to follow Jo downstairs and find out whatever she might know.

15. FRUSTRATION

The floorboards under Isaac's feet protested a loud creak with every step. The cold had seeped into every crevice of the house, and despite the diligent efforts of the servants flitting from room to room with wood, Mason Manor's many fireplaces did little to stave it off. He rubbed his hands together as he walked, exhaling occasionally into his clasped palms in an effort to bring the color back to his extremities.

He descended the main staircase slowly to the first floor. Reaching the foyer, he saw that his mother had made good on her promise to Josephine. Jo was sprawled out on the floor in the parlor to his right, gently stroking the brown tabby cat who usually lived in the barn. The cat was napping peacefully on the hearth in front of a blazing fire, a small bowl of milk not far from its side.

Isaac sat on the stiff sofa nearest Jo and she looked up at him with a relaxed smile. "Ma gave the kitty some milk while I took my bath."

"I see that," Isaac replied. "He must be relieved to get out of the cold." As Isaac spoke, the cat stretched out its paws and released a small contented sigh. Isaac wished his own problems could be so easily solved.

He thought for a moment about how to broach the subject of the presence. He wanted to be careful not to scare Josephine with the possibility of the house being haunted, but he needed to find out if she'd had any encounters with the woman he'd been seeing. He decided to use the book of ghost tales in his study to break the ice.

Isaac cleared his throat in a way that he hoped sounded natural. "I read a spooky ghost story while you were in the bath."

Jo perked up, her eyes wide. "What was it about?"

"About a woman who died in a big white farmhouse and haunted the new family who moved in."

"Ooooh." Jo was mesmerized. "Was she a mean ghost?"

Isaac pretended to think for a moment. "Well, not exactly. She never tried to hurt anyone, but she did appear out of nowhere and scare them sometimes."

Jo leaned in toward Isaac, whispering, "What did she do?"

Isaac leaned closer in and paused to build the suspense. Talking in a low voice, he said, "She would sneak up behind them… and when they least expected it… she would say… Boo!"

Jo jumped at his exclamation, then giggled wildly. The cat peeked at her with one eye and promptly went back to sleep.

"You scared me!" Still laughing, she punched him lightly in the shoulder.

Isaac smiled. "It was only a story."

"But maybe it was a real story!"

"Maybe it was in this very house!"

Jo squealed. "That would be so creepy! I'm glad I've never seen a ghost."

It didn't sound like Jo had had any experiences with the presence, but Isaac decided to press a little further to be sure. "Well maybe she hasn't decided to show herself to you just yet. In the story, sometimes the ghost would slam doors or knock things off the table when no one was looking. Did you ever notice anything strange happening in our house?"

Josephine screwed up her face in thought, then finally shook her head. "I don't think our house is haunted, Isaac. I think you're just trying to scare me!"

Isaac laughed. "I told you it was only a story. You're the one saying it's real."

"Well I changed my mind."

"Okay." Isaac smiled and rumpled her hair.

Jo returned his affection with a begrudging half smile. "Even if it was real, I wouldn't be afraid of any old ghost."

"I know you wouldn't." Satisfied, Jo turned back to the cat, tracing the long black stripe down its back with her fingertip.

Isaac hoped she'd never have to confirm that theory. He knew from experience that even when the ghost was a gorgeous young woman, it was still terrifying. There was just something so unnatural about a person appearing and disappearing at will that it was hard to feel anything but unnerved in her presence.

Jo stroked the cat for some time and Isaac watched her in silence, reflecting on how he might try to contact the presence. Suddenly Jo looked up at Isaac with an earnest face and asked, "Isaac, are you going to get married soon?"

Isaac was taken aback. "Wherever would you get that idea?"

"Because I heard you the other day, talking about a woman."

Isaac thought back – had he mentioned the presence to anyone else? No, he was certain he hadn't. How could Josephine know about her? "When? To whom?"

"A couple days ago. I came by your room in the morning to see if you were up yet, and you were talking in your sleep. You kept saying her name."

"What name?"

"Alessa."

Now Isaac was beyond confused. He didn't know anyone named Alessa. He didn't think he'd even heard that name before. Why would he be uttering it in his sleep? He didn't even remember having any unusual dreams lately. "That's odd. I don't even know anyone by that name…"

"Are you sure you're not fibbing me?" Josephine narrowed her eyes accusatorily.

Isaac reassured her. "How could I be secretly courting a woman? I never even leave the grounds!"

Jo considered for a moment and nodded her head in concession. "I guess that's true. You just sounded… I don't know. You sounded like you loved her."

Isaac smiled soothingly. "I promise, I don't know any Alessa and I'm not going anywhere anytime soon."

"Good. I don't want you to go."

Isaac's chest panged with guilt. More gently he said, "I have to go someday, Jo."

"But why?"

"Well, everyone has to grow up sometime. I may want to go to university and study science and become a great inventor. I couldn't do that if I stayed here, could I?"

"No… But why can't you just run the farm like Papa does?"

"I could, but… I just, well, I don't know if that's what I *want* to do. Don't you ever yearn to see the city?"

Jo scowled. "I like the farm."

"I like it, too. But I may want to spend a few years away, to work on my studies and find myself a wife. Wouldn't you like to have a sister?"

Looking down at the cat, Jo replied, "Only if she was fun."

Isaac smiled and took her small hands in his. Jo looked up at him. "Of course. And you know that when I go, I will miss you dearly and I will come back to visit you often."

Josephine loosed a small smile and appeared satisfied. Isaac let her go back to playing and headed up the stairs towards his study. He wondered again where the name Alessa might have come from. He tried to recall any dreams he'd had lately, but nothing came to mind.

Alessa. He rolled the name on his tongue and oddly enough it did feel familiar. *Had* he met an Alessa at some point? Perhaps he had read the name in a book or the newspaper. He couldn't pinpoint any particular instance, but obviously this name had gotten lodged in his subconscious at some point. Isaac made a mental note to keep an eye out for any Alessa references he might come across, in hopes of finding the source.

Alessa. No, that name just wasn't ringing any bells.

16. ANXIETY

Alessa cleared her throat audibly. She was standing at the open doorway of the office of the librarian, Mary Brighton. As might be expected for someone who chose to devote her life to books, she was engrossed in a thick volume and didn't seem to notice Alessa's presence. "Excuse me?" Alessa piped.

"Oh! Sorry, dear, I didn't notice you there." She gently closed her book and set it down on the desk. The librarian seemed to recognize Alessa. "Are you back to work on your paper about 33 Mason Manor?"

Alessa smiled brightly. "Yup. I finished going through the record books the other night and I was wondering if you knew of anywhere else I could look for information...?"

"As a matter of fact..." Mary Brighton shuffled some papers on her desk and pulled out a thin manila folder. Inside was a piece of lined paper with a series of numbers jotted down in a neat cursive hand. "Ah, here we go. I had a feeling you might be back, so I took the liberty of checking the microfilm archives for newspaper articles about the Masons, the family that owned the property. Here's a list of reel numbers and slide positions for the articles I found." She handed Alessa the paper across the desk. There were two lines of numbers carefully recorded on the page. "All of the film and the reader machines are on the fourth floor. They're relatively easy to use, but feel free to come get me if you run into any trouble."

"Thanks again for your help." Clutching the paper, Alessa turned to go. This was already far more than she had been hoping for and she was eager to see what the articles contained.

Ever since her encounter with Isaac in the bathroom a few days prior, Alessa's obsession had taken on a new heat. He'd finally seen her. She was no longer an invisible bystander, but a fully acknowledged player in this strange game. By the look on his face, Alessa surmised that he had been just as surprised about this turn of events as she had.

After he'd vanished the instant before she reached him, Alessa had slammed her arms into the water in frustration, streaking the walls with a splash of bubbles. The situation was infuriating to Alessa. She'd been *so* close to a breakthrough, and then nothing.

She wondered what he had seen when he looked at her. Did he realize he was dead? If he'd been wandering that house alone for almost 100 years, she could only imagine what a shock it would be to turn around and find someone else there. Did he know who she was? Did he think she was another lost soul? She hadn't a clue how to find out, but she was determined to try.

She hadn't been able to stop replaying the scene in her mind, wishing she'd had the courage to move faster, or the insight to realize sooner that he'd been looking at her. She *had* to be ready to act the next time she saw him, and in the meantime, she needed to do everything she could to learn more about him.

Alessa took the stairs two at a time up to the fourth floor and followed the signs to the microfilm archive. The shelves of film were neatly organized and clearly numbered, and it was only a matter of moments until Alessa set her eyes on the reels that the librarian had indicated.

The microfilm projectors had instructions posted nearby and Alessa was able to load the first reel easily enough. She turned on the scanner's backlight and booted the attached computer, double-clicking the icon for the scanner program on the desktop.

The first slide popped up immediately. It was an issue of the local paper, *The Courier*, from 1916, the year before Isaac's house had changed hands to his uncle. Alessa checked the list Mary Brighton had given her and navigated to the suggested slide.

Alessa gasped. There in black and white was Isaac, dressed smartly in a dark suit and grinning with pride. She'd never seen him so cheerful. He was standing alongside two well-heeled middle-aged adults, who Alessa guessed were his father and mother, and a young girl who must have been his sister, Josephine. In the photo, a man behind a podium was handing some sort of plaque to Isaac's father while they looked on, smiling. The headline on the article indicated that he was being presented with an award by the local Chamber of Commerce. Alessa continued to read.

MASON MANOR HONORED FOR MERCANTILE ACHIEVEMENT

On August 10th, Albert Mason, owner of Mason Manor, was recognized by the Chamber of Commerce for Outstanding Achievement in Production and Trade. Mason Manor was one of 11 local businesses nominated for this year's award. Remarks from Chamber President Thomas Browning indicated that Mason Manor was selected for continuing economic achievement. "This growing season, Mason Manor is producing a variety of crops at record levels, marking our township as a popular center of commerce for traders throughout the region. The Mason family has been an influential member of our town for many generations and we are proud to honor Albert Mason for his service."

The article was only a stub, but the photo was more valuable than any words could have been. Alessa couldn't take her eyes off of Isaac. It was surreal to see him here, to have clear evidence that he actually *existed*, that he was once a person with a life and a family and hopes and dreams. Affection bloomed within her chest. She longed to see Isaac as he once was – whole and happy and alive.

Alessa took a screenshot of the photo and article and logged into her webmail, attaching the screenshot to an email addressed to herself. On second thought, she added Janie to the email as well.

Alessa sat back in her chair, still gazing in awe at the photograph on her screen. The hair, his build, those eyes – they were all the same as the figure she'd been seeing. Isaac, her ghost, was *real.* There was no question in her mind anymore that she'd imagined any of it.

Alessa's head was swimming. She'd had her suspicions about the ghost's name and what had happened to him, but there was always that voice of doubt in the back of her mind, whispering that none of this made any sense. But now Alessa knew for certain that the ghost was once an actual person. Now she had genuine proof. Without a doubt, the ghost was Isaac Mason.

Alessa's hands trembled with excitement as she removed the first film. She didn't know what she would find in the next article, but she was certain that whatever it was would give her a fuller picture of Isaac's life, and help her to better understand who he was and maybe even why he had appeared to her. She fumbled with the second reel while attaching it – she felt like she couldn't move fast enough.

Alessa paged through the slides with a hunger, finally stopping on the spot the librarian had designated. It was the front page of *The Courier* from the 14th of April, 1917. Alessa's eyes greedily scanned the page, impatient to find the next bit of information.

She didn't have to look far. It was blared across the main headline, in big bold letters:

MASON FAMILY PERISHES IN TRAGIC FIRE

Bile rose in the back of Alessa's throat. The blood drained from her head and her vision blurred as she tried to digest what she'd just read. The whole family had died in a fire. No. All of them? Isaac and his parents and little doe-eyed Josephine? The thought of that much loss was too terrible to entertain.

The strength of Alessa's reaction surprised her. She'd *known* Isaac was dead, and she'd already guessed that something tragic had happened to the family. But it hadn't felt real before. In this moment, it didn't feel like Alessa was reading a sad story that happened to some long-gone family over a century ago. She felt like she was reading about people she loved.

She felt like she was reading about her parents.

Alessa's realization took her right back to the night her parents had died, standing in the doorway as it dawned on her why the police had knocked on her door in the middle of the night. The nausea, the dizziness, the denial. It was the same. Alessa sucked down air as she struggled to stay upright in her seat. She felt like someone had opened her up and scraped out her insides, leaving her empty and exposed and cold.

She took a moment to steady herself before she read the article, each word a searing stab in the chest.

MASON FAMILY PERISHES IN TRAGIC FIRE

Mason Manor was the site of a tragic barn fire which claimed the lives of all four members of the prominent Mason family yesterday evening, including Albert, 42 years of age, Martha, 41, Isaac, 17, and Josephine, 9. The Fire Department and Sheriff are still investigating the official cause of the fire, but witnesses on scene speculated that it was likely due to an unfortunate accident.

The Masons' housekeeper, Henrietta Jameson, was the first to notice the blaze. As she explained, "I was in the kitchen preparing supper and I saw little Miss Josephine heading out toward the barn. A few minutes later, I smelled smoke, and when I looked up, the entire barn was aflame. I called to Mr. Mason and he and the Missus ran outside to help."

The Masons and their household servants doused the barn with buckets of water and were able to free many of the horses that were trapped inside. After a short while, they heard young Josephine Mason calling for help from inside the barn. According to the housekeeper Ms. Jameson, "When we realized Miss Josephine was in the barn, that's when things really got bad. She always loved to play in that hayloft and I suppose she was up there when the fire started and got trapped."

Mr. Mason rushed to his daughter's aid. Eyewitnesses report that shortly after he entered the barn, a section of the wall collapsed, but as far as they could tell from the outside, Mr. Mason had not been hurt.

At that point, the family's son, Isaac Mason, had noticed the blaze and come out to join the firefighting effort. When he learned from his mother, Mrs. Martha Mason, that Albert and Josephine were inside, Isaac too dashed into the inferno.

A tearful Ms. Jameson recounted his last words. "He turned to Mrs. Martha and said, 'No, this is all my fault.' Then he just leapt into the flames the same as Mr. Mason had done."

At the time Isaac entered the burning barn, the building was showing signs of severe structural damage and instability. Witnesses report that shortly after Isaac disappeared from view, two walls and the roof of the barn collapsed inward. All three Mason family members inside were killed.

Though Mrs. Mason was safe from the blaze, she was severely affected by the emotional trauma of the incident. Not long after the barn collapsed killing her husband and two children, she suffered a heart attack and doctors were unable to revive her. Mrs. Mason was known for many years to have had a weak heart.

The tragic and sudden loss of this well-known local family has left many in a state of disbelief. The Masons were best known for their successful agricultural business and were recently honored by the Chamber of Commerce in August of last year. The Masons are survived by Albert's brother, William, a prominent local businessman, and will be honored in a ceremony at St. Anthony's Church later this week.

Tears splattered onto the keyboard in front of Alessa with a soft whap. The sound pulled her back from the article and she remembered where she was. She wiped her face self-consciously and glanced around. Mercifully, there was no one nearby to see her weep.

Alessa hung her head in her hands, mentally reviewing the devastation of the article. A barn fire, Josephine trapped in the loft. Albert rushes in to save her, then Isaac comes outside and learns what's going on. It's "all my fault," he says, and runs into the burning barn. Isaac's mother watches helplessly as her family is burnt alive, then dies from the shock of it all. It was a wonder that Isaac was the only ghost she was seeing. It was just too horrible to contemplate.

Alessa felt physically sick. She knew she should have expected something like this, but she'd been completely blindsided by the article, especially coming off the high she'd felt after finding Isaac's photo. Isaac's entire life had flashed through her mind in the span of only a few moments, and it was more than she could handle. Alessa felt like her chest had been ripped open and now only an empty hole remained where her heart had been beating moments before.

She wanted to do something to comfort Isaac, but what could she do? Having lost her own family, she well understood the intense emotional pain he was experiencing when he had died; she was still feeling it over a year later. There was no way he could have accepted his loss in the few moments he had before the barn collapsed, and so he'd gotten trapped between this life and whatever came next. He'd probably been reliving that horrific night over and over again for a century, a fate far worse than death.

How could she help him move on? She knew now that Isaac was more than just a figment of her imagination. He was a real person, and one she felt as obligated to as if he were her own family. She *needed* to do something. The only question was, what?

17. DESPERATION

Alessa frantically rapped on Janie's bedroom door. "Janie, are you in there?"

"Yeah, yeah, one sec!" Janie called from inside with a hint of irritation. She opened the door with her hair in a towel, one hand holding her bathrobe closed. She caught the look on Alessa's face and her expression changed to concern. "What's wrong? Are you okay?"

"No," Alessa moaned as she pushed past Janie and sat down hard on the bed. She leaned forward with her elbows on her knees and her head in her hands, sniffling, her long hair falling in front of her face. She tried to breathe deeply through her nose but only succeeded in clogging it further.

Janie closed the door behind her and stared at Alessa's hunched form with concern. She tied the belt of her bathrobe and pulled her desk chair around to face her friend. She sat down directly in front of Alessa and placed her hands on Alessa's knees, mirroring her position in sympathy.

"Less, tell me what happened. You're scaring me."

Alessa took another loud sniffle and brushed her hair back, looking up at Janie with glassy red eyes that still shined from the tears she'd shed on her walk back from the library. "I know how they died, Isaac and his whole family. It's terrible, Janie."

Janie clenched her jaw and waited for Alessa to continue.

Alessa took a quivering breath. "It was a fire. In a barn. Isaac's sister was trapped inside." She snatched a tissue from the nightstand and blew her nose. "Then his father went in to save her, and Isaac followed, and then it collapsed on all three of them. His mother watched everything from outside the barn then died of a heart attack later that night."

"That's horrible," Janie agreed, though she didn't look nearly as shaken as Alessa. "How did you find out?"

"From some old newspaper articles in the library archives." Alessa wiped her nose again.

Janie rubbed Alessa's shoulder in an effort to console her. "I'm sorry, Less, that's really sad."

Alessa just sniffed again.

"Didn't you expect that it would be something like this?"

Alessa nodded. "Yeah. I don't know… It just brought back a lot of feelings, from when I lost my parents."

Janie got up and retrieved a bottle of water from the fridge, which she held out to Alessa.

Alessa accepted the bottle and took a swig, clearing her throat. After a moment she added, "I found a picture of him. It's in your email."

Janie snatched her laptop from the desk and plopped down on the bed beside Alessa, opening the attachment in Alessa's email. She stared at the photo as Alessa watched her reaction.

For a brief moment, Alessa saw what looked like recognition – and maybe relief? – cross Janie's eyes. Puzzled, Alessa was about to ask Janie what she was thinking but then her odd expression was replaced by curiosity and approval. Alessa thought she must have misread Janie's initial reaction.

Still eyeing the photo, Janie said, "Well, I can certainly see how he snagged your attention. I wouldn't mind this guy popping up in my bedroom from time to time, either."

Alessa leaked a small smile. Janie always knew how to lighten her mood. Exhaling, Alessa rubbed her eyes and wiped the tears from her face. "Sorry I'm such a mess. It was just such a shock, to see him there in that photo and finally know for sure that he was *real*, and then minutes later read about this horrible thing that happened to him." She shook her head.

"It must have been hard." Janie squeezed Alessa's hand.

They sat in silence for a few moments, each lost in their own thoughts.

Then Janie asked, "Do you know how the fire started?"

"Not really. The article was from the day after and just said they were still investigating, but that it was probably an accident. Though it did also mention that Isaac had said something about it being his fault before he went into the barn."

"That's odd. I wonder what he meant."

"Yeah, me too." Dejectedly, Alessa added, "I'm sure we'll never find out."

"Well…" Janie paused to assess Alessa's condition before continuing, concerned about adding more turbulence to Alessa's already difficult day. "I don't want to get your hopes up or anything – because it's a long shot – but I was thinking about the ghost theories you were telling me about, specifically the time warp theory…"

Alessa cocked her head in interest.

"Did you do the reading for our next unit in physics yet?"

Alessa signaled that she hadn't.

"Well, it's about electromagnetism, and there was a sidebar in one of the chapters about how spikes in the planet's naturally occurring electromagnetic waves can cause weird changes in perception in certain locations. So I was thinking, what if our house is on one of these spikes? Maybe that could cause some sort of 'wrinkle' in the space-time continuum which is allowing you to see into the past?" Janie rolled her eyes at herself and chuckled. "I sound like some nerd from a sci-fi movie or something."

Alessa smirked in agreement, but stayed quiet. She was eager to hear more of Janie's theory.

"Anyway, I was thinking that maybe there's some scientific explanation for why you keep seeing Isaac, something about our times crossing paths. And I thought that maybe if we can figure out what's causing it, you might be able to contact him."

Alessa perked up. She thought she knew where Janie was going with this. "You think… I could warn him?"

"Maybe… I don't know. It's just a guess. I have no idea *how* to go about doing this, of course."

Alessa's mind was racing. Maybe this was why Isaac had appeared to her. Maybe she really *was* supposed to help him. Maybe she could save him.

Janie interrupted her reverie. "Less – don't get too excited. Remember that much smarter people than us have been trying to solve the problem of time travel pretty much forever and they've made almost zero progress. I don't think we're going to have much better luck."

Something Alessa had read during the fog after her parents' deaths surfaced in her mind. "No, no – Janie, that's it. They *have* made progress. Do you remember the news that came out last fall about those scientists who had created a particle accelerator that could move things faster than the speed of light?"

"Yeah, so what? Didn't they only do it with subatomic particles? It's not like they can do it with people."

"Well, that's sort of time travel, right? At least we know it's not impossible."

"So, what, your plan is to break into a particle accelerator and try to crawl into it or something?"

"Don't be ridiculous. It's just… an idea."

Janie raised her eyebrows. "Okay. Well, let's try to think of some *other*, more plausible ideas as well."

Alessa conceded that the particle accelerator idea was far-fetched, but it was the best she had to go on at the moment.

And it was far better than nothing. Alessa felt hopeful for the first time since she had read the article about the fire.

At least she had a plan for what she needed to research next. "Okay. I'll see what I can dig up about time travel theories and any scientific studies that have been done. Who knows, maybe we'll get a lucky break."

"Okay, sounds like a plan."

Alessa sprung up from the bed with a renewed sense of determination. She *would* find some way to help Isaac. She had to.

The next day passed by painfully slowly. Alessa had crammed in some quick research about time travel in between – and sometimes during – class, but she hadn't managed to turn up anything very useful.

Using the academic journal database on the library's website, she was able to find the research journal where the results of the particle accelerator experiment were published, but she could barely comprehend anything written in the report. The journal was targeted toward a readership of other scientists, not laypeople, and it assumed a level of understanding about quantum physics that Alessa simply did not possess. She saved a copy of the article, but it wasn't much use to her at the moment.

After that she had decided to try a wider search of the internet for time travel theories. There was plenty of information, but she soon discovered that it was difficult to distinguish between science fiction and science fact.

She found an abundance of elaborate crackpot hypotheses that went way over Alessa's head, but even respectable sources reported findings that seemed fantastical. One article by a noted physicist explained that scientific studies had nearly proven that there were actually 11 dimensions – the three dimensions of space, the fourth dimension of time, and seven other "dimensions" that Alessa could not seem to visualize in any way.

Alessa could not fathom how one might go about proving such a thing, but she read that supposedly all of these dimensions are wound together and sometimes folded up in ways that might allow a jump from one point of a dimension to another, for example, from today to a time in the past or future. According to the article, these tiny "wormholes" in time are apparently constantly opening and closing all around, but they're just so small that they can't be detected.

Theoretically, if one could capture and enlarge a wormhole, that would create a tunnel that a human could pass through to reach a different time.

The article went on to explain that this would create opportunities for paradoxes – for people to change the past in ways that would affect the future – which should be a physical impossibility due to the laws of cause and effect. There wasn't much understanding of how this could be possible or what consequences it might have, but Alessa was intrigued nonetheless.

Perhaps there was something about her house that was causing these naturally occurring wormholes to expand, and that was why she and Isaac were able to see each other for a few moments until the hole closed again.

When she returned home from class, her mind was spinning with the possibilities. She'd never given much thought to the idea of time travel, which she had assumed was an aspiration firmly lodged in the realm of fantasy. But the day's research had shown her that real, legitimate scientists were pursuing this field of study, and it gave her hope that she might somehow be able to warn Isaac and prevent the tragedy from happening. And if she could help Isaac, maybe someday she could save her parents as well.

Back in her room, Alessa took a long look at herself in the mirror. Was it possible that the Isaac she was seeing was not a ghost, but a glimpse of the real Isaac during the past? If this was the case, could she really help him? It seemed risky to meddle with the flow of time to save him, but her eyes burned with conviction. She had to try.

At almost the same moment that Alessa resolved to move forward with her investigation, she noticed a twitch behind her in the reflection of the mirror. She turned around just as Isaac finished materializing in front of her, not four feet away.

Her body trembled as the familiar wave of emotions washed over her, the fear and the sorrow and the longing. But she refused to succumb to the turmoil that threatened to overwhelm her. Now was her chance. She had to act.

He was looking straight at her, his jaw slack. He seemed to be waiting for her to make a move, but Alessa struggled to find her voice. She managed to choke out, "Isaac."

Isaac concentrated on Alessa's face and leaned in slightly, as if listening closely. Had he heard her?

"Isaac, there's going to be a fire."

He shook his head, looking bewildered, as Alessa continued speaking. Finally he pointed at his ear. She realized he couldn't hear what she was saying.

"Fire! Fire!" Alessa shouted the word, desperately hoping he would understand.

It was clear that he didn't.

What else could she do? She groped for ideas and decided to try to mime it to him – striking a match, mimicking a small blaze with her fingertips, putting it out with a fire extinguisher. She felt ridiculous; she'd never been good at charades. Did they even have fire extinguishers back then?

Isaac looked baffled. This exercise was hopeless.

Alessa threw her hands to her head. Think. Think. She racked her mind for ideas, frenziedly searching for a way to make him understand. A solution occurred to her.

She darted to the desk and scribbled one word on an open notebook: "FIRE." Tossing the pen, she ripped the page from the spine and turned, holding it up for Isaac to see. But he was already gone.

18. DILEMMA

Isaac crouched behind the corner of the cool gray wall, taking slow measured breaths as his heart pounded in his throat. He tried to calm his nerves, but he knew he was in more danger than he had ever been before. He needed to perform now. If he was caught, there was no telling what they might do. And it wasn't just for himself that he feared.

Isaac looked back at his companion, who crouched next to him beside the wall. He looked up at Isaac, flashing striking blue eyes not unlike Isaac's own. He had Isaac's light brown hair as well, but a more robust muscular frame.

"Just a minute, Isaac," he whispered. "I think it will look suspicious if we're both carrying heavy packs." His partner was unloading a large canvas sack of stolen food into the various pockets of his cargo pants and worn woolen coat. He crumpled the empty knapsack and tossed it behind him. "Okay, I'm ready. Do you remember the plan?"

Isaac nodded, but fear surged through his veins. This was his opportunity to prove himself, to show the world that he was worth something. If he could do it, maybe someday he'd be able to make up for everything he'd cost his loved ones.

His partner seemed determined as well. "Put the backpack on now. If they catch us, you pretend that you have no idea what's going on. Don't try to play the hero – there's no sense in both of us going down. If I'm captured, I need you here to take care of Less."

Isaac gulped and nodded again. He was determined to swallow his fear. He *would* make his partner proud.

As if he'd heard Isaac's thoughts, his partner placed a hand on Isaac's shoulder and offered a reassuring squeeze. "Listen, you're going to do great. Just act casual. We'll waltz across the compound, meet the others in the alley to make the drop, and no one will notice a thing." As usual, he exuded a showy air of confidence that Isaac could only ever hope to achieve.

Isaac peeked around the corner, a light breeze rousing the dust from the frozen ground. They were only steps away from safety, but first they had to cross 40 open yards in full sight of the guards. Other residents of the compound milled about the square; Isaac just needed to blend in. He took another deep breath. "Okay, let's do it."

Isaac and his partner stood up. They stepped out from behind the building and strolled through the center of the clearing, looking straight ahead. They were more than halfway across when Isaac noticed a light thwacking against the side of his boot and realized his shoelace had come undone. He decided to ignore it; he would just have to walk more carefully.

As they neared the alleyway which held the door to their destination, Isaac heard someone call out from behind them. "Hey, you! Be careful – your shoe is untied!"

Isaac swore under his breath. He couldn't ignore the entreaty without arousing suspicion. He glanced quickly at his partner, who nodded. "Thanks!" Isaac casually called out behind him.

He bent over to lace the offending shoe, his heavy pack slumping forward against his neck. Before Isaac could react, a single shiny red apple rolled loose from the side pocket of his knapsack and hit the ground with a thud. Then all hell broke loose.

Six guards emerged from their concealed posts and came rushing at Isaac and his companion from all directions. Isaac panicked. His eyes searched for somewhere to run, but they were blocked from every side, except forward. They couldn't go that way without giving up their meeting place.

Isaac's companion grabbed his wrist and gave him a meaningful look, and Isaac remembered what he was supposed to do. As three pairs of hands grasped his shoulders and roughly forced him to the ground, Isaac let a glazed look slide over his face and he feigned a dull confusion.

His partner, meanwhile, was flailing wildly, bellowing and fighting off the three guards who had descended on him. Food flung from his pockets in every direction. "Leave him alone! He doesn't know anything! I put the backpack on him! Let him go!" He landed one good punch that sent a guard reeling, but Isaac could see in his eyes that he was resigned to his fate. The fight was all for show – his partner knew he was done for.

Inside, Isaac was screaming. He cursed himself – how could a simple shoelace bring them to this? And why wasn't that pocket on the backpack secured? It was all his fault – again – and now his companion was paying the price for Isaac's stupidity. An overwhelming guilt impelled him to act, but his partner had made it clear what duty Isaac had to fulfill now.

He needed to stay quiet, he needed to remain calm, and he needed to do whatever it took to convince the guards that he was innocent. Isaac fought back tears as one by one the guards released him and joined the others in mercilessly beating his partner.

With one sickening final crack, the guards stood up and began to drag his companion away. He felt the bag of food being torn from his back and heard it thump against one of the guard's shoulders a few yards ahead. Isaac knew that nothing he could do would be of any use. Even if his partner managed to survive the ordeal, he'd likely be tossed in prison, lost to Isaac forever.

Isaac had never felt so alone.

Isaac woke slowly, his neck stiff and crooked to one side. He stretched slowly, pushing through the pain as he cracked his neck to the other side. He surveyed his surroundings as he shook off the viscous sense of dejection that still clung to his mood.

He was slouched in his favorite red chair in his study; he must have nodded off. Isaac tried to remember what he had been dreaming about. Something about getting caught, feeling guilty and hopeless and alone. He breathed slowly and waited for the flood of depression that had washed over him in his sleep to slowly dissipate as reality set in. It was only a dream.

Isaac stood up, still feeling slightly shaken from his nightmare. It had been so vivid, but already he'd lost most of the details, and the more he tried to remember the dream, the faster it slipped away.

Isaac was relieved to be awake and back in his own home. Intending to refresh himself with a glass of water from the kitchen, he turned towards the door but halted in place. The phantom woman had materialized not more than a couple arms' lengths away.

Any lingering thoughts of his strange dream were quickly eclipsed by her appearance. She was facing away from him, her long thick hair spilling down her back. She spun around quickly to face him and locked her startling green eyes on his face. Isaac's chest was hammering.

She spoke, but all Isaac could hear was silence. He tried to make out what she was saying, but he was no lip-reader. She looked frantic, like she was shouting something over and over again, but she might have been locked in a soundproof box for all the good it did Isaac. He pointed to his ear, trying to signal that he couldn't hear what she was saying.

She seemed to understand. Instead of talking, she began making gestures with her hands, striking one hand across the back of the other and waving her fingers in the air, then mocking holding something in her fists. Isaac had no clue what she might be trying to show him.

She threw her hands to the sides of her head in frustration as Isaac looked on. Whatever she had to say was obviously very important to her, and he was anxious to learn what it was. He just didn't know what to do.

Finally, she dropped her arms with an expression of realization on her face and dashed to the side. Isaac thought perhaps she had figured out how to convey her message and he watched her eagerly. But as she stopped in place and started to lean over, her form vanished.

Isaac sunk back down into the armchair, reviewing the encounter in his head. What was she trying to say? She had looked so desperate, shouting and gesticulating wildly. He couldn't make sense of any of it. He'd had no luck making out any of the words she'd been saying to him and whatever she'd tried to mime had been completely lost in translation as well.

Isaac gritted his teeth. He was glad to have finally caught her attention, to know that she was as aware of him as he was of her, but their inability to communicate was a major hurdle. She looked like she'd been on the verge of a breakthrough, but she'd faded before he could see what she was doing. Now all he was left with was a slightly sick feeling in the pit of his stomach.

Something was wrong. Isaac wondered what could have made her so frantic. Was she trying to tell him who she was and how she had found him? Did she need his help? What was this message that she was so determined to share?

Isaac worried that he had missed something important. He just couldn't dismiss the sense of urgency that her actions had conveyed. It didn't seem at all like she was just trying to connect, to say "hello." It seemed like a plea. Or a warning.

Isaac felt anxious. His heart was still fluttering in his chest and he could feel the adrenaline surging through his limbs. He felt alert and wary, primed to defend against an attack.

Yes, her expression had been unmistakable. Someone was in danger. Maybe it was her, or maybe it was Isaac himself. But he didn't know who or what threatened them and he was powerless to find out. Without a clear understanding of the woman's message, Isaac was held hostage by his own ignorance.

19. TRAGEDY

Days after his last encounter with the woman, Isaac was still on edge. His life had been pervaded with a deep sense of foreboding and he found himself feeling jumpy, even the slightest noise causing his body to tense in anticipation. He couldn't seem to shake the feeling, and it was making him irritable.

Isaac was sitting in the parlor attempting to focus his attention on the record playing on the phonograph. He couldn't seem to pick up more than a few notes at a time. He closed his eyes to drown out the distraction of the room, but then all he could see was the woman feverishly gesturing at him. The music couldn't compete with the silent cacophony in his head.

He felt so inadequate. Why couldn't he understand her message? It'd been all Isaac had thought about for days, but he still couldn't make any sense of her signals. What had she been trying to say?

Josephine came sauntering in from the foyer and woke Isaac from his dark meditations. In each hand she carried a long unlit candlestick unceremoniously wedged into a silver candlestick holder, the carved wooden pony he'd given her yesterday peeking out from her pocket. She smiled at Isaac as she crossed the room towards the blazing fireplace, but remained respectfully quiet to avoid interrupting the song.

Isaac suspected that Josephine had noticed the change in his demeanor, as she'd mostly avoided him the past few days. Isaac felt bad – he knew his sister was as bored as he was with nothing to do but wander around the big empty house – but at the same time, he was glad to have her out of his hair. If the ominous feelings he'd been having were to come to fruition, he'd sooner have Jo out of the way.

Josephine knelt on the hearth and held the two candlesticks over the flame. The wicks caught one after another, and a drop of wax sizzled as it dribbled into the fire. Jo backed away from the fireplace and placed the candlesticks side by side on the low table in front of Isaac, plopping onto the sofa next to him.

Josephine wet the tips of her thumb and forefinger in her mouth then closed her fingers over the wick of the first candle with a quick motion, extinguishing the flame with a hiss. She'd learned the trick from one of the servants and now she practiced it whenever she was bored. She used the second candle to relight the first, then extinguished it once again. Isaac watched as she repeated the cycle six times, still struggling to listen to what the phonograph was playing.

On her seventh attempt, Josephine clumsily knocked the side of the candle and spilled a few drips of hot wax onto the table. Isaac's patience had been low to begin with, and he was not in the mood to clean up Jo's mess. He gave her a reprimanding look and waited for the dribbled wax to dry so that he could scratch it from the hardwood surface.

"Josephine, you know Mother is going to punish you if you damage any of the furniture with your stupid trick."

She gave him a hurt look, but continued on with her game in silence. Isaac had been harsher than he'd meant to be, but he just couldn't take her disruptions in addition to everything else he was dealing with.

After a few moments she knocked the candle again and it spilled outright across the table.

"Jo!"

"It was an accident!" She had jumped up and was trying to mop up the wax with her sleeve, succeeding only in spreading it further.

"You're just making it worse! Go do that somewhere else!" Isaac felt some remorse at her wounded expression, but he knew that if he wasn't firm with her, she'd never leave him alone.

"Fine." She gathered up the lit candle in one hand and the fallen candlestick in the other and stalked out of the room.

Isaac sighed once she was gone. He hated to be cruel to his sister, but she was liable to burn down the house with her little diversion, and he didn't want to be responsible for it, especially not at that moment.

After he'd finished picking the wax from the tabletop, Isaac gave up on the the record and turned the knob to switch the player off. He just couldn't concentrate today. He decided to go upstairs and splash some cool water on his face. Hopefully the shock of it would wake him up from the fog he'd been rambling around in.

Reaching the bathroom, he perched his hands on the edge of the countertop and paused to peer in the mirror above the sink basin. He looked haggard. He'd been plagued by more and more unsettling dreams since his last encounter with the presence, each leaving Isaac feeling a disturbing mix of fear and confusion and guilt. He hadn't been sleeping well as a result.

He turned the knob and filled the bottom of the basin with an inch of cold water. He unbuttoned his sleeves and rolled them up over his elbows. Bending over the sink, he scooped the water into his hands and splashed it gently on his face. As he'd hoped, the chilly water stung his cheeks and sent shivers down his back.

Isaac looked up, refreshed. The color had come back to his face and his blue eyes sparkled as droplets fell back to the basin from his eyelashes. He still felt anxious, but at least his mind didn't feel as cloudy as it had.

He pulled the drain plug and turned to the towel hung by the door. Isaac gently dried the moisture from his face then hung the towel up on the rack and rolled his sleeves back down. He was securing the buttons at his wrist as he headed for the door when he noticed something in his peripheral vision.

It was the woman. Isaac jumped back with a gasp and nearly smashed into the wall. She was standing by the sink with a similar expression of shock on her face. But her dismay was soon replaced with determination.

Isaac watched as she dug into a pocket in her snug denim trousers and withdrew a small swatch of paper. Her image was already beginning to fade as she unfolded the sheet and held it up to him. There was writing scrawled across the page, but as her image rapidly grew fainter, Isaac had time to read only one word before she vanished completely: "FIRE."

As suddenly as she had appeared, she was gone. Fire. The word echoed over and over in his mind as he paced to his study. Fire. What was she telling him? Was it some kind of warning? Or was she sharing something about her own experience?

He stood at the window pondering her meaning when he noticed something. An acrid smell stung the back of his nose and he thought he heard a faint yelling in the distance. Then it dawned on him. Smoke. Fire.

Isaac raced down the back stairs to the kitchen. Was this what the presence had been warning him about? Was the house on fire?

He skipped the last three steps and bounded into the kitchen. Everything looked in its place except for the fact that it was deserted – usually one of the servants would be preparing dinner by now. He stepped further into the room to see if he could find anything amiss, and that's when he saw where everyone had disappeared to.

Beyond the window, smoke was rolling across the lawn towards the house. It spewed from the barn, which was engulfed in massive flames. A group of servants were standing in a line from the water pump to the barn door, passing buckets which they were frantically pitching onto the burning building. Isaac could see that it was no use. The structure shuddered visibly from the intensity of the blaze.

Isaac dashed out the back door and up the hill towards the barn, pumping his legs faster than they'd ever taken him. The escaped horses reared wildly in the commotion and whinnied over the shouts of the servants. Isaac was shocked at the heat from the inferno; he could feel it from 30 yards away.

He had difficulty seeing through the smoke, but he soon found his mother clutching the housekeeper, Henrietta, and sobbing violently. Isaac gripped her shoulders and tried to get her attention. "Mother, what's going on? How did this start?"

She just bawled harder, crumpling to the ground in a heap of desolation. It hit Isaac that things might be much worse than they first seemed.

He turned to Henrietta. "Where's father? Where's Jo?"

The distraught housekeeper shook her head vigorously, tears in her eyes. She sobbed out a reply. "We heard Miss Josephine calling for help from inside. Your father went in after her."

No. "When? When?!" Isaac's throat burned from the smoke. He could see that part of the barn had collapsed already and the rest was due to go at any moment. His body threatened to faint as the blood rushed from his head with one monumental realization.

This was all his fault. He had sent Jo away with those candles, told her to get out of the house. Where else would she have gone? The hayloft was her favorite place. She must have climbed up there after Isaac had yelled at her, and of course it would go up in flames the first time she knocked over that candle, littered as it was with dry straw. She was only a child – she would never think twice about the danger. And now his father was trapped inside with her.

Isaac couldn't believe his own foolishness. The people he loved most in this world were facing a fiery death and it was entirely his fault. He'd been too distracted to see what was right in front of his face, to recognize what the presence had been trying to warn him of the whole time. He had not only ignored those warnings, but had actually prompted his sister to accidentally set the fire that might kill her. Isaac felt acid rising in his throat, but he choked it back down. He needed to think.

Henrietta continued to cry and tear at her own hair as his mother shuddered on the ground. He couldn't just stand there and watch his family die. He had to try to save them.

His heart pounding, he hastened toward the open barn door where the soot-covered servants were still splashing water, trying to clear a path for Isaac's father and sister to escape. The heat intensified as he neared and sweat soaked his brow. Isaac knew that it was now or never. He dashed through the doorway into the blaze.

The fire inside wasn't as widespread as he'd expected, but he started choking immediately and squinted his eyes against the smoke to get a better view. His father and sister were nowhere to be found. He stretched out his arm to try to feel his way toward the hayloft, but he could barely see his own hand. He tried calling out to them and could not even hear his own voice over the roar of the blaze.

Isaac shook from head to toe as he stepped deeper into the barn. He heard a crackling and suddenly a large flaming beam from the ceiling crashed down behind him, blocking his only exit. He had no choice but to go forward.

He crept cautiously towards the back of the barn, crouching to see through the thick smoke. Isaac called out again and he thought he might have heard a faint coughing. He headed in the direction of the sound, gasping against the suffocating heat.

Isaac almost stumbled over a pile of smoldering wood, then he thought he heard the coughing again. Isaac looked closer and realized what he was seeing. The hayloft had collapsed and he was standing beside the rubble. Was Josephine still here?

He tore at the heap of wooden boards, straining as the lack of oxygen burned his lungs. The walls shuddered around him and he could hear the building roar as the supports gave way. The ceiling around him began to collapse.

Isaac caught a glimpse of blond hair under the debris and he knew he'd found his sister. But it was too late. In a moment she'd be gone, and Isaac was going with her. He'd never experienced such an aching despair, such an overwhelming sense of hopelessness. There was nothing he could do now.

Isaac sunk to his knees, his sight growing dim and his head swimming as his body gave in to the stifling effects of the smoke. He collapsed onto his side, his hand reaching out for Jo as tears streamed from his face. He mouthed a silent apology to his sister and his mind wandered one last time to the mysterious woman and her fateful warning.

And then his consciousness faded into oblivion.

20. FISSURE

8:32 AM. Alessa sighed and dropped her eyes from the bedside clock, carefully surveying her room once again. She didn't know what she was looking for exactly – some sort of sign. But so far, everything appeared to be exactly the same as it always had.

Alessa had been playing at this for almost 12 hours now, to no avail. After seeing Isaac in the bathroom while getting ready for bed the night before, she'd had difficulty sleeping and had woken up every few hours expecting… she wasn't sure what. *Something* to be different. Maybe to wake up in a different room, in some building that wasn't Isaac's house, since if his family didn't die, maybe the university never acquired it? Isn't that how changing the past was supposed to work?

She wasn't sure if Isaac had gotten the message, but she *thought* he might have. After the frustration of their last encounter and her pathetic attempt at charades, Alessa had made sure that the next time she and Isaac met, she'd be prepared. But she wasn't quite sure how she would know if she'd been successful.

She'd been diligently carrying that scrap of paper in her pocket for days, and was still keeping it close at hand, just in case. Alessa plucked it from the nightstand and unfolded the well-worn creases to scan the message once more. "FAMILY IS IN DANGER – BARN FIRE." She'd emphasized the last word with red pen and underlining. Alessa hoped that the message was clear and concise enough that he would be able to read and remember it even if they only had a few seconds to connect.

As it was, the encounter had been much shorter than usual and Alessa was glad she had thought to keep the message short. She was fairly certain that she had wrangled the paper from her pocket in time, but she wasn't positive. Isaac had started fading almost as soon as she'd unfolded her message, so she hadn't been able to get any confirmation from him.

Alessa flopped her head back to her pillow and stared up at the ceiling. How was this time travel business supposed to work, anyway? If she somehow got a message to Isaac in his own time and he did something different as a result, shouldn't that mean that something in the future would change to reflect Isaac's actions? At the very least, shouldn't the newspaper article about his death no longer exist?

Alessa's mind was spinning. The whole concept of manipulating time was more than she could wrap her head around at the moment. There were just too many possibilities and no way to predict how changing one thing – like whether Isaac's family lived or died – might affect everything else.

Alessa had read on the internet that some physicists claimed that all of time was happening at once, that every possible choice and every possible outcome had already happened and was still happening at every moment. As a result, any change in the "past" would not affect the "present" since, according to this theory, everything was happening simultaneously already. The idea was baffling, and Alessa just couldn't process it.

She wondered if perhaps she was making a mistake by trying to affect events that had already happened. Assuming that changing the past *did* affect the future, presumably, the results *could* be catastrophic. Though in this particular case, Alessa couldn't imagine how Isaac's family surviving might negatively affect anything. She tried to think through the different scenarios in her mind.

One scenario in particular caused her a moment of panic. If the Masons lived, they would likely have continued passing the estate down through subsequent generations, which meant that it might never have been sold to the university. That meant Alessa would never have lived on the property, and would therefore have never crossed paths with Isaac. So if her plan worked and she all of a sudden woke up one day in a different place, she might not even *remember* things ever having been the way they are now. Did that mean that if her plan succeeded, she might never even know?

Alessa shook off the thought. She hadn't considered the possibility of losing all memory of Isaac before, and she wasn't keen on the idea. He had become such an integral part of her life in recent months that she couldn't imagine losing him, having never even known of his existence. The idea of continuing on the path she was on before Isaac first appeared – of struggling to recover after losing her parents with nothing but schoolwork to distract her – was just too bleak.

But perhaps that wouldn't be how it happened. Just because Isaac's family survived didn't necessarily mean that the house would never become university property. Even if it took decades after Isaac's family's lives ran their courses, there were myriad ways that the house might somehow eventually land in the university's hands. And if the reason Alessa could see Isaac was, as Janie hypothesized, due to the natural physical properties of the house – as opposed to his becoming a ghost after dying under tragic circumstances – then maybe Alessa would have seen him anyway. In fact, maybe this was how things were meant to happen all along. Maybe Alessa was always meant to save Isaac's family.

Alessa decided to put all this conjecturing out of her head. It was too early in the morning to be trying to unravel the mysteries of time. Plus, she had an ethics assignment to do before her late morning class.

After a short trip to the bathroom to freshen up, Alessa was settling in at her desk and flipping open her ethics reading when Janie poked her head in.

"Morning, Less." Her cropped hair was bedraggled and she had noticeable bags under her eyes.

"Hey, Janie." Alessa noted the exhaustion etched into Janie's face. "You feeling okay?"

"Yeah, I'm fine, thanks," Janie yawned.

Alessa wondered what could have kept Janie up. She'd been half asleep watching a movie on her laptop in bed last night when Alessa had burst into her room to tell her about giving Isaac the warning.

"So, any more developments with the Isaac thing?" Janie asked casually.

Alessa shook her head. "No, nothing yet."

Janie nodded thoughtfully, then added, "Do you think it worked?"

"I'm not sure… I don't know how I would even know. I keep trying to figure out how things might be different now if Isaac lived, but it's all so confusing."

"Yeah, I was thinking about that…" Janie hesitated for a moment. "Alessa, are you sure you're doing the right thing?"

Alessa grimaced as a small knot formed in her stomach. "What do you mean?"

"I mean, if it didn't work this time… maybe you should just let it go."

Alessa swallowed. "Why?"

Alessa had already buried the doubts that had been nagging at her all morning, and she hoped Janie wasn't about to bring up the same concerns; she wasn't eager to think about it again.

"I don't know, Less. It just seems like maybe you're messing with something you shouldn't. Who knows how saving Isaac might change things? Maybe things already happened the way they were supposed to…"

Alessa understood where Janie was coming from, but at the same time, she felt betrayed. Janie was the one who had suggested the whole idea of a time warp and using it to contact Isaac to begin with. Why the sudden about-face?

"Less? Come on, don't make that face. I know how badly you want to help him. I'm just… scared."

Against her better judgment, Alessa felt a sudden flush of anger well up inside her. "Janie, if you're so scared, why did you suggest the idea to begin with?"

She knew it wasn't fair to be irritated with Janie, but some part of her felt like Janie had given her a shiny new toy and then promptly taken it away. If it wasn't for Janie's suggestion, Alessa probably wouldn't even have considered the possibility that her encounters with Isaac weren't with a ghost but with his past self. Janie had gotten Alessa's hopes up that maybe she might be able to *do* something about his fate, and now she was dashing those hopes to the ground. Alessa knew she was being childish – Janie was probably right about the consequences of meddling with time – but she wasn't ready to give in yet.

"I wouldn't even have thought of trying to warn him if you hadn't said it first," Alessa added.

Janie's face blanched and she recoiled, sputtering a retort. "Well, I wish I hadn't said anything. It was a dumb idea. I'm sorry."

For some reason Janie's apology made Alessa's aggravation boil over. "You know, Janie, I don't think you *do* know how much I want to help Isaac, because if you did, you would be supporting me instead of trying to hold me back."

Any remaining traces of color drained from Janie's face. "Alessa… I –"

Alessa held her hand up. "Just save it, Janie. My mind is made up, and nothing you say is going to change it. I'm going to warn Isaac, and I don't care about the consequences. I couldn't live with myself if I didn't try."

Janie looked like she was about to argue, but she let it go. "Okay, fine. I have to go to the library now, but we can talk later. Just… don't do anything rash," she pleaded.

Alessa just gave Janie a stony glare. She could see the hurt on Janie's face and felt a pang of remorse, but she just couldn't seem to let the anger go.

Janie turned and left, closing the door cautiously behind her, and Alessa dropped into her desk chair. She was shaking with rage from head to toe.

Alessa knew she was being irrational, but she wasn't in the mood to be sensible. Janie's concerns were perfectly reasonable – the same thoughts had occurred to Alessa herself – but Alessa had invested too much in the possibility of saving Isaac. She wasn't willing to let it go without a fight.

Alessa realized that having the opportunity to make a difference in Isaac's fate had given her a taste of empowerment for the first time in months. After her parents had died, she'd sat idly by while her life spun out of control, feeling powerless to fix anything. Even the simplest task – doing her homework, getting dressed, cracking a smile – had seemed beyond her reach.

When Isaac started appearing to her, Alessa had worried at first that their distressing encounters would unhinge her completely, but much to Alessa's surprise, Isaac's presence had had the opposite effect. She felt a deeper connection to him than she had with anyone since her parents had died, and her fixation with resolving his mystery had given her focus and provided her with something to strive for after so many months of drifting.

It'd seemed so hopeless at first, but after uncovering Isaac's identity and proving his existence to herself, she'd felt a deep sense of satisfaction. It reminded Alessa that she *was* capable, that she *could* control her own fate, that she wasn't alone. But now everything was threatening to slip away.

Alessa wasn't ready to give up on Isaac yet, but as she reflected on her conversation with Janie, she supposed it wouldn't hurt to wait a bit longer and think through her strategy.

Alessa sighed, her face flushing with chagrin as she remembered the accusatory tone she'd used with her best friend. None of this was Janie's fault. Of course she was just trying to look out for Alessa, and Alessa had thrown it in her face.

Regretting her behavior, Alessa resolved to apologize to Janie as soon as possible. Their physics lecture later that morning would likely be her first opportunity.

With a groan, Alessa turned back to her ethics book, already counting the minutes until she could set things right with her friend.

21. FORTUNE

For the first time that season, Alessa could see her breath fog in the air, each puff evident of winter's creeping arrival. Butterflies fluttered in her stomach as she briskly strode to class, the heat within her chest a strong contrast to the chilly weather.

Alessa had spent the last few hours grappling with her ethics assignment in between bouts of agony over her argument with Janie. By the time that Alessa had hit the print button on her short composition, it was clear that she had taken an indefensible position in accusing Janie of intentionally standing in her way.

Alessa realized that her desperation to feel like the master of her own life once again – a sentiment she hadn't felt since losing her parents – had become unhealthily wrapped up with her desire to help Isaac. The thought of losing the opportunity scared Alessa deeply, and she had inappropriately taken her angst out on Janie. She was anxious now to set things right with Janie, but at the same time was nervous about how Janie might react in the wake of that morning's quarrel. She certainly had every right to be angry with Alessa.

Upon entering the physics lecture hall, Alessa scanned the auditorium for Janie's face but was crestfallen to see she wasn't there. She tried not to let the disappointment get to her quite yet. Janie was certainly known to run late more often than not, so Alessa chose a seat near the door that would allow Janie to make an inconspicuous entrance when she arrived. If she arrived.

The professor commenced scrawling on the blackboard, and when Janie still hadn't shown up ten minutes into the lecture, Alessa's chest tightened with the intuition that her absence was probably Alessa's fault. Janie must be even more upset than Alessa had anticipated. Alessa shifted uncomfortably in her seat and attempted to concentrate over the next hour on the remainder of Professor Liu's oration.

As class ended, Alessa powered down her laptop and packed it into her bag, slinging the backpack over her shoulder with a heavy sigh. It would be hours before she got another chance to remedy things with Janie, and she wasn't looking forward to having the argument hang over her head the rest of the afternoon. It was going to be a long day.

Alessa turned towards the door, but her departure was interrupted when the professor called out to her. "Ms. Khole? Do you have a few moments?"

Alessa contorted her face into a smile before replying. "Sure." She'd been hoping to look for Janie in the cafeteria before ethics, but now she probably wouldn't have enough time to talk even if she did find her.

Professor Liu smiled good-naturedly and removed his round-lensed glasses, folding the wire frames into a pocket of the white lab coat that tugged just a bit too tightly around his slightly pudgy frame. Alessa waited for him to continue.

"I've been looking for a research assistant to help out in my lab and I was wondering if you might be interested."

Alessa was slightly taken aback by the request. This was only the third occasion she'd traded words with the professor – including the time he had reprimanded her in front of the entire class – and she was surprised that he would extend this kind of offer. But on the other hand, she supposed it was hard to get to know students in such a large class, and she *had* done quite well on the midterm.

All the same, Alessa wasn't really interested in doing research and was scrambling to think of a reasonable excuse to politely decline the offer. To buy time, she decided to ask for more details. "What kind of research are you doing?"

"Are you familiar at all with theories about wormholes?"

Wormholes? That was an interesting coincidence. "Actually, I read an article about them the other day."

The professor clapped his hands together. "Great. My research is in the area of using electromagnetic fields to manipulate the wormholes that open and close imperceptibly around us all the time. I'm trying to see if I can isolate one and stretch it large enough to pass an atom through."

Alessa's heart raced as she processed what the professor had just said. She responded cautiously, "Isn't that sort of like… time travel?"

Professor Liu smirked mischievously. The expression made him look much younger. "Potentially…" He leaned in conspiratorially, shielding his voice from the few students who were still filing out of the auditorium. "The research is confidential and very exciting. If we can do it, we'd be the first lab to ever successfully pass an atom through to another dimension. I'm not sure yet if it will end up in another time or another place or somewhere else entirely, but regardless, we're not quite there yet. At the moment, I'm just running the machines constantly and trying to isolate a wormhole so that we can experiment with manipulating it."

Alessa concealed her astonishment behind a thoughtful nod as she considered the implications of getting involved with the experiment. Could this be her chance to warn Isaac? She'd had no idea such advanced research was going on at ESU, led by her very own physics teacher no less. "Sounds… fascinating. So, what exactly would you need me to do?"

"At the end of the month, I'll be taking leave for a few weeks – my wife is expecting – and I'm looking for someone to just check on the lab every day and let me know if we've caught a wormhole."

"How would I know?"

The professor considered for a moment. "Oh, it's not difficult. You have to know what to look for, but I can teach you. It wouldn't be a significant time commitment, either.

You'd just need to stop by for a few minutes once a day. Unfortunately, I don't have enough grant money to pay you… but I could put your name on the report when we publish the findings…" He looked hopefully at Alessa.

"Oh, that's no problem. I've been… looking for an opportunity like this, to beef up my resume." Alessa felt guilty deceiving the professor, but the opportunity seemed too good to pass up. "I'd be happy to help."

Professor Liu's face softened with relief. "Excellent! If you have a few minutes now, I could bring you by the lab to orient you with the procedures?"

Having given up hope of finding Janie before ethics, Alessa had some time and nothing to do except brood over their argument, so she happily obliged. "Sounds great."

Following the professor up to the lab on the second floor, Alessa couldn't contain her excitement over her good fortune. If Janie's theory about the house's natural electromagnetic fields was right, she might be able to use the professor's equipment to amplify the effect and open a wormhole directly to Isaac's time. Forget the particle accelerator – this could be exactly what she needed. Who knew doing well on one midterm would open such a monumental door?

The professor unlocked the unassuming entrance and ushered Alessa inside. Surveying the room, she noted the marked contrast between the dated workspace and the shiny new equipment strewn across every available surface. The professor led her to one corner of the room and began pointing out the functions of each part of the wormhole manipulator.

The apparatus consisted of three silvery spheres mounted on foot-long poles which were set equidistant in a triangle on the tabletop, a glowing strand of electricity connecting each globe. The professor explained that the poles were placed in precisely the right relative positions to maximize the amplification of the electromagnetic fields in the center of the triangle.

The idea was that if a wormhole opened in that position, as popular theory suggested one eventually would, the strong fields would trap it there and allow the researchers to vary the settings on the device to try to enlarge it. A computer monitored the apparatus to detect any changes in the fields within the triangles. The graph on the screen was flat except for one small blip about a month into the three month project.

Professor Liu motioned at the graph. "That was the closest we've gotten so far. A wormhole opened up within the triangle, but it wasn't directly in the center, so the fields weren't strong enough to capture it."

Alessa thought it seemed like this experiment would require a lot of waiting – what were the chances that a wormhole would appear in exactly the right spot anytime soon? "Is there anything you can do to broaden the effective area of the triangle? Can you increase the strength of the fields or anything?"

"We could, but it would require a lot more energy and this old building just isn't equipped for it. I'm working on securing another grant which will allow us to move to a more advanced lab, but in the meantime, this is the best we can do."

Alessa nodded. Assuming there really was a spike in the natural fields around her house, if she could get this equipment back there, it might serve the same purpose as pumping more electricity into the system. And the entire setup was small enough that she could fit it all into a large duffle bag to smuggle it home…

Alessa could barely believe her own gall. Only moments after entering the professor's lab, she was already contemplating strategies to steal his equipment. Perhaps she was going too far, but the temptation was too strong to resist. When would another opportunity like this ever fall into her lap? On the other hand, Professor Liu was so trusting that it just seemed wrong to take advantage of him.

She could always put everything back, though, once she'd gotten through to Isaac. That way, she rationalized, she would only be borrowing. And if she did it while the professor was on leave, he would probably never even know. Plus, if her experiment worked, she could even devise some way to suggest the idea to Professor Liu – that would advance his research by months, maybe even years. Alessa felt slightly better about her duplicity. If she really thought it through, it might be a win-win for her, Isaac, *and* the professor.

Professor Liu continued with her orientation. "We run the machine continuously, night and day, but we need to check it every day since occasionally there are surges in the power lines which cause it to overheat and turn off. We don't want it to be offline for any significant period of time since we might miss our opportunity, so if you find it turned off when you come in to check on the progress, just flip this switch in the fuse box and it should come back on." He tripped the fuse to show how the machine turns off and back on.

After concluding the tour of the lab, Alessa agreed to start coming by twice a week to continue her training until the professor went on leave, at which time she would transition to daily responsibilities. She was already anticipating the start of his vacation. "So, when is your baby due?"

"Second week in December," he beamed.

Great, Alessa thought. That would give her a few weeks to figure out how she could smuggle the equipment into her house without alerting campus security. "That's wonderful," she smiled back.

Professor Liu held up a set of keys to the lab and presented them to Alessa with a genuine smile. "Welcome aboard, Ms. Khole! It will be nice to have another helping hand around here."

Alessa snatched the keys from his hand, grinning from ear to ear. "Thanks again for the opportunity. The experiment sounds really riveting." Far more riveting for her, in fact, than the professor could possibly imagine. "I can't *wait* to get started."

22. REVELATION

By the time Alessa had gotten through that afternoon's ethics seminar, her anticipation was palpable. The entire way home she fought the urge to run, until it finally overtook her as the Zeta Epsilon Pi house peeked into view. Dashing up the stairs, Alessa headed straight down the hall and burst into Janie's room.

"Janie! I know you're mad at me and you're right – I was totally out of line and I'm sorry. But I've got something to tell you." Alessa spat the words out as fast as her lips would take them, gesturing emphatically with her hands.

Janie, who had been hanging laundry in her closet, turned quickly in Alessa's direction, a look of relief on her face. "So you decided to take my advice and think things through a little before you try to contact Isaac again?"

Alessa deflated. "Well…" She wasn't sure how to continue.

All of a sudden, Alessa wondered if sharing the news of the research position with Janie was a mistake. She hated the idea of lying to her best friend – or even keeping a secret from her – but at the same time, this was something Alessa knew she had to try and she didn't want it to come between them again.

"Well, what is it?" Janie demanded.

After a moment of consideration, Alessa decided to be honest. She needed Janie to understand why she felt compelled to push on. "Professor Liu asked me to assist him in his lab."

Janie looked puzzled. "I didn't think you had any interest in doing research…"

"I didn't…" Alessa smirked. She really couldn't contain her excitement. "…until he explained that he's trying to manipulate wormholes to open a door to another time."

Janie's face flushed. "Less, this is a terrible idea."

Alessa was expecting this reaction, but it still stung. "What is? I haven't even told you yet!"

"You don't have to! You're thinking of using whatever technology he has to try to contact Isaac, obviously." She swore audibly. "You're so bullheaded! Why can't you just *let it go*?"

Alessa was taken aback by the venom in Janie's voice. She wasn't angry anymore, but hurt. Janie really must not understand how important this was to Alessa. Staring at the floor, she sulked, "Janie, he's the only thing I have left." Looking up into Janie's eyes, she added, "I have to try."

Janie shook her head and flung the pair of jeans she was holding. They hit the wall with a whap. "The only thing you have *left*? How about *me,* Alessa? How about *your life*? You're willing to throw all that away just to take a gamble on this ridiculous idea?"

Alessa started to recoil but threw her shoulders back in defiance. "Yes, actually, I am. Because I think *you're* being ridiculous. How could I live with myself if I knew I had a chance to save someone I love and I didn't even try? I would do the same for you."

Janie closed her eyes and shook her head, as if she were trying to drown out Alessa's appeal. "Less, listen to me." She glanced around the room warily then hissed, "Don't you think the timing of this offer is just a bit… convenient?"

Alessa cocked her head to one side and regarded Janie with curiosity. Slowly, she uttered, "What do you mean?"

"I mean…" Janie bit her tongue, shaking her head again. "What I mean is that this is just totally out of character for you. You've always been a *paragon* of levelheadedness and now you're acting like a crazy lady, like some sort of *plague* crawled into your head and is holding you *hostage*." She looked at Alessa expectantly for a moment, then continued more softly. "I just think you need a little more time to think about this. I promise I will support you in whatever you decide to do –" she reached for Alessa's hands. "– because I *do* know how much Isaac means to you. I just don't want you to rush into it."

Alessa allowed Janie to take her hands, but inside she was still resistant. It was clear that Janie had more to say and Alessa couldn't understand why she was holding back, especially after Alessa had been so forthcoming with her own feelings. She was tempted to press her further, but something in Janie's expression told Alessa that it would be futile to ask. Janie obviously wasn't ready to share whatever it was that she wanted to say.

Instead, Alessa tried to reassure her friend. "I won't have an opportunity to act until the professor goes on paternity leave in a few weeks, so I'll think it over between now and then. But I'm pretty sure I already know what my decision will be."

Janie nodded and seemed pacified. "That's all I ask. Just take some time to think things through."

Alessa departed for her own room, her sense of exhilaration much dampened from earlier in the day. Despite Janie's reassurances, Alessa wasn't sure that she'd be able to count on her friend for support if she did decide to move forward with her plan to steal the equipment. And the fact that Janie was obviously withholding her thoughts bothered her even more. She hoped that – as Janie suggested – more clarity would come with time.

The next morning, Alessa felt more conflicted than she ever had, and her frustration with Janie had reached an all-time peak. She couldn't imagine why Janie wouldn't just come out and say whatever she was trying to insinuate during yesterday's conversation. The growing rift between them troubled Alessa deeply, and it was making her reconsider everything. Was saving Isaac really worth the risk of losing her best friend?

All of this indecision had left Alessa with a stronger appetite than usual, so she'd decided to fix herself an egg sandwich before her morning class. After downing the sandwich, she found that the hearty sustenance did indeed help to fortify her outlook. She just hoped her housemates wouldn't notice the absence of the ingredients she'd borrowed.

Striding down the first floor hallway from the kitchen, Alessa heard a muffled noise, like a heavy lock clicking, from the other side of the wall to her right. That was odd – she didn't remember there being a room on the other side of this hallway. She stopped in place and eyed the wall. Sure enough, it was blank. Alessa was about to chalk up the disturbance to a figment of her imagination when she noticed a narrow fault running most of the length of the wall from top to bottom. As she looked closer, she could see other fine slits adjoining the first – the outline of a door.

Before Alessa had time to consider what she was seeing, the door swung inward and a hand extended out, yanking her by the collar into a small, dark room.

It took Alessa's eyes a moment to adjust. The room was no larger than a supply closet, and the only source of light was the blue glow from hundreds of security monitors that were mounted to the walls in every direction. She saw images of the quad, the science building, the outside of her house. The Z-E-Pi kitchen. Inside her bedroom? Alessa's mouth dropped. Had the university really taken the security cameras that far? Wasn't that a violation of some kind of privacy right?

As she watched, one by one the screens flickered and replaced their crisp images with a single error message. "CAMERA OFFLINE." The room glowed brighter as each monitor flashed the error on a vivid white background, and gradually Alessa could make out more detail.

The security monitors were unlike anything Alessa had ever seen, shiny glass panels hung in neat rows across every surface of the room. The screens were almost paper-thin; Alessa hadn't even known such technology existed. In the corner, she saw what she believed was a control panel, with various glowing buttons seemingly floating in midair alongside a continuously updating list of text. She made out the first couple lines.

```
Camera 1753. Status: offline. Cause of malfunction: unknown.
Camera 8237. Status: offline. Cause of malfunction: unknown.
```

Now that she could see more clearly, Alessa glanced around alertly looking for whoever had pulled her into this disturbing little closet. With a gasp of surprise, Alessa saw that it was Janie. She was watching the monitors attentively and turned to Alessa as the last one flicked to the error screen, a fevered look in her eyes.

"Alessa, we don't have much time, so I need you to listen to me. Don't repeat *anything* I say here – otherwise we'll all be in great danger. Do you understand?"

Alessa just nodded her assent, her heart in her throat. She could tell that Janie was dead serious, and Alessa was clutched by fear. What was going on?

"Okay. I need to know how much you remember." Janie stared intently into Alessa's eyes.

Alessa shrugged her shoulders. "Remember about what?" she croaked.

"About the war? The outbreak? Losing our family? Starting over in Paragon? The rebellion? *Anything*?"

Alessa had no idea what Janie was talking about. She just stared at Janie in bewilderment.

Janie groaned with frustration and put one hand to her temple, looking off to the side. "It's worse than I thought," she muttered to herself. "I hoped the dreams might have triggered something, but her stitch seems to be holding strong."

Janie continued to stare into space, and Alessa realized she was listening. In fact, Janie wasn't touching her temple, Alessa saw, but her ear. Was she wearing some sort of concealed earpiece? Janie nodded in response to whatever she heard on the other end of the line.

Turning back to Alessa, Janie grabbed her shoulders and looked her directly in the eyes once more. "How about Joe? Do you remember Joe? Do you remember the day he was captured? How you and Isaac became close after his death?"

Alessa couldn't keep up. Each thought felt like a trudging step through thick, viscous goo. Some of these names – Joe, Paragon – sounded familiar, but she couldn't place why. Her mind still catching up, a thought occurred to her about Janie's initial line of questioning. "Wait, did you say '*our* family?'"

Janie exhaled a deep breath, tears welling in her eyes. "Alessa. I'm your sister."

Alessa shook her head, her heart pounding. She didn't know how it could be true, but something inside told her it was. She felt faint. "How…"

Janie brushed off the question and continued at a rapid pace. "Alessa, we're almost out of time, so I'm going to get to the point. Nothing beyond this door –" she gestured at the hidden door Alessa had entered through, "– is real."

Alessa still felt ten steps behind. "What?" she whispered.

"The university, these people, your memories, Isaac's apparition – they were all deliberately chosen to create the illusion of an early 21st century college where a girl, you, falls in love with a ghost. It's 2114, Alessa – almost a 100 years later than you think it is. Isaac *is* real, but he's not a ghost and he's not in some other time. He's as alive and present as you and me. He's just on a different set."

"Set? Wait, Janie, slow down. I can't –"

"There's no time, Alessa. The dramas, please try to remember," Janie pleaded.

Alessa just stared blankly, shaking her head in disbelief.

"This is all the set of a TV show, Less. You've been, well, brainwashed essentially – we call it 'stitched' – to think that you *are* your character, and so has everyone around us. But in reality, we're all prisoners here."

Alessa's mind was racing. This didn't make any sense.

Janie continued. "The memory wipe technology – the stitch – they used on us isn't perfect. There are certain things they couldn't erase, like your name and your feelings for certain people. So the producers worked those things into the plot, then they used a selective perception tool on you to smooth the edges around their deception, helping you miss the clues that might alert you that this wasn't reality. The idea is that the more real *this* world is to you, the more you'll forget who you really are, and the less likely it will be that you'll rebel again."

Janie paused, waiting to see if Alessa was following. She continued softly, "Do you see? That's why you feel all those things when you see Isaac. You *love* each other. None of that is made up. But you were both captured and separated months ago, and held prisoner while they did – who knows what? – to you both. You probably thought he was gone forever. *I* didn't know what had become of either of you for months. Then finally our spy within the production team taught me how to resist the stitch and helped me infiltrate the show.

"But Isaac isn't gone, Alessa. We're going to save him. And not just from some bogus special effects fire, but for real. We're working on a plan to help you both escape. We just need a little more time."

23. RECONCILIATION

Grabbing Alessa's shoulders once more, Janie beseeched Alessa to be cautious. "Less, we're almost out of time, so I'm going to emphasize once more how *critical* it is that you don't let on that you know *any* of this."

Alessa had never seen Janie look so frightened. She still couldn't process most of what Janie had said, so she just nodded quickly in response.

"Say it. Promise me you'll be careful." The reflection of a hundred tiny screens glowed eerily in Janie's wide eyes.

Shaken by Janie's frenzy, Alessa stuttered, "I… I promise. I won't let anyone know."

Janie dropped her hands from Alessa's shoulders with a visible sigh. "Just remember that if you're not careful, we'll both end up like Nikhil."

"Like Nikhil?" Alessa remembered the night they almost kissed, watching those security officers drag him away into the dark. She whispered hesitantly, "What happened to him?"

"He was the star of another show that they're filming on campus, but his show wasn't supposed to intersect with yours. So the producers had him taken away..." She shook her head. "I honestly don't know what they did with him. No one has seen him since."

Alessa gasped quietly. Her stomach felt queasy as she realized that the violent tussle she'd seen really *had* been her fault.

Janie grabbed Alessa's hand. "I know what you're thinking, and it's not your fault. None of us could have known." She paused, her eyes clouding, then continued slowly, "Well... maybe *I* could have, but I didn't know about him meeting you until the night of the party. I thought the producers were introducing a love triangle – I never imagined he was from another show until I learned what happened from my contact a couple days later."

Janie's reassurances made Alessa feel slightly better, but not entirely. She wasn't even sure if she could *believe* everything that Janie had revealed, but regardless, she suddenly felt petrified. Maybe she hadn't been living the *happiest* life for the past year – or however long she'd been part of this charade – but she *had* at least felt physically secure. Alessa would never have guessed that her seemingly normal everyday life was so fraught with danger, that one misstep could end it all. She felt on edge, and then she realized with a start that the feeling was all too familiar.

"Janie, how long have I been here?"

"On the set? Since the start of the semester – all of your memories before that are fake. But you were being held prisoner for months before that, over a year actually."

Alessa rubbed her eyes with her hands, willing herself to wake up from this nightmare. She didn't.

Janie tried to reassure her. "I know it's a lot to process. I'm sorry. And I'm sorry for my behavior the past few days. It's just that, I didn't realize that time travel was the plotline the producers had in mind – I thought it was too out there – and then when I suggested it to you, I unwittingly set you on that path and fast-tracked the story. I knew that when you finally reunited with Isaac, the show would be over and we'd lose our best chance at getting you both out. So I was just freaking out. I hadn't been able to get in touch with my contact and I thought I was going to lose you. But it's okay now, we're working out the plan."

As Janie finished, one of the monitors flashed back to life – students milling around the cafeteria. Then another, and another, their pace accelerating. Janie swore.

"Okay, you have to go, *now.* We've been in here for a couple minutes, so you can't just reappear in the same spot you were when the cameras went off." Janie snapped her fingers rapidly as she assembled a quick plan in her head. "Oh! Got it – run over to the stairs and walk down them as if you had gone up to your room one last time before going to class. That should account for your whereabouts during the blackout."

Alessa nodded, her heart railing against her rib cage. She wasn't ready for this yet.

The screens were popping back on at a rate of two or three per second now, and Janie was visibly panicked. She turned Alessa around and pushed her towards the door. "I'm sorry, it's time. We'll talk again soon. Just remember your promise and *act normal* in the meantime. Okay? You can do this."

She opened the door with one hand, the other on Alessa's back, the room flashing with each resurrection of a camera. "Oh, and Less? One more thing. I love you." And Alessa felt herself shoved from behind back into the hallway of Z-E-Pi.

The sunlight filling the hall was blinding after the dimness of the security closet. Alessa could feel the adrenaline surging through her body; she knew what she had to do. Feeling her way along the wall, she ran as quickly as she could to the foyer and halfway up the stairs. Grasping the rail, she took a couple deep breaths to steady herself, then turned around and began descending. She hoped she'd made it in time.

As she exited the sorority house and briskly made her way down the path toward the quad, Alessa suspected that she hadn't given the producers any reason to be suspicious. Even the security guards she passed didn't give her a second look.

As her heart rate began to slow, Alessa was able to dismiss the threat of immediate danger and try to wrap her head around Janie's revelations. Her mind was reeling. A thousand questions popped into her brain in rapid succession, each thought raising another before she could even begin to ponder the answers.

Trying to remain calm and maintain a normal walking pace, Alessa shook the myriad ambiguities from her mind. Now that she could *think* instead of just reacting, she focused her thoughts on one question: what evidence could she find to support Janie's radical claims?

Glancing around, Alessa reasoned that everything looked pretty normal – students bundled up in the cold hurrying to and fro, a maintenance worker raking leaves into a pile. The ivy-covered walls, the professors in their tattered tweed jackets, the mousy little librarian and her dusty old tomes…

Come to think of it, maybe everything was a little *too* normal.

Then there were the cameras, of course. The university's claim that they were for security wasn't *completely* unreasonable, though the fact that they were apparently hidden even in Alessa's bedroom did point towards there being something unseemly going on. And the monitors in that closet were certainly more advanced than anything Alessa had ever seen. Even if such technology *did* exist today, she couldn't imagine the school budgeting *that much* money for fancy equipment when regular old flatscreens would have done just fine.

And then there was the closet itself. Alessa had walked down that hallway in Z-E-Pi countless times and never *once* noticed a doorway there. And once she finally did see it, it wasn't like it was cleverly hidden or anything. Yes, it was the same color as the wall, but the outline of a door was plain to see. It felt almost as if she had been wearing fogged up glasses without realizing it, and then the fog was wiped away and she could finally see clearly. She wondered what else she had missed.

Entering the econ building, she looked around the lobby and noticed another hidden door similar to the one in her house. She stood in place for a few moments, pretending to fiddle with something in her bag, and casually watched the other students filing into the building. Not a single one seemed to notice the door, or anything else around them for that matter – they all just walked straight to class, their eyes fixed on their destination. Were they acting? Alessa remembered what Janie had said – "We're all prisoners here." Had Alessa been wandering around in the same daze as everyone else?

Alessa thought back over her experiences. Were there red flags that she should have caught? It did seem odd that Isaac and Alessa only ever saw each other. If he really was a ghost, why hadn't anyone else ever seen him? Or if their house really was stuck in some sort of time warp, shouldn't everyone who lived there be affected at some point? Why hadn't she seen any of Isaac's other family members or, for that matter, anyone else who had ever been there before or after Isaac's or Alessa's times?

And what about the more bizarre claims that Janie had made, for example about all of Alessa's memories before ESU being constructed? Losing her parents felt so real that Alessa couldn't imagine those memories being artificially implanted in her. It was pure agony to know that her family was gone, an almost physical pain. But then again, why didn't she have a single photo of her parents? Janie had said something about the memory wipe – the "stitch" she called it – not being able to erase certain feelings, and also that they had lost their – Janie and Alessa's – true family. Maybe the feelings were real then, and her memory had just been altered to apply those feelings to a different circumstance?

If that was true, though, did that really mean that Janie was her *sister*? They did look somewhat alike, she supposed. By no means twins, but they shared the same dark hair and sharp features, and Alessa had always *felt* like she'd known Janie forever, even though they supposedly only met a few months ago…

It suddenly hit Alessa that she didn't even know Janie's last name. In months of conversations and emails and shared classes, it had somehow never come up, and Alessa had never thought to ask. She felt that familiar foggy feeling, the thought beginning to slip away almost as soon as it had occurred.

Quickly, Alessa pulled out her notebook and jotted "Janie's name" in the corner of a sheet. Tearing the page from the book, she marched into her econ lecture, taking a seat toward the back of the class.

As she unzipped her backpack, Alessa had the frustrating feeling that she'd forgotten something. She strained to remember what it was. Homework? No, she was certain she'd done the reading… Did she bring her laptop? Yes, there it was in her bag…

And then Alessa noticed the crumpled piece of paper that she was clutching in her hand. Unfolding it, she saw her own writing in the upper right corner – "Janie's name." Alessa shook off the fog once more as her line of thought came flooding back. She didn't know Janie's last name.

Before she lost the thought again, she opened her laptop and navigated to the student directory. Searching for Janie, only one listing came up:

```
Khole, Janie.  Freshman.  33 Mason Manor (Zeta
Epsilon Pi), Rm. 2E
```

Alessa's head swam as she quickly closed her browser and shoved the paper to the bottom of her bag, hoping no one had noticed what she'd been doing.

So it was true. Janie was her sister. Something clicked in Alessa's mind, and she knew she wasn't going to lose that fact again.

Alessa wondered why the producers would take the risk of listing Janie's real name in the directory. She remembered Janie explaining that the stitch couldn't separate a person from key facts about themself, like their name. Alessa supposed that if she had looked herself up and saw a different last name in the directory, she would have immediately recognized that something was wrong. So given that the producers thought Janie was stitched as well, it made sense that they wouldn't try to change it. And until today, their selective perception technology had worked like a charm to hide these little inconsistencies – it seemed as though anything that caused dissonance in Alessa's mind would be forgotten the moment after she recognized it.

Alessa calmly turned her notebook to a new page and began taking notes on her professor's lecture. But inside, her mind was racing and her emotions swelled. She teetered between biting fear and the blackest despair.

If Alessa had had any doubts that what Janie had said was true, her jarring discoveries since leaving the security closet had quelled them completely. How much time had Alessa lost to the producers' games?

ESU was most definitely *not* the idyllic collegiate environment she thought she'd been inhabiting. Far from it.

Yes, it appeared that Alessa had stumbled upon some fantastically twisted kind of hell.

24. RECOLLECTION

Alessa slid her tray onto the long table in front of her and squeezed onto the bench, smiling at the handsome young man across from her. He flashed his bright blue eyes and returned her grin.

"Hey, Joe." Tossing her hair behind her shoulders, she threw back a long sip of milk and released a satisfied sigh. "How's your day going?"

Joe swallowed a bite of his apple. "Not so bad. I'm on landscaping duty, so I've been enjoying this weather."

Alessa wished she'd been assigned landscaping as well. Butterflies wheeled in her stomach at the thought of being able to spend the day side by side with Joe, not to mention that it was a gorgeous summer day, sunny and warm but blessed with unusually low humidity. As it was, she was stuck inside on kitchen cleanup.

Joe took a tentative look around and leaned in, whispering conspiratorially. "So, have you given any thought to joining me tonight?"

Alarmed by Joe's indiscretion, Alessa glanced up and down the long bench checking to see if anyone else was looking. They were all clad in the same dull cotton jumpsuit as Alessa and Joe, slowly eating their lunch and making idle chitchat. Alessa noticed with envy that the hot food today was fettuccini alfredo. She was tempted to steal a bite, but then she noticed the glazed look on her neighbor's face as the drugs in the food took hold. Scowling at her undressed salad, sometimes Alessa wished she could just forget what she knew about the colony.

Ever since the day she'd gotten ill a few weeks ago, Alessa had been careful not to eat anything rich which could hide the bitter taste of the drugs. She still wasn't sure exactly when – or why – Paragon had started drugging the food, but when she'd recovered from her sickness, her mind had felt clear and sharp for the first time in months. After 24 hours of not being able to keep anything down, her system had finally cleared the drugs and she'd been determined to keep it that way ever since.

Alessa's alarm had grown when she returned to her work shifts and noticed the zombie-like behavior of her younger sister, Janie, and her best friend, Joe. Being under the influence of the drugs herself, she hadn't discerned the change in her loved ones until she could think with some clarity. Once she realized what was going on, Alessa had covertly steered them away from the items she suspected contained drugs, and after a few days, they'd begun to return to their normal selves.

Since then, they'd been subsisting mainly on produce and nuts, which was difficult since the colony's communal dining halls served only a limited supply of fresh fruits and veggies. Mercifully, it seemed that the milk was left untainted, so that had provided them with a consistent and nutritious source of calories. But even so, Alessa and her friends were quickly dropping weight.

It still wasn't clear to Alessa what exactly the point of the drugs might be. As far as she could tell, Paragon was an orderly and peaceful society, everyone contributing to their share of the work and, in turn, provided with everything they needed to live a comfortable life. It had certainly been a relief from the chaos they'd been plunged into before the colony – after the constant threat of nuclear war and then the pandemic that had killed almost everyone she knew, including her and Janie's parents and kid brother, Paragon had been a sanctuary.

Alessa still wasn't sure how she and Janie had survived the devastating outbreak, some mutated strain of a fast-acting plague that seemed to viciously chew up its victims from the inside out. No one even knew how it had all started – whether it was a biological attack from one of their enemies in the Eastern Allies, or just some sort of horrible mistake at a lab. But regardless, the disease had spread rapidly and it had been merciless.

Alessa's family had spent weeks barricaded in their home, watching friends and neighbors fall sick one by one. When the government finally announced a safe quarantine area, they had carefully traveled there together, only to be separated at the gate. Coughing and wheezing, the condition of Alessa's parents and brother betrayed to the guards that they had contracted the virus en route. As a result, only Alessa and Janie would be allowed inside. The sisters despaired at leaving their loved ones behind, but their parents had insisted that they continue on to safety, promising to find them once their ailments were cured. They never saw their family again.

Alessa had been only 17 at the time, Janie 14, and the two of them clung together in their new home as the outbreak continued to ravage the population beyond the quarantine zone. Eventually communication with the outside world was lost – as far as they knew inside the quarantine area, no one outside was spared and it probably wouldn't be safe to leave within their lifetime. A temporary government was established to keep order and they named their new home Paragon. Paragon was supposed to have been a beacon of equality, a community where everyone shared the labor and cared for each other and worked together towards a common goal: survival.

At first the idea seemed to have been working. Yes, there were sacrifices – limited food, the bland but functional government-issue jumpsuits, grueling menial labor assignments that everyone had to endure. But in return, they were safe. And Alessa and Janie at least had each other.

Being in the same age group, Alessa, Janie, Joe, and Joe's brother Isaac were all assigned to the same "efficiency unit" – the complex where they slept, worked, ate and socialized. As orphaned teenagers looking after their younger siblings, Alessa and Joe had become fast friends, bonding over the burden they shared and prodding each other with amusing banter to lighten the load. Before long, Alessa very much hoped that they would someday become *more* than friends, but she hadn't yet had the courage to express those feelings.

And so despite everything that had happened, Alessa had been doing okay. After a few years in Paragon, she had adjusted to her new life and had fallen into a comfortable routine. Each day she received her work assignment, reported for meals when they were served, and spent her free time with Janie and Joe, watching the engrossing TV dramas that aired in the evenings. She had even been happy. And then she'd discovered the drugs.

Now Alessa was more scared than anything. She suspected she was breaking some sort of protocol by not ingesting the mind-altering substances, but at the same time, she wasn't even sure who she should be hiding from. As an egalitarian society, there were no clear authority figures in Paragon. Obviously *someone* was in charge, making the decisions about who lives where and does what jobs, and also apparently what drugs go in the food. But Alessa didn't know who that was, and some instinct told her it would be a bad idea to start asking too many questions.

Worse, Alessa wasn't even sure when the drugging had begun. Her sense of time was skewed, one day running into the next with only the passing of the seasons to break up the year. It was easier now that her mind was free, and she knew it'd only been a month or so since she'd stopped taking the drugs. But she wasn't sure how much time had passed before then. It could have been months, or it could have been years.

After weaning Janie and Joe off the drugs, Joe had been the first to notice that there were a handful of other people eating a similar diet in the cafeterias, dishing the hot entrée onto their plate and pushing it around to make it look like they'd eaten it, but never taking a bite. He'd cautiously mentioned his observation to one of them, and shortly after he'd received a covert invitation to a secret meeting with some sort of underground organization. He was to meet with them for the first time that night, and he'd been urging Alessa to join him.

"Alessa."

Joe's voice snapped Alessa back to the present.

"What do you think? Are you going to come with me?"

She looked down at her plate. "I don't know... It just seems kind of risky." Joe had always been the more daring of the two – it was something Alessa found appealing about him, since boldness was a quality she lacked. She couldn't even work up the nerve to tell Joe how she felt about him, let alone sneak out of her bunk in the middle of the night.

"Don't you want to know why this –" Joe motioned at their dazed dining hall companions "– is happening?"

"Of course I do," Alessa hissed. She continued under her breath. "But you don't even know who these people are. How do you know you can trust them? You're putting yourself in danger."

Joe sat back, resigned. "Fine. I understand your concerns, but if I don't take this opportunity, we may never know what's going on. I've got to try."

Alessa sighed and shoveled a forkful of dry lettuce into her mouth. At the very least, maybe these rebels might have more insight into exactly which food was drugged so that she could resume eating something other than salad.

"All right," she groaned through her teeth. "I'm in."

Later that evening, Alessa was lying in bed in the pitch dark, the soft sounds of her dozing bunkmates wafting around her. Alessa glanced in the direction of her sister, but couldn't make out her face in the dim light. She hadn't told Janie what she was planning for fear that she would want to come along, so she'd waited until Janie had fallen asleep then pulled out the clothes hidden under the bed and dressed silently in the dark. Now she was just waiting for Joe to show up.

A quiet tap on the open window signaled his arrival. Luckily, Alessa was bunked on the ground floor and the windows were all propped open due to the heat, so sneaking out wasn't as complicated as she had anticipated. She simply slipped out the window and followed Joe across the compound's dark courtyard to an unmarked door in the alley between two buildings.

Inside, Alessa and Joe found a group of six people scattered about a supply room, some perched on boxes while others leaned against the dusty walls. The man Joe had reached out to in the cafeteria was present, along with a few other individuals that Alessa recognized from around the compound, plus one tall striking blond about Alessa's age whom she'd never seen before. All of them seemed to be waiting for a signal from a middle-aged woman with cropped dark blond hair who sat rigidly in the sole chair in the room. Alessa thought she looked familiar as well.

Alessa and Joe awkwardly shifted their weight and looked around, afraid to be the first to speak. Then finally, the woman stood up from her chair and addressed the group, "Thank you, everyone, for joining us this evening. Carlos, would you put out a seat for our newcomers?"

A sturdy Latino man in his thirties who'd been standing near the door crossed the room to pluck a storage container from a shelf and gently placed it beside Alessa and Joe. When Alessa tried to adjust the angle of the box with her foot, she was surprised to find that it was so heavy that she couldn't get it to budge. She left it alone and sat down, but Joe remained standing.

The woman continued. "Before we can go any further, we need to know who you are and how you found out about us."

Joe cleared his throat. "I'm Joe and this is Alessa." Alessa waved tentatively, feeling intimidated. "A few weeks ago, Alessa came down with a mild virus which left her unable to eat for about 24 hours. In that time, the effects of the drugs in the food wore off, and she realized what was going on. She got her sister and me off the drugs, then I did the same for my brother. Since then we've been eating a restricted diet, and when I noticed him –" he pointed at the man he had approached in the cafeteria "– doing the same, I mentioned it to him and well, here we are."

Studying Alessa with a slightly alarmed expression on her face, the woman demanded, "Did you go to the infirmary when you were sick?"

The atmosphere turned tense as they waited for Alessa to answer. "N-no," she stuttered. "I –" she looked down at her hands, ashamed. "I was afraid it might be, you know, *the* virus, so I just hid out in the bunk. I was too scared to tell anyone."

There was a collective release in the room. "I apologize for the interrogation. I was worried you might have attracted notice during your illness, in which case they might still be following you – we can't be too safe, you understand."

The thought of being tailed for the past month sent shivers down Alessa's spine. She didn't think that kind of thing happened in Paragon.

Joe took half a step forward. "Listen, we just want to understand what's going on. Why are they putting stuff in the food and when did it start? *Who* is doing it? And how did this whole secret organization come about?"

"All in good time. First, I believe introductions are in order. We are the inner circle of the Rebel Alliance. My name is Regina Green."

No wonder she looked familiar – before the outbreak, Regina Green was the CEO of one of the largest media companies in the world. Alessa had seen her face on television and magazine covers, but certainly never expected to meet the woman herself. In person she looked much older than Alessa remembered, with more gray hair than she had first noticed; maybe Paragon just had that effect on people.

"This is my daughter, Elizabeth." The voluptuous young blond stepped forward, the shapeless standard-issue jumpsuit somehow perfectly hugging her svelte body.

"Call me Lizzie," she said. Alessa noted with a pang of envy that she addressed her remark to Joe, who hadn't been able to peel his eyes off her.

Regina briskly continued. "You've already met Carlos. He's a former police commander and head of our underground militia." Carlos nodded.

Militia? Alessa had assumed that the entire rebel movement was in this room. Apparently there were more people involved in this than she had thought.

"Alicia and Sato lead our medical and mechanical teams, respectively." Regina gestured at two women perched side by side on a storage container. The first, Alicia, was a lean dark-skinned woman with a genial smile, her narrow face framed by a halo of natural kinky hair. The second, Sato, was a tough-looking Asian woman, her sleeves rolled up to reveal a bevy of tattoos on her forearms. Sato nodded almost imperceptibly, her expression impassive.

"And finally, I believe you already know Michael." The portly middle-aged man Joe had approached in the cafeteria stepped forward to shake Alessa's and Joe's hands.

"I'm a social psychologist. Nice to officially meet you both."

"Likewise," Alessa replied.

As Michael took his seat, Joe addressed Regina. "I didn't know there was an organized rebel movement. How did this all come about? And who exactly are you rebelling against? Is there something more going on than just the drugs?"

Regina nodded. "It's a long story, but I'll give you the short version." She paused and took a deep breath. "I first learned of the Ruling Class when my daughter, Lizzie here, showed up on my doorstep about 18 months ago." She looked at Lizzie, tears welling in her eyes. "I'd thought Lizzie had died in the outbreak, since we were separated at the gate when she tested positive for the disease. It turns out the test was a lie. They were keeping her for something worse."

Alessa caught her breath. She and Janie had been separated from their family at the gate as well. Was it possible that her parents and brother were still alive? Her heart fluttered madly as she considered the possibility, but she dismissed the thought almost as soon as it had occurred. With some measure of relief, Alessa remembered that her family members had all begun showing symptoms of the disease well before reaching Paragon. As much as she wished them to be alive, she had an ominous feeling that whatever Regina was about to reveal would make her glad they were gone.

Regina continued. "Paragon is not the perfect society we've been led to believe it is. We're all being exploited for our labor, in the service of an upper class of bureaucrats who are running everything behind the scenes. And beyond wasting resources and lying to us about pretty much everything, they're also exploiting us in… other ways."

Lizzie took her mother's hand and picked up the story. "I wasn't sick. On the contrary, I was young and healthy and somehow unlucky enough to have caught the eye of one of the bureaucrats. They…" she looked down and took a deep breath, fighting back tears. "They sterilized me and then they forced me to serve as a concubine. For two and a half years, I endured their abuse day in and day out…"

Alessa felt physically sick as Lizzie continued her hideous tale. She'd had no idea such atrocities were taking place. "… until one day I finally had enough. I attacked one of my… patrons…"

Regina took over, pained but proud. "The Ruling Class likes their women compliant, and my Lizzie is anything but."

His face pale, Joe whispered, "How did you get away?"

Regina held out her hand to signal that she would get there. "I have an old friend on the inside. As you might know, before all of this I used to head a media empire. One of my old producers was recruited into the Ruling Class and assigned to lead production on the dramas. When Lizzie was jailed for her insurrection, she was cast in one of the shows.

"My friend knew they were testing memory wipe technology on the 'actors' since they were all prisoners who wouldn't otherwise be willing to comply, and he had ethical qualms about it to begin with. Then they tried to feed him some garbage about how the prisoners were endangering society, but he knew Lizzie and he knew it couldn't be true, at least in her case. He was able to speak to her in private and when he learned what she'd been through, he started looking more closely at what was going on. He learned that I was alive and helped her escape to me."

Alessa was shocked to learn that the actors on the dramas were really prisoners, people like her who had been stripped of their free will. She had watched those shows every night, even after the effects of the drugs had worn off; she'd *enjoyed* them. Once again she felt sick. She couldn't believe the atrocities in which she had unwittingly been complicit.

Regina sat down, clearly drained from reliving her horrendous story. Alicia stood up to continue. "By that point, some of the workers in certain efficiency units had gotten wind of something dubious going on – rumors of people secretly living in luxury, that sort of thing – and workers were starting to openly rebel. Shortly before Lizzie escaped, they began drugging the food and airing the dramas. We don't have the right equipment to do a positive identification, but we believe the drug is some sort of sedative that dulls the senses and induces a mild state of euphoria. The idea was that if we were all kept happy and our minds were occupied with entertainment or work at all times, that they could keep us under control.

"We've since learned that most of the people within the Ruling Class don't realize how bad things are. Only a small subset of people know about the drugging, and everyone else thinks that the workers are well aware of the existence of the bureaucracy and that they support the Ruling Class in their mission to 'design a perfect society.'

"They don't know that people are being exploited while the Ruling Class lives in comparative luxury, devoting their minds to intellectual debates about how things in Paragon should be run. Like Regina's friend, many of them are good people who would be appalled to learn what's going on, and we are slowly recruiting those people to our cause.

"I think in the beginning the Ruling Class was intended to be a temporary installation, just until the leaders figured out how to make a truly egalitarian society work. In the aftermath of the outbreak, there were thousands of people crowded into this quarantine zone with little order or direction, and once we lost contact with the outside, I think whoever was in charge realized we would need a more permanent solution in order to survive for much longer. So they plucked a collection of the best and brightest and asked them to figure it all out. That's when they started handing out the work assignments and organized everyone into efficiency units – I'm sure you both remember.

"But Paragon is still a work in progress, and as you can imagine, designing a perfect society turned out to be a bit trickier than they expected; from what our allies within the Ruling Class have shared, it sounds like it was difficult to get consensus on pretty much anything. And then – as always happens when you give a group of people power over another – things just got out of hand. They may have started with good intentions, but at the first sign of conflict, a few bad seeds wielded people's fear to steer things in the wrong direction, and that's how we ended up where we are today."

Regina nodded in assent and took the lead once more. "Our mission is to end the exploitation and bring down the

Ruling Class once and for all. We've been covertly recruiting soldiers for about a year now, and we can use as many people as we can get. It's not easy, and it's not safe, but it *is* serving the best interests of everyone here."

Regina paused and looked Alessa and Joe each in the eye in turn before she brought her discourse to its conclusion. "The question then, for you, Alessa, and you, Joe, is are you willing to join us?"

25. CONVICTION

Alessa woke in her bed at Zeta Epsilon Pi. For a moment, she felt content and well-rested, enjoying the bright sun falling through her window. And then she remembered. The vivid dream she'd just stirred from – the outbreak, the colony, the rebels – was not a dream at all.

In the last 24 hours, Alessa's world had been shaken entirely to its core. Alessa was not a college student, and Isaac was not a ghost. This campus was not real. And suddenly Alessa had far bigger concerns than how she would fare on her exams this semester. Her every move was being watched, and one foul step could mean the end. It was a rude awakening to learn that her comfortable bed was, in reality, no better than a cold prison cot.

Alessa thought over her detailed dream and the others like it that she'd been having all semester long. She knew now that they were far more than they appeared. They were memories, buried in her subconscious and pushing their way to the surface, little seeds of truth that had taken root long ago and refused to stay dormant any longer.

In her head, Alessa tried to piece her various dreams together to figure out the timeline. She guessed that the latest dream had happened earliest, since the others all involved being captured and imprisoned, or discussing upcoming missions. How long ago had this all happened? How old was she really?

She tried to picture Joe, but all she could conjure was Isaac's face. In her dream, she had felt so close to Joe. He had been a huge part of her life – her confidant, her co-conspirator, even her crush. Alessa rolled over to ease the guilt that was crushing her chest. How could she have forgotten him?

Willing herself out of bed, Alessa plodded to the bathroom to brush her teeth. She was standing at the sink when Lizzie strolled in, flashing her bright perfect teeth in Alessa's direction. All of the envy she'd felt toward Lizzie melted away, replaced by compassion and respect. Alessa would never again begrudge Lizzie her beauty; it had cost her far too much. For the first time, Alessa responded with a genuine smile. She wondered how Lizzie had ended up on the show, and if she had any recollection of reality. She wondered if Regina even knew where Lizzie was.

Returning to her room, Alessa sat down at her desk and checked her email, hoping for a message from Janie. Her inbox was empty. Of course, it would be stupid to put anything in writing, especially on a network that was probably being monitored by the producers. Now that bits and pieces of her former self were coming back, Alessa was eager to tell Janie of her progress and to ask her the million questions that were circling in her mind. But she would have to wait.

In an effort to keep up her ruse for the producers, Alessa grabbed her ethics book and moved to the bed to feign some reading. She opened the book and allowed her eyes to scan the page, not taking in a single word. Instead, she concentrated on trying to remember how she'd ended up here.

She tried once again to concentrate on Joe, on remembering who he had been to her. Thinking back to her dream and all the things she'd felt, she conjured an outline of the person she thought he might have been. Good-natured, handsome, strong, honorable. Caring and protective, but playful, even a little bit mischievous. She closed her eyes and repeated his name to herself, visualizing a different version of Isaac, pushing herself to re-forge those connections that her brain had lost.

And then, suddenly, she remembered.

Alessa was pacing in her bunk, a knot in her stomach. She had slunk off from her afternoon work duty to steal a glance at the courtyard, hoping to get a glimpse of Joe as he finished his assignment. Joe had only been working with the rebels for little over a year, but he'd proven himself a valuable asset, and today he was executing his most dangerous assignment yet. She was eager to see him safely returned.

Alessa shivered and pulled her scratchy sweater tighter over her bony shoulders. Like many of the rebels, the recent cold front had been difficult on Alessa. With winter approaching, they were all starting to feel the effects of malnourishment from the restrictive diet they kept to avoid ingesting the drugs. As such, Joe and Isaac had agreed to steal some extra rations of food from the supply kitchen on behalf of the rebel forces.

Peering out the window to check if Joe and Isaac were on their way toward the meeting spot, she noted that the courtyard appeared perfectly sound, with only a handful of residents milling about. But Alessa knew better. Rebel intelligence showed that there were at least four guards posted in the area in concealed positions, waiting to quash any sign of rebellion. The residents of Alessa's efficiency unit had no clue that they were under almost constant surveillance by the Ruling Class. Alessa thought wistfully of the days when her ignorance shielded her from the truth as well.

Movement at the far corner of the courtyard caught Alessa's eye, and she was relieved to see Joe and Isaac strolling casually together across the open square. They were almost to the alleyway where Alessa knew they would be passing their plunder to another rebel team when one of the residents resting in the plaza called out to Isaac. Alessa couldn't make out what they said, but she saw Isaac stop and bend down, as if tying his shoe. As he reached forward, something shiny and red – an apple? – shook loose of the side pocket on his backpack and landed on the ground, kicking up a small cloud of dust around the point of impact.

Alessa held her breath, and then out of nowhere, the guards appeared. They rushed towards Isaac and Joe, tossing Isaac to the ground while Joe flailed and screamed, various foodstuffs flying from his pockets as he tried to draw their attention. It worked. The guards abandoned Isaac, who lay placid in the dirt, and turned on Joe.

Alessa's heart dropped – she ducked lower behind the window, clutching the sill in a death grip as she watched Joe fight for his life. There were just too many of them, landing blow after blow after blow. He collapsed to the ground and they fell after him, merciless.

After a few interminable moments, the guards withdrew, peeling the knapsack from Isaac's back and dragging Joe's listless body behind them. Alessa brought her hands to her mouth to stifle a cry. She was shaking from head to toe, her body urging her to fight, but she knew that nothing she could do would be of any use. Joe was gone.

Isaac was still lying on the ground, the glazed look in his eyes matching that of the vacant onlookers who had withdrawn into themselves at the first sign of violence. Bitterly, Alessa observed that the drugs had done their job.

With the guards out of sight, she saw Isaac slowly get to his feet and head toward the nearest entrance to the bunks. She knew the guards were probably still watching, but she couldn't let him weather this alone. That was the last thing Joe would have wanted.

Alessa grasped the windowsill and unsteadily hoisted herself up, running down the hall towards the entrance that Isaac had been heading for. Isaac rounded the corner, dazed, and Alessa nearly plowed him over in her haste. When he saw her, he broke down.

"It's my fault. It's my fault. It's my fault." Isaac muttered to himself as Alessa pulled him into an empty room, closing the door behind them. Isaac sank to his knees with tears streaming down his face, and Alessa held him to her chest, gently hushing his cries. He was 21 years old, almost a man now, but in her arms he wept like a child. Alessa was only two years older than him, but she'd never felt more protective of anyone than she did in that moment.

"It was an accident, Isaac," she whispered. "It's okay, it's okay. It's going to be okay."

Isaac heaved and clung to her. After a few moments, he regained enough composure to look Alessa in the eyes. "I'm so sorry, Alessa. It's my fault. I just bent over and – and I killed him… I killed them all." Isaac collapsed into himself again, burying his face in his hands.

Alessa stroked his hair and held him once more. "Shh, Isaac, it was a mistake. I saw everything. It was a mistake. There was nothing you could have done." Excruciating pains seared through Alessa's chest, ripping through her like she'd been stabbed in the heart. She wanted to wail and thrash and cry out for justice, but she knew she had to be strong for Isaac now. He didn't have anyone else left.

She looked down at Isaac and wiped the tears that streaked his dust lined face. "I know you're hurting. I am too. But we can't let them see. They would know immediately that we're not on the drugs and we'd both be taken away. Joe would want us to be strong. Okay? I need you to breathe."

Alessa took slow, deep, rhythmic breaths to show him and Isaac followed suit, clutching her hand all the while. After a few moments, they both appeared calmer, at least outwardly.

"Okay, Isaac. That's better. We have to go back to our shifts now. We have to act like nothing happened. You did a great job pretending out there, and now you need to do it again. I'll come find you tonight and we can talk, but for now, we've got to go on."

Isaac gulped and nodded. "Thank you, Alessa, for being here. I… I don't know what I would have done. I promise I'll be stronger, for you, from now on."

Alessa tenderly cupped his face with her hand. "What you did today – laying still while they took Joe away – that was the strongest thing you could have done. I don't know how you did it. I don't blame you for what happened, Isaac. Please don't blame yourself."

He just looked down.

And with that, they both straightened up and parted ways, bonded perpetually by their loss.

26. ELICITATION

Alessa sat up and dropped her ethics book into her lap, a blistering pain surging through her head. The memory of losing Joe seemed to unleash a floodgate.

Alessa's vision swam as the rest of her memories finally came back in a rush of images and sounds and emotions. An odd stitching sensation surged through her head, like thousands of tiny needles weaving in and out of her brain, pulling her neurons back into place with a firm and unwavering hand. The pain was searing.

Alessa fought through it and placed the book to the side as gently as she could, struggling not to attract the producers' attention. She curled up under the blanket, hoping that the production team would interpret her actions as boredom with her studies. Once safely under the covers, she pressed her hands to her temples, tears leaking from her eyes as she grimaced from the pain. She stifled a cry as the throbbing in her head grew more intense and waited for the agony to end. But the onrush of memories persisted, unrelenting.

"That was close." Still breathing heavily from their mad dash across the compound, Isaac locked the door, a satisfied smile settling across his face.

Alessa struggled to suppress her ragged breaths, anxious to attract any notice.

Stepping deeper into the small room, Isaac fingered a long, neat row of uniforms hanging on a rack. "Looks like our intel was good."

"Let's just change before anyone finds us here," Alessa advised. Alessa had only been in the service of the Rebel Alliance for a few months now, and this was one of the most daring assignments she'd been on yet. It was one thing to risk getting caught outside the bunks after curfew for a basic reconnaissance mission – at least she could make up some excuse in that case – but if they were discovered stealing wait staff uniforms and sneaking into a meal at the headquarters of the Ruling Class, she didn't know what explanation could possibly get her out unscathed.

Isaac smiled reassuringly. "Don't worry, Less – this isn't my first attempt at this, and it's always worked out fine." Handing a uniform to her, he added, "Here, this one looks like your size."

Isaac's confidence did much to assuage Alessa's fear – she trusted that Isaac knew what he was doing. In the aftermath of losing Joe, Isaac had become one of the rebels' most admired crusaders, flawlessly executing dangerous missions and covertly winning the rebels supporters and allies amongst the workers and the Ruling Class alike.

But in the wake of Joe's death, Alessa had been in shock at the brutality with which Joe had been apprehended. She still couldn't wrap her mind around the finality with which he'd vanished, as if he had never even existed. But after witnessing Joe's fate, Alessa knew she could no longer entertain any delusions that Paragon's rule was benevolent. Whoever was behind Paragon's secrets had made it clear that they were not about to let anyone stand in their way, and their show of force with Joe had finally convinced Alessa that something truly sinister was lurking below the surface of their peaceful little settlement.

Watching Isaac honor his brother by fighting back, Alessa had been inspired to finally join hands with the rebels in earnest. And she'd been relieved to find that her missions allowed her to channel her grief over Joe into rage, a rage that had helped her find a courage inside of herself that she hadn't known existed.

Taking a deep breath, Alessa mustered that courage and accepted the uniform from Isaac. At any rate, it was too late to turn back now. Unzipping her jumpsuit, she turned modestly from Isaac's view. Isaac smiled sheepishly before considerately moving to the other side of the rack to afford her some privacy.

In the months since they'd lost Joe, Alessa had been training with the rebels to become a stealth soldier like Isaac, and though they'd initially assigned her another partner, Alessa's sense of responsibility toward Isaac had led her to ask if he could train her instead; after what Joe had told her about Isaac's tendency to blame himself for every misfortune that befell his loved ones, she wanted to be able to keep an eye on him. Over the course of their missions, though, Isaac and Alessa had had ample opportunity to reminisce about Joe, and their shared grief had brought them closer than either of them had expected.

As Alessa got to know Isaac's quirks and values and dreams, she could feel the beginnings of something deeper blossoming towards him. She was surprised to see how quickly Isaac was growing into a man, emulating all the good qualities of his brother while adding his own brand of kindness and humor and intellect. She'd never thought she'd fall for someone younger than her, but Isaac had been through enough to mature him well beyond his 21 years, and Alessa respected him immensely.

And as much as Alessa tried to ignore it, there was something else there lately as well, a maddening fluttering in her chest that she couldn't seem to quell whenever Isaac was around. Peeking through the rack of uniforms, Alessa caught a glimpse of his broad bare back, the taut muscles in his shoulders rippling as he slipped on the stiffly starched uniform shirt. Alessa could feel something stirring inside her, something she hadn't felt since… well, since Joe.

Feeling guilty, Alessa knew she should look away, but her eyes lingered on Isaac just a moment longer. He began to turn in her direction and she quickly turned aside. Reddening, she hoped he hadn't caught her spying.

"Ready to go?" Isaac peeked around the rack and Alessa smiled in affirmation.

"Ready as I'll ever be."

Isaac led the way back out into the hallway, striding calmly but purposefully towards the location of the main dining room. Pausing at the threshold, he tossed one quick glance over his shoulder to confirm they'd found their mark and continued in.

Alessa rounded the corner behind Isaac and her eyes bulged as she took in the magnificent room before her. She'd known the Ruling Class was housed in what was once a lavish hotel, but she hadn't been prepared for the opulence that now barraged her senses.

The room itself was exquisite, a massive ballroom bedecked with intricate wood moldings and extravagant sparkling chandeliers hung from high arched ceilings. Unlike the other structures in Paragon – most of which struggled to maintain even their current level of shabby disrepair – this room gleamed and shone from every surface. Even before the war, Alessa had never seen anything so grand.

Hundreds of well-heeled guests sat poised around long tables, beautiful women – attentive and smiling – silently flitting amongst the bevy of mostly older men who slurped their goblets of wine and eyed the women greedily. Laid out before them all was a sumptuous meal of roasted meats and hearty cheeses and vibrant fresh vegetables. Alessa's mouth watered at the smell of hot bread and garlic wafting in the air.

Alessa had heard rumors that the Ruling Class was living a more comfortable life than did the workers, but this was beyond even her wildest imagination. Compared to this feast – which Alessa had been led to understand was a normal everyday meal – most of the people of Paragon were living in what could only be described as abject squalor. Alessa hadn't known that this much food even *existed* within the colony's borders, let alone that an upper class of bureaucrats was gorging themselves on it on a daily basis. She was appalled – there was no other way to describe it.

After a quick nudge from Isaac, Alessa realized her jaw was hanging open and she quickly snapped it shut. Following the lead of the other waiters, Alessa and Isaac cleared empty plates and refilled wine glasses, staying as inconspicuous as they could. Alessa did her best to muffle the rumbling of her empty stomach so that she could listen in on as many conversations as possible.

What she heard aligned well to her expectations – some mild debates about housing policy, discussions of proposed job assignment procedures, one pair of guests arguing vehemently over how many children each family should be entitled to have. And all the while, the lovely, impassive concubines passed new platters of delicacies and popped fresh bottles of wine, their expressions eerily dead-eyed despite their unbroken smiles.

From what the rebels had learned, these men were tasked with determining suitable laws and policies for Paragon's society, but even years after the compound's gates had been closed, little progress had been made. And given what Alessa was seeing, she could easily understand how the Ruling Class had ended up in this state – who *would* want to resolve these disputes when every minute they delayed saw them plied with more food and drink and flesh than any man could want?

As the meal concluded, Isaac and Alessa hurried back to the supply room where their jumpsuits were stashed. Locking the door behind him once more, Isaac turned to Alessa.

"So what'd you think? Was it what you were expecting?"

Alessa just shook her head and swallowed – the scent of roast beef clung to her nostrils as she closed her eyes in envy. She couldn't put her feelings into words.

Isaac understood. "Sickening, isn't it? The rest of us are practically starving out there, laboring 12 hours a day to haul their trash and dig their wells and clean their city. And these people barely even know we're alive, stuffed as they are with bacon and brie and cabernet." Isaac was practically spitting.

His bitterness was mirrored in Alessa's gut, which roiled uncomfortably. Alessa had really believed that the rumors were exaggerated; she'd even been willing to concede that perhaps if these people really *were* working for the benefit of everyone in Paragon, that perhaps they deserved some special perks. But not like this. This was just an insult.

"Those women…" Alessa looked up at Isaac. "Are they all… like Lizzie?"

Isaac sighed wearily. "Did you see their eyes, Less?"

Alessa shook the memory away; she was afraid she might throw up.

Isaac tentatively took her hand. "Come on. We need to go report to Regina what we heard."

Still curled under the covers in her bed, Alessa clutched her shoulders as her memories continued to surface. Gradually, the onslaught slowed and her headache began to subside.

She and Isaac had spent the next two years taking on ever more dangerous reconnaissance missions in an effort to gather the information they would need to bring their enemies down. Isaac continued to be Alessa's constant partner, and together they had become some of Regina's most trusted soldiers.

But despite their many small triumphs, Regina and the other leaders of the movement soon realized that they were fighting a losing battle. Some devastating losses throttled morale within the ranks, not the least of which was Lizzie Green's recapture, which forced Regina to go into hiding to escape the Ruling Class's subsequent investigation. One by one, important rebel affiliates seemed to disappear, occasionally cast on the TV dramas in a thinly-veiled effort to provoke those who were still undercover.

Without being able to wage open mutiny, the rebels were limited in their resources, and the threat of discovery put them in constant danger. In order to take down the Ruling Class and free the people of Paragon from further manipulation, the rebels needed to escape the confines of the colony and create their own stronghold. But with the deadly virus still potentially lurking outside the gates, it wasn't clear if the rebels could survive an exodus.

To determine the feasibility of escape, Isaac and Alessa had been entrusted with a mission to sneak offsite and conduct reconnaissance, looking both for any remaining traces of the plague and for a suitable new home for the rebels. Janie – who had by this point become enthralled with the Rebel Alliance despite Alessa's best efforts to keep her from getting involved – supported the leaders' decision to send Isaac and Alessa. She was convinced that fleeing was their only long-term means for survival, and there was no one she trusted more to carry out this crucial mission.

But something had gone awry the night that Alessa and Isaac had set out on their fateful mission, and they'd been apprehended while trying to steal across the compound's borders. Painfully, Alessa remembered that their detainment had almost been her undoing.

Tap, tap. Tap tap tap. Tap.

Alessa listened closely to each cue, the code Isaac had taught her during her early training days proving immensely useful now that they were locked up down the hall from each other and under constant surveillance by the prison's guards.

After four weeks in Paragon's penitentiary, Alessa and Isaac had figured out the prison's routines and pinpointed the weaknesses in its security procedures. They'd been able to communicate coded messages to the other prisoners during mealtimes and recreation, and they had a plan in place to break free. Now they were only waiting for their chance.

Alessa had been shocked to find that the detention center was surprisingly primitive, with the same cinderblock cells and iron bars and metal cuffs that'd been used to keep people locked up for hundreds of years. Only the high-tech locking mechanisms that secured the bolts of her cell door – and the clinical white interrogation rooms decked out with shiny monitors and insidious mechanical torture devices – marked this place as a modern dungeon. But what the guards hadn't figured out yet was that a regular old steel lock would have been far more effective than the fancy fingerprint scanners they currently employed.

Tap, tap, tap. Tap.

That was the signal – two guards were working their way down either end of the hall to release the prisoners one by one for the evening meal. Isaac was planning to delay the guard at his end of the cellblock until the guard on Alessa's side reached her cell. Already, she could faintly hear commotion stirring from Isaac's direction.

Tugging at his rifle strap with only mild interest in the disturbance at the other end of the hall, the guard approached Alessa's cell and gave her a quick once-over before reaching for the scanner pad. The locks banged, and the bars slowly slid up. Alessa rose from her cot and strode tentatively towards the cell door, in the same manner she had every day for the past four weeks. The guard didn't suspect a thing.

The moment she was through the threshold, Alessa loosed a vicious, spine-tingling cry, alerting Isaac that it was time to make their move – "Now!"

Simultaneously, Alessa and Isaac each took out their guards with a couple quick diverting jabs and one powerful blow to the head. The guards hit the floor with a simultaneous thump, to raucous applause from their fellow inmates.

Heaving the unconscious guard over her shoulders, Alessa dragged the bulky man towards the security station in the center of the hall. For the first time in weeks she locked eyes with Isaac; he mimicked her movements from the opposite side of the hall and worked his way towards their meeting point. Seeing Alessa, Isaac's face lit up, a smile Alessa knew he reserved only for her, and Alessa's heartbeat skipped in response. The uprising was almost complete, and soon they would be together once more.

In just a few more steps, Alessa and Isaac would meet at the security station and swipe both guards' fingerprints, releasing the master lock on all of the cells in their wing and unleashing hundreds of riotous inmates on the prison. In the chaos, Alessa and Isaac would be able to slip through to freedom.

Grunting, Alessa slogged up the hallway, lugging the weight of the guard as best she could. Isaac was already at the security station, waiting for her. Alessa puffed with each stride, reaching out toward Isaac's gleaming blue eyes. Just… one… more… step…

Alessa slumped the guard against the wall and brought his fingertip to rest upon the scanner pad. Almost instantly, the hall reverberated with a hundred clanks as the locks on the cells unlatched and the cell doors began to slide open. Alessa flashed an ecstatic grin in Isaac's direction.

Still holding the guards in place to complete the release of the doors, Isaac reached towards Alessa, wrapping his arm around her waist and pulling her close to his side. He beamed down at her, his sapphire eyes filled with pride. Her eyelids fluttering shut, Alessa reached her lips towards his, craving his touch after so many weeks apart.

But as Alessa closed the space between them, her lips met nothing but air. Opening her eyes with alarm, she found Isaac crumpled on the floor, a massive snarling guard looming over her holding a heavy baton.

"Isaac!"

Alessa dove to the floor on top of Isaac, shielding him from the guard's oncoming blows.

"…Alessa?" Isaac croaked. His whisper was almost inaudible over the din of the cell locks slamming back into place. Alessa could see that Isaac was dazed, just coming to after being knocked unconscious by the guard's powerful strike, but before she could react, she found herself soaring.

Another guard wheeled her through the air, carrying her effortlessly away from the racket of the uprising. Before she could get her bearings and resist, she hit the floor with a thud and heard the slam of a heavy door. All she could sense was blackness and silence and cold.

Scrambling to her feet, Alessa felt for the metal of the door and pounded furiously against it. Bang, bang, bang, bang. No reply. Realizing her frantic knocking was futile, Alessa lashed out in frustration.

"Isaac! Isaac! ISAAC!" She screamed until her throat was raw, but a heavy, pervasive silence was the only response.

Sinking back to the floor, Alessa cringed as a wretched sob rang throughout her lonely cell, almost inhuman moans of fury and desolation. She realized with a start that they were her own.

Following the uprising, Alessa had suspected that she would never see Isaac, or Janie, again and she couldn't have imagined anything worse. That's when she'd started overhearing the torture.

For months, the muffled wails of her fellow inmates were the only sounds to penetrate Alessa's thick-walled cell. She'd known it was only a matter of time until they came for her.

But when they finally did, it'd been nothing like she had expected. She'd been prepared to be battered and abused, but a guard had simply immobilized her as a lab coat clad doctor injected something into her arm. At first she thought it might be some sort of tranquilizer, but then she noticed an odd tingling in the back of her head, almost a knitting sensation, gently at first but growing more intense. And then the pain had kicked in, sharp twinges coursing through her brain as she screamed and writhed and begged for it to end.

And the next thing she knew, she'd woken up in this very same bed, on her first day of class at ESU.

Alessa had certainly suffered in her life, but her memories of solitary confinement were the most excruciating of anything she'd yet experienced. All those months alone in the dark,

Isaac's absence had become a constant panging throb that had replaced her heartbeat, leaving a gaping hole in her chest where Isaac should have been.

And suddenly Alessa knew it, viscerally, could feel it deep within her core. Isaac was hers. He was as much a part of her as her own blood, as the oxygen that seeped through her lungs.

No wonder the last months had been so agonizing. The teasing glimpses of him had torn her apart, left her feeling hollow and empty. They might as well have taken her innards with the void his absence had left inside her.

If there was one thing Alessa was sure of, it was that she needed Isaac to be whole again. And she would do *everything* in her power to have him once more.

27. OPPORTUNITY

Over the following days, time roiled tumultuously for Alessa, each moment seeming to alternate between dragging on listlessly and whizzing right by. After regaining so much of her memory, Alessa was eager to tell Janie of everything she'd recalled and she waited anxiously for an opportunity to speak with her shielded from the camera's ever-watchful eye. But with the producers monitoring Alessa's every step, she was frustrated to find that that opportunity had not come, and every minute she was forced to wait seemed to last an eternity.

At the same time, with her memories flooding back, it was almost as if Alessa was living in double time. Her mind was constantly flitting back and forth between life as a college student at ESU and life as a rebel in Paragon. She was startled on more than one occasion to look up and find that over an hour had passed while she daydreamed about some past event. But in the present, Alessa could feel every single second ticking by.

The knowledge that she was under constant surveillance was disconcerting, to say the least. Suddenly, every decision she made was a matter of life and death – she was constantly coaching herself to look "natural," to act "normal," to make sure she stuck to whatever she knew of the producers' planned storyline. To do otherwise – as Nikhil had regrettably discovered – would be to put herself, and Janie and Isaac, in mortal danger.

Knowing that cameras were trained on her at all times, even the most routine tasks became stressful. It took all of Alessa's strength not to hesitate when getting undressed in her own bedroom; though she yearned to scoot out of the camera's sight, she forced herself to change in front of the closet as she always had. Even the notion of falling asleep felt eerie, with thousands of pairs of eyes pricking her back as she lay on her side facing the wall. Just preventing herself from tossing an errant glance in the direction of any of the numerous cameras on campus was a constant battle. Alessa had thought she'd been mentally and emotionally exhausted before, after her visits from the "ghost." She realized now that she hadn't even known what exhaustion meant.

Alessa had been cataloguing questions in her head, trying to prioritize what was most crucial to ask Janie the next time she got the chance. She knew it was likely they would only have a few moments together and there were so many things she wanted to know. How did Janie manage to resist the stitch? Of all the shows that were filming, how did she manage to get placed on *this* one, and cast as Alessa's best friend no less? And where exactly was Isaac? Most importantly, how were they all going to get out of this alive?

At the time that Alessa and Isaac had been caught, Janie had been only marginally involved in the rebel resistance. Worried for her sister's safety, Alessa had made sure that the extent of Janie's involvement was limited to eating the right diet to stay away from the drugs and keeping her head down as she went about her business.

At first Alessa hadn't even *told* Janie about Joe's clandestine meetings with the rebel units, which Alessa herself had attended only on occasion. Wanting to believe that Paragon's leaders had good reasons for the decisions they'd made – that they had everyone's best interest at heart – Alessa had had reservations about being actively subversive, and for a year she'd watched from the sidelines as Joe took on a bigger and bigger role within the rebel organization.

But Janie had been too sharp for Alessa's ploy. She'd noticed Alessa slipping out with Joe for what she assumed were midnight trysts, and she'd grown steadily more upset when her sister neglected to share her secrets. When she had finally confronted Alessa about her furtive rendezvous, Alessa had chosen to reveal the truth rather than lie to her sister once again.

Janie, of course, was enthralled with the whole idea. Much like Joe, she had a daring streak that drove her to take what Alessa considered unnecessary risks, and on top of that, she had always hated being excluded from anything that Alessa did. To placate her, Alessa had kept Janie informed about what she learned from Joe, but she had prohibited Janie from becoming directly involved. Janie was still a teenager at the time and Alessa knew that her judgment was clouded by the romanticism and adventure of it all, that she just wasn't seeing the danger. And so Alessa had put her foot down.

Even after Alessa had fully devoted herself to the cause following Joe's loss, she'd managed to keep Janie out of it for the better part of two years. But Janie had remained resentful of Alessa's embargo on her participation, and as Alessa had grown more confident in her own role and abilities, she'd realized that perhaps it was time for Janie to get involved as well. Alessa had just begun training Janie a few weeks before she and Isaac were apprehended.

From what Janie had said during their meeting, it'd been over a year since her and Isaac's imprisonment, and in the interim, Janie had obviously developed her talents and become quite influential within the rebel order. Alessa couldn't imagine what Janie had gone through to successfully infiltrate the show and make it this far intact, after being tossed in a jail cell and probably tortured and subjected to the excruciating stitch procedure. Alessa wanted to know how she'd done it. She wanted to ask Janie how she'd made it through all of that alone. She wanted to tell her sister that she was proud of her.

But for the time being, Alessa had to keep these sentiments to herself. As far as the production team knew, Alessa and Janie still were not speaking to each other after their fight almost a week ago, and Alessa had kept her distance in an effort not to arouse any suspicion. Janie had said she needed time to work with her ally within the producers to sort out the escape plan, and Alessa was going to give it to her. This scheme had to be flawless; they couldn't risk being caught again.

Despite Alessa's patience, however, the schedule was still tight. Training for her research position was starting the following day and after two weeks, her professor would be going on leave and the producers would expect her to execute her plan to steal the "wormhole manipulator" and travel to Isaac's "time." From what she remembered about the dramas she'd watched, the show always seemed to end when the main characters finally achieved their goal – which in her case was reuniting with Isaac in the "past" to warn him about the fire. And Janie had said that her intel led her to believe the same, so a little over two weeks was probably all they had before the producers started getting antsy. And who knew what might happen when they took matters into their own hands.

As Alessa exited the history building after her afternoon class, she was surprised to find the ground blanketed with inches of a wet, heavy snow. There'd been talk of an impending snowstorm – the first of the season – but with everything that was happening, Alessa hadn't really paid attention to the forecast. Despite the early hour, the sky was quickly approaching dusk and the lamps lining the quad already shone brightly, reflecting off the sparkling layer of white that sheathed every tree branch right down to the smallest twig.

Watching each breath rise in a festive puff as she trudged her way home – averting her eyes from any cameras she passed

– Alessa felt a small flutter of delight stirring within her. The snow-encased trees bowed enchantingly, and for a moment at least, the campus felt like a winter wonderland, instead of the dungeon she knew it to be.

By the time Alessa reached Z-E-Pi, her shoes were soaked through and the tip of her nose had turned a startling shade of red. She was relieved to cross the threshold into the warmth and slip off her wet sneakers in favor of a cozy pair of woolen socks. This prison certainly had more creature comforts than her cold cell in Paragon's penitentiary, that much she had to admit. She realized with a pang of regret that in a couple weeks, whether the plan succeeded or failed, she would no longer have this warm bed to return to each night.

Alessa sat down at her desk. She intended to check her email, but the moment she opened her laptop, the screen went dim and the lights switched off, plunging her into near-darkness.

Sitting in the twilight, Alessa's heart began to race. What was going on? Was this it? Were they coming for her? How had she blown her cover?

She scrambled for a plan and scanned her room for a weapon, settling on the heavy flashlight by her bedside. Clutching it at her side, she stood rigid, waiting for whatever was coming next.

A bright beam of light shined through her open door. Alessa pinned herself to the wall beyond the beam's initial sweep, straining to see past the source of the light.

A tentative whisper pierced the silence. "Alessa?"

"Janie?" Alessa flooded with relief.

The light shone in the Alessa's direction. "Is that you?"

"Yes!" she hissed. "What's going on?"

Janie pointed the light upward, illuminating the room. "We knocked the power out. A tree went down at the far end of campus, taking a power line with it, and though it actually didn't affect this building, we tripped a fuse to make it look related. Once they've got the power up, we'll have to turn it back on, but it should be at least 10 minutes or so."

"Oh, thank God." Alessa dropped her flashlight on the bed and ran to her sister, embracing her. "Janie, I've been dying to talk to you. I remember everything now. I'm so sorry I forgot, I don't know how…" Tears welled in her eyes as she looked at her sister for forgiveness.

Janie just hugged her tightly. "It's not your fault, Alessa. That's exactly what the stitch was supposed to do – they injected you with some kind of substance that literally rewires your neural pathways, breaking down your memories and putting new ones in their place. You couldn't have known how to resist."

"But you did, Janie. How?" she searched her sister's face.

"We figured it out a few months after you were caught. Some of the prisoners proved resistant to the stitch, so our allies within the Ruling Class sought them out to ask how, and it turned out to be so much simpler than we ever thought. They said that after they were injected, instead of thinking about the pain, they concentrated on a single thought – something that was meaningful to them, like a memory of a loved one – and somehow it blocked the wipe from rewiring some of their neurons. Since they didn't lose their grip on reality entirely, everything else quickly came back to them."

"So that's what you did?"

"Yeah. Once we figured that out, it was a no brainer. We knew we needed to get you and Isaac out – with Lizzie getting captured and Regina going underground and then you two being detained, morale within the ranks had taken some big hits, and we really needed a win.

"Our agent on the inside heard about you and Isaac being cast for this show after they couldn't seem to get either of you out of each other's heads, and when I approached Regina with the idea of infiltrating the drama, she reluctantly agreed that it was worth the risk. I deliberately got captured, repelled the stitch while pretending that it worked, and then our inside guy worked his magic to have me cast as your friend, ostensibly for the same reason as you and Isaac – since we were so close, it was easier to work me into this false world than try to get rid of your memories of me altogether."

Alessa was overcome with gratitude; she couldn't believe her little sister had risked so much for her. She wanted to be mad at Janie for putting herself in danger, but she couldn't seem to muster any anger. "Janie, it's brilliant. I don't know how you pulled it off…"

Janie shrugged off Alessa's praise. "It was nothing, really. Well, I mean, prison was kind of –" her eyes clouded for a moment "– terrible… But here, well, besides the cameras, this is the most comfortable place I've lived since before Paragon. It's almost like a vacation."

Alessa laughed at the absurdity of Janie's assertion. This was certainly unlike any vacation she'd ever heard of.

Janie continued. "So anyway, I'm so glad to hear you finally got your memories back, and you seem to be doing okay. I want to update you on where we are with the plan, but before I get to that – when the lights go on, we should assume the cameras are back. Just pretend like I came in here looking for a flashlight and that we're finally making up, ok?"

Alessa nodded. "Got it."

"Okay, so, the plan. I think I told you that Isaac is on another set nearby, right?"

"Right."

"Okay, well, he's basically living in a replica of this house inside a big dome a few miles away. The campus was already here from before the war, so they just spruced it up a bit and then they built his set separately. Since they were planning the stunts with the fire, they needed an environment that offered a little more control – no snowstorms or rain unless they allowed for it, that sort of thing."

Alessa interjected with a question. "So how have we been seeing each other then?"

"Holograms. There are projectors hidden all over the house just like the cameras," she motioned at the ceiling, "so whenever they feel like it, the producers turn on the projection for one of you so that you can see the other person, or they turn it on at both ends if they want you to see each other. It's all happening in real time, which is why he keeps disappearing before you can tell him about the fire. To build the suspense, you know?"

Alessa nodded – she would need some time to digest all that. "And what about Isaac? Does he know what's going on? Does he know who I really am?"

Janie shook her head. "As far as I know, he has no idea that any of this is fake and he thinks you're some kind of apparition. He doesn't even know your name, though apparently he's been saying it in his sleep."

Alessa wasn't sure how she felt about that. Part of her was disappointed that Isaac didn't remember her, but at the same time, she supposed she hadn't remembered who he really was, either. And who knew, maybe he *did* remember and was just keeping it to himself like her and Janie.

Janie interrupted Alessa's thoughts to continue her report about Isaac. "The producers actually already filmed the fire scene – it was all pyrotechnics, but I heard it was really convincing. They made it look like Isaac passed out from the smoke and then the burning barn collapsed around him. Really the whole thing was rigged, though. According to our mole on the production team, they just gassed him and put him back in his cell to wait it out until you come to save him – once you do, they're just going to reset his stitch to the day before the fire, as if it hadn't happened yet."

Alessa winced, thinking of Isaac undergoing another agonizing stitch. She shook off the thought. There was nothing she could do about it now, and she still had a list of other questions for Janie.

At the time Alessa had been captured, there still was not much known amongst the rebels about the inner workings of the dramas or, for that matter, the objectives of whoever was running Paragon. Alessa turned over the list in her head and decided to start with the simple questions. "What about everyone else here? Isaac's family and the other students – are they all in on it?"

Janie shook her head. "Oh, no, no, they're all like us. Some are rebels, like Lizzie..."

"Yes, I remembered that…" Alessa cringed at the thought of whatever unfortunate turn had landed poor Lizzie back in the hands of the Ruling Class.

"Some are just people who got unlucky, stumbled across things they weren't supposed to see."

"How many of us are there?"

"Hundreds, I think. There are all these different plotlines happening on the same set and a bunch of people from the Ruling Class editing behind the scenes. They're careful to show each drama only to efficiency units where no one should know the actors. Even with the drugs, I'm pretty sure I would have noticed if my own sister was on TV," Janie explained, "so they try to avoid those situations by being deliberate about where they broadcast which dramas. And of course, if there are any mishaps, that just means they have a new actor."

"Why don't they just kill us?"

Janie thought for a moment. "That's a good question. We really haven't found a good answer for that yet."

"Okay… What about their ultimate motives? Do we know exactly what the Ruling Class is doing or why they're keeping a blindfold over the workers?"

Janie shook her head. "Not really. It seems like it's a small subset who's behind all the bad stuff. We've learned that many – most – of the people within the Ruling Class just think they've been elected by the workers to design a new constitution for our society. They too watch the dramas, but they think they're just entertainment, and they don't know about the drugging. They just live in this comfortable little bubble and don't seem to realize that someone is orchestrating all this exploitation right under their noses."

Janie loosed a weary sigh, obviously troubled by the challenges the rebels were facing. "The problem is that no one has really figured out *who* is engineering everything, so our allies have been hesitant to spread the word of the resistance because they don't know who to trust. Plus, it would be hard to convince anyone in the Ruling Class that anything is amiss, since they're all living in the lap of luxury, and disappearances and that sort of thing are much less common and much better covered up than they are for us."

Alessa was surprised at how much and how little had changed. Though the rebels had managed to recruit and train some talented new people, like Janie, it seemed that they were still no closer to answering some of the most basic questions about their enemies. Most of this information was known when Joe first started with the rebels, and that was almost three years ago.

Alessa decided to refocus on their immediate situation. "So, how are we getting out of here?"

Janie hesitated for a moment before she continued. "As you've probably figured out by now, the producers are giving you an opportunity to steal Professor Liu's 'time machine' and use it to get to Isaac. What will really happen is that when you bring it here and turn it on, they're going to gas the room so that you pass out, and when you wake up, you'll be somewhere on Isaac's set. What we're still figuring out is how to get you two *off* his set once you're there. There are a bunch of hidden utility tunnels and things like that since his is not a real house like this one, so we're thinking maybe you can sneak out that way. But it's going to be tricky. We're still working on finding the right path."

Alessa rolled the plan over in her mind. "And where will *you* be during all of this? How are you going to escape?"

Janie averted her eyes. "We're still figuring that out," she looked up at Alessa reassuringly, "but it will be fine, don't worry."

Alessa was wary of Janie's nonchalance, but she supposed it was unfair to expect her to have all the details before the plan was even complete. Alessa wanted to thank Janie more explicitly for everything she'd done and tell her how full of pride it made her feel to see Janie so strong and independent and sharp. But before she got the chance, she was blinded by a sudden flash from the lamp. The lights had come back on.

Janie slipped right back into character, switching off her flashlight and handing it to Alessa. "Well, I guess I don't need to borrow this anymore. I'm sorry, again, for the way I've been acting. It was just stress with school and everything. I'm sorry to have taken it out on you."

Alessa squeezed her sister's hand and tried to convey her appreciation in her eyes. "It's okay, Janie, really. I'm just glad to have you back." Alessa hoped Janie caught her meaning.

Janie smiled. "Okay, I'm going to get back to work on that paper. Let me know how things go with your first day in the lab tomorrow."

And with that, Janie exited, leaving Alessa to ponder her memories and her questions on her own once more.

28. INTROSPECTION

Over the following weeks, Alessa counted down the days to Professor Liu's departure with anticipation. She played along with the producers' games, diligently visiting the lab every few days to receive her training, and in the evenings she and Janie huddled together, conspiring on plans to steal the equipment as soon as Alessa had the lab to herself.

Knowing that their "time travel" plot was only a ruse took much of the pressure off of Janie and Alessa's plotting. Though they debated the merits of different strategies and feigned distraction with their assignments and classes, they knew that whatever path they chose, the producers would ultimately make sure that their pilfering was successful.

Internally, however, both sisters anxiously fretted over their *true* plan: how they would orchestrate their upcoming escape. They knew this would be their best – and probably only – chance to shake loose of Paragon's crushing grip, and so *this* plan truly needed to be flawless. It was a dangerous undertaking, and they knew they could surely count on the producers to try to thwart them at every turn.

Janie still had not received word from her rebel contacts about the details of their strategy, or if she had, she hadn't gotten an opportunity to communicate that to Alessa. As the date loomed closer, Alessa harbored doubts that the rebels would be able to pull together a reliable plan in time. But in the end, she had no choice but to wait, trusting in their allies to deliver them to freedom.

In the interim, Alessa found herself with plenty of time to reflect on her situation, and she found that she was grudgingly impressed with the cleverness of the producers' ploy. They had so skillfully woven her character's background with her true thoughts and feelings that, until Janie's revelation, she had never once questioned her experience. She'd been so utterly convinced that she had even readily dismissed the flashbacks of her true life that had come to her in dreams. It was beyond frightening to consider what could happen if this type of memory-altering technology was used on a larger scale.

It still amazed Alessa how willingly her emotions had transferred from their true sources to the producers' constructed ones. Shifting her feelings of sorrow at losing her real family in the outbreak to her imaginary parents in their car accident wasn't too dramatic of a jump, but transforming her distress at losing Isaac into distress at seeing his ghost – without triggering her memory – was certainly a more complex feat.

Now that Alessa could remember her real life, the wave of emotions that had overcome her whenever she saw the ghost felt all too familiar. The fear, the hopelessness, the despair – these were Alessa's constant companions during her time held captive in solitary confinement.

Listening to the cries of the other prisoners as they were interrogated had tormented Alessa, images of Isaac bloody and lifeless flashing before her eyes with the sound of each ragged wail. In her hours of idle time, she'd worried endlessly about what would become of Isaac, wondering what terrors they were subjecting him to and how, if either of them managed to make it out alive, they could ever move forward without the other by their side. It only made sense that these emotions would come back to her whenever she saw him, almost like a conditioned response.

And then, of course, there was the strange but powerful desire that had undercut even her most ravaging fear. A deep sense of allure had always drawn Alessa to Isaac's "ghost" despite the troubling feelings that his presence had evoked, and this aspect of her reaction had been the most confusing to her. She'd been able to rationalize the anxiety and sorrow as natural responses or projections of the ghost's, but the physical pull she felt towards him had always been somewhat of a mystery.

Until, of course, she recognized Isaac for who he really was. Just as their romance had emerged slowly from the ashes of Joe's demise, so had a smoldering passion that had only grown more intense as their relationship progressed. And like a glowing ember, all Alessa had needed was a little touch of kindling to reignite that fire.

Alessa fumed at the way the producers had manipulated her emotions, using the attraction that burned between her and Isaac to drive her participation in their plot. If she hadn't felt that attraction to Isaac, she probably would have reacted to the ghost by moving to a different dorm, just as any normal person would have done, and the show would have been over right there. But the producers had known that some deep part of Alessa would thirst for Isaac, and they'd used that knowledge to trap her in their game.

Even the general aura of depression that had settled on her in recent years had been convincingly worked into her character's backdrop. Before her memories resurfaced, Alessa had thought she'd been disappointed in her college experience and frustrated with her own inability to take control of her future. In reality, these were feelings she'd developed while living in Paragon.

The collapse of life as she'd known it – and especially the loss of her family – had left Alessa questioning whether she even wanted to be alive at all. But as everyone in Paragon had settled into a routine, she'd allowed herself to be swept up in the comfort and predictability of structure. Those early years that she and Janie had shared together in Paragon had almost been happy. Alessa had come to accept that it was a different life, but an okay one.

However, once she'd discovered the drugs and started working with the rebels, Alessa's contentedness had evaporated into thin air. With no one else to turn to, she'd trusted the society of Paragon to take care of its people. That betrayal had left her disillusioned and distraught. Then, after losing Joe, she'd valiantly fought alongside Isaac for justice, but inside, she'd privately grappled with the enormity of her task.

Someone had masterminded this plan to convert a simple government quarantine zone into a highly controlled multi-class civilization, which most of the inhabitants didn't even realize they were living in. Alessa knew that she was outmatched, and with every setback that rattled the rebels, her confidence had eroded further.

Alessa *did* feel powerless and *did* feel alone, but not for the reasons she had thought. It wasn't because, as she'd reasoned when she believed herself a student, the death of her parents had unraveled her plans for the future. It was because she *had* no future, and neither did anyone else she loved. If Paragon had any say in it, she was destined to live out her days in the same drab jumpsuit, eating the same lackluster food, working the same monotonous jobs to support some privileged upper class who barely even knew she existed.

And the knowledge that Paragon was not the refuge that everyone around her assumed it to be left her isolated and demoralized. She'd dutifully fallen in line each day with the medicated zombies around her, shuffling mechanically from work assignments to meals to nightly drama airings, and collapsing at the end of each long day into a stiff bed in her crowded bunk. But inside she was crying out.

She'd yearned to race from one citizen to the next, shaking them from their stupor and rallying them to the cause. But Alessa had known that that would only get her killed. Instead, she'd kept her head down and resisted Paragon's schemes in subtler ways, like the careful diet she and her friends kept to evade the drugs.

But sometimes it all felt futile. After all, no amount of salad that she consumed was going to bring down whoever had put her here. Some days it seemed like it would have been better to just give in to the temptation of the hot entrée, to allow her mind to become vacant once again and finally accept her fate.

But she had pressed on.

Now that Alessa knew what Paragon was truly capable of – the nightmarish prisons, the indifferent use of mind control, the elaborate deceptions just to keep the populace subdued – she was torn between rage and despair. Something had to be done to right these wrongs, that much she was certain of. But how? Their enigmatic enemy had proven cunning and determined; taking down this opponent would be no small feat. Was *Alessa* really the one to do it?

The truth was that the rebels were failing. They had been for months, and when Alessa and Isaac had set out to scout for an escape, Regina had placed all of the alliance's hopes on the shoulders of their mission. Now it was months later, and as far as Alessa knew, no progress had been made. If the plan to break them out failed this time, it could mean the end of the rebellion. It could mean the end of liberty for everyone in Paragon, whether or not they knew.

These thoughts weighed heavily on Alessa as the semester's final days of class rolled around, bringing with them a sense of impending finality. Alessa privately relished her last days of comfort – she knew that once she went for Isaac, there would be no warm fluffy bed to return to, no closet filled with cozy sweaters, no cafeteria with tray after tray of satisfying food. They would be on their own, and there would be no turning back.

Finally, the day before Professor Liu was scheduled to leave, Alessa received word from Janie that the plan had been set in motion. As she stood near Janie's shower stall brushing her teeth that evening, Janie whispered a hushed message through the plastic curtain, her voice concealed from the producers' mikes under the cover of the spattering water.

"We're executing tomorrow, so be ready. You'll find a map of your escape route in your pocket when you wake up on Isaac's set."

Alessa continued to shimmy her toothbrush, listening carefully for Janie's words. She felt unexpectedly calm.

"Be careful, Alessa. I'll see you on the other side."

29. EXECUTION

At the completion of her afternoon ethics seminar, Alessa zipped her backpack and headed off towards the science building to meet Janie. Jangling the keys to Professor Liu's lab in her pocket, Alessa wondered what the producers had in store for her next. With any luck she would be on Isaac's set by nightfall, but she knew from experience that things rarely went as planned in Paragon.

Janie had proposed that they smuggle the "wormhole capturing apparatus" out of the lab by daringly hiding it in plain sight, and as Alessa approached the front of the building, Janie was waiting for her and clutching a large box that was labeled "broken equipment."

Noticing Alessa's approach, Janie smiled wickedly. "Let's do this."

Alessa led Janie up to the lab and unlocked the door. Once inside, they worked quickly in silence to disconnect the power and load each piece of the machine into the container. Sealing the top with tape, Alessa and Janie hoisted the box between them and strolled out of the building.

Alessa was surprised at how nervous she felt, her entire body shaking with adrenaline as she and Janie waltzed through the quad, doing their best to look unassuming. She knew the producers needed her to get to Isaac's set to fulfill the climax of the show, but she just didn't expect them to make it this easy for her. She kept waiting for the other shoe to drop.

At the edge of the quad, Alessa and Janie turned onto the wide cobblestone path that led to Z-E-Pi. Alessa's heart skipped a beat as she noticed a security guard up ahead. She made to turn off the path and let him pass, but before she could nudge Janie in the right direction, the guard looked up and noticed them.

Janie swore under her breath and panic rose in Alessa's chest. The guard was headed right for them. Had the producers changed their plans? Maybe they wanted Alessa to get caught, had decided to draw the show out longer. If that was the case, there was nothing Alessa could do but play along. She braced herself as the guard approached them.

"Good evening, ladies."

"Hi," Janie responded cheerfully.

Alessa just kept her mouth shut and tried to steady her racing heart.

"That's an awfully large box you've got there – hope that's not elicit contraband or anything." The guard smiled.

Alessa just laughed nervously in response.

"I'm just kidding. Do you need any help carrying that thing?"

Janie jumped in. "Oh, how nice of you to offer. No, thanks, I think we'll be okay – not too much farther to go."

"All right, then. You have a good evening."

"You too," Janie replied. When the guard was out of earshot, Janie added, "Way to keep it cool, Less."

Alessa exhaled. "Sorry."

They continued quickly home and deposited the box on the bed in Alessa's room. Closing the door, Janie turned to Alessa.

"So, where should we set this baby up?"

Alessa hadn't really given this much thought – she suspected that the producers would make the device work no matter where they used it.

"How about right here?"

Janie frowned. "What if someone walks in? We should do it in the attic bathroom where no one will notice us."

"Yeah, but I only had one encounter with Isaac upstairs – I've had tons in here. I think we're more likely to snag a wormhole where they most often naturally occur, which means wherever I see him most, and that's here."

"Okay, fine," Janie relented. Alessa knew of course that the whole dispute was for show – this close to the end, it was essential to stay in character to keep the producers' suspicions at bay.

Unloading the three electromagnetic poles, Alessa positioned one on the bed. She placed the second on her desk and handed the third to Janie. "Put this in the other corner while I hook the power up, will you?"

Janie perched the final pole atop the fireplace mantle across the room while Alessa connected the power cord and plugged it into the wall.

She took a long look at Janie. "Well, here goes nothing…"

Janie nodded and Alessa flipped the power switch.

Alessa wasn't sure what to expect when she turned the apparatus on, but if she'd been hoping for special effects, she wouldn't have been disappointed. At first the device looked the same as it had in the lab, with waves of electric current – what Alessa had suspected was really another hologram – circling the globes mounted on each pole and connecting them in a triangle formation.

And then all of sudden sparks began to crackle at various points around the triangle, and a tiny dot appeared in the center, suspended in midair. As Alessa watched, the dot began to grow, slowly at first but quickly gaining speed, the edges of the expanding circle reaching toward the floor and ceiling. Through a long oval which now stood as high as Alessa, she could see what looked like the back of her house, only different, newer. Isaac's house.

Again, Alessa marveled at the convincing visuals that the producers' holograms could construct; she really felt like she was looking through a window into another time. Even though she knew it was an illusion, Alessa felt the urge to reach through the ring, to see if what she was looking at was real.

And then she heard a quiet hiss and her head started to spin. Were the producers flooding the room with gas? The wormhole continued expanding outward, reaching ever closer to Alessa and growing at a faster and faster pace. Out of the corner of her eye, Alessa saw Janie duck for cover against the wall. The last thing Alessa remembered before losing consciousness was the side of the hole racing toward her.

Alessa woke up face down on the lawn outside her house, or rather, Isaac's house. Coming to, the first thing she noticed was the poke of a folded piece of paper tucked into her pocket – the map Janie had promised their ally would deliver.

Still sprawled on the ground, Alessa's heart raced as she considered the magnitude of the task in front of her. She needed to convince Isaac to follow her, sneak off the set while avoiding the production team's grasp, and set out into the wilderness beyond Paragon's walls – where a deadly virus may still be lurking – to find *something* that would revitalize the rebel movement and give them hope for the future. She wasn't quite sure how she would be able to manage all of this without getting killed, but she supposed it was too late to back out now.

Alessa stood up to take in her surroundings. The ground was bare, with no hint of the snow that blanketed the actual ESU campus. As Janie had expected, it seemed the producers had landed Alessa in what Isaac believed was springtime, the day before the fire to be exact – perfect timing for a dramatic conclusion to the show. But little did the production team suspect that they were about to get an even more dramatic ending than they'd hoped for.

She was alone in the backyard at dusk, a light shining from the kitchen of the nearby house. Peering in the window, she found Isaac sitting at the table whittling away against a block of wood.

The blood rushed to Alessa's head as she registered that Isaac was only steps away. She watched him greedily for a few moments, fighting the urge to burst through the door and scoop him up in her arms right then. Her breathing quickened as she stretched her fingertips on the glass of the windowpane, struggling to contain her overwhelming desire to touch him.

First things first – she knew she needed to get a good look at the map before she could lead Isaac to their escape. How could she steal a peek without attracting the producers' notice?

Just then the lights flickered, giving her the opportunity she'd sought. Perfect timing – Alessa guessed that her ally had somehow disrupted the power supply, but she knew that the producers would be scrambling to restore the cameras before they missed her reunion with Isaac. She hurried to unfold the map before they could.

Hidden in the shadow of the house, Alessa stole a quick glance at the plan and noted that her starting point was the foyer closet. Hastily shoving the map back into her pocket, Alessa choked down her fears and readied herself for what came next.

30. AWAKENING

Isaac stood at the kitchen window examining the small block of pinewood in his hand in the fading evening light. He switched on the overhead lamp to get a closer look, searching carefully for knots and noting each of their locations in turn. Satisfied, he withdrew a small, sharp knife from a drawer and made his way toward the heavy wooden table.

Even an hour after the servants had put the last clean pot back on the shelf, the hearty aroma of dinner still lingered in the air as Isaac sat down to begin his carving. He wasn't much of a woodworker, but he hoped that keeping his hands busy for a few hours might help his mind to focus on something other than his last encounter with the mysterious presence.

Though three days had passed since he'd last seen her, he'd had no success in shaking the troubling feeling that had settled in his gut after he'd failed to grasp the meanings of her frenzied gestures and frustratingly silent shouts. He'd replayed the scene over and over in his mind, but could not make sense of anything she'd tried to convey. All Isaac knew was that she was desperate to tell him *something*, and he was eagerly anticipating their next meeting in hopes of learning what that something was.

Isaac turned the block over in his hand as he considered what shape this particular piece of wood might best take to. With his mind so preoccupied over the past few days by his exchange with the woman, Jo was certain to be feeling snubbed, and he thought she would appreciate a gift.

Isaac withdrew the knife from its thick leather sheath and starting chipping at one corner. The soft wood gave readily under his steady hand and within a few minutes, a rudimentary resemblance of a horse had emerged. He held it up to the light to examine it and was pleased with his handiwork. However, with a painful cramp slowly creeping into his hand, he opted for a short break before continuing.

Carefully sliding the blade into its case, Isaac set the knife on the table. He allowed his mind to wander as he massaged the heel of his palm with his thumb to loosen the cramp. As usual, most of his thoughts revolved around the presence.

The strange woman had taken hold of him like nothing he'd ever experienced. For months now her mystery had dominated his waking thoughts, and he'd devoted an inordinate amount of time to anticipating their next encounter. He had hoped that he'd be able to learn more about her by now, but frustratingly, he was no closer to understanding who she was than he had been at the start.

After their last exchange, however, Isaac felt certain that he was on the verge of a breakthrough. She had tried to communicate with him, and it was only a matter of time before they figured out how to break down the barriers that stood between them. His body tingled as he remembered her burning emerald eyes and wondered idly what it would feel like to run his fingers through her thick, glossy hair.

A flicker from the overhead light interrupted his reverie. Isaac wondered if there was some sort of outage coming – after all, the power lines running to the farm weren't exactly reliable. He stood up with the intention of checking the electricity in the rest of the house, but he was interrupted by a sudden swing of the back door.

Standing in the doorway was the woman.

Isaac gasped. He'd been anticipating this moment for days, but her unexpected appearance left him breathless nevertheless. He froze in place as his mind scrambled to compute a course of action.

As they locked eyes, time seemed to slow and Isaac was able to perceive her more clearly. She somehow seemed more *vivid* than she ever had before, flushed and radiant, with gleaming hair and glowing skin and shining sea-green eyes. And then he realized what it was. She was solid.

Isaac gaped as comprehension dawned on him. The woman wasn't just some transparent figment, but alive, and here, standing in full flesh and blood right in front of him.

"Isaac!"

The peal of her voice reverberated in his ears. *Finally*, he could hear her. As he registered her words, confusion replaced his relief. She knew his name? "How…"

She paced toward him, her hands reaching out for his, and he prayed that she would not disappear again. She didn't. As her fingers closed around his, the heat of her palms pressed through him, strangling the words that had been rising in his throat.

"Isaac…" Tears glistened in her eyes as she squeezed his hands.

All Isaac could think to say was, "…Who are you?"

She took a deep breath and looked up at the ceiling, steadying herself. Then she trained her startling green eyes on his. "It's me, Isaac. Alessa."

Isaac's head spun. Alessa? Wasn't that the name that Jo had said he'd been uttering in his sleep? He tried to make sense of it. How could he have known her name? Did they know each other somehow? If so, he couldn't imagine how he could have forgotten her…

Alessa grasped his hands tighter, pulling him back to the moment. "Isaac, I know you're confused. But you need to listen to me. I have something very important to tell you."

The lights continued to flicker, but Isaac barely even noticed. All he could concentrate on was her – her eyes, her skin, her scent – there was nothing else.

"I'm here to warn you, Isaac. There's going to be a fire that will kill you and your family, but I think you can avert it."

Isaac's jaw dropped. "How could you know this?"

"I'm…" Alessa paused and took a slow breath. "I know how this sounds, but the truth is, I'm from the future. I live in this same house, a hundred years from now, and I've been seeing your ghost."

"From the future? But how is that possible? I thought *I've* been seeing *your* ghost, or something like it, anyway."

Alessa shrugged her shoulders. "I don't fully understand it, either. All I know is that I dug up some old newspaper records and I found articles saying that your entire family died on April 13th, 1917."

Isaac released Alessa's grasp and brought his hand to his chest to steady himself. "But that's tomorrow!"

Alessa placed her hand on his shoulder to reassure him. "That's plenty of time! I know the fire was started by Josephine in the barn, so you just need to keep her away from there for the next 24 hours and I think everything should be okay…"

Isaac's heart pounded as he tried to process what she was saying. He and his family would die tomorrow, but she'd found a way to warn him in time. He just needed to make sure that Jo didn't leave his sight.

He placed his hand gently but firmly on Alessa's shoulder. Only inches away now, he gazed solemnly into her eyes.

"Alessa, I don't know how to thank you." He paused for a moment to let the magnitude of his appreciation sink in. "You've been the only thing I've thought about for months, but I couldn't seem to contact you. It was the most frustrating thing I'd ever experienced."

Alessa smiled softly. "I know, Isaac, I felt the same. I just felt…" she searched for the right word, "…drawn to you. When I learned what happened to you – what *would* have happened to you – I just… I couldn't live without knowing I'd tried to warn you …"

Tears welled in Alessa's eyes as she looked up at Isaac, invoking a tenderness inside him that yearned to comfort her in any way he could. He could feel the current buzzing between their bodies, a compulsion to hold her. He withdrew his hand from her shoulder and gently cupped her face, tentatively at first. Her breath caught and she seemed to melt into his touch.

Emboldened, he threaded his fingers through her thick, soft locks, releasing his other hand from hers and resting it on the curve of her hip. His body throbbed with the closeness of her, his heart bursting with affection and gratitude and desire as he leaned in.

As Isaac pulled Alessa closer, he could feel her gripping his shoulder tighter. She slipped her free hand around his waist and pulled hard, closing the space between their bodies. Anticipation flared in her eyes, razing the last shreds of his inhibition. Her eyelids closed at the same moment as his, and Isaac drew a hurried breath.

As he leaned his face towards Alessa's, Isaac knew at once that he'd been here before.

Dirt and leaves clung to Isaac's skin as he lay huddled in the thicket. Even hours after the sun had set, the heat and humidity of the day refused to subside and the air felt thick and heavy. And being sidled up next to Alessa in such close quarters – the bare skin on her long, taut limbs glistening in the moonlight – certainly wasn't helping.

Isaac had partnered with Alessa on countless reconnaissance missions in the six months since they'd lost Joe, but this was the first that had placed them in such close physical proximity. In that time, his feelings for Alessa had grown and evolved in many ways, but tonight the only feeling he could concentrate on was that of her body pressed next to his.

He'd always found Alessa's beauty undeniable, but knowing how his brother had felt about her, it had always seemed best to push those feelings aside. And as Isaac got to know Alessa, he came to appreciate her on a much deeper level.

After losing Joe, she'd become Isaac's lifeline. Given that they needed to hide their grief in order to avoiding arousing suspicion, Alessa was the only person he could talk to about what he was feeling. Their clandestine assignments for the rebels provided their only opportunities to talk freely about their shared pain and their uncertain dreams for the future.

In addition to her emotional support, Isaac had also grown to admire Alessa for her efforts in the rebellion. Ever since the tragedy with Joe, Alessa had invested herself completely in the cause and had quickly proven talented. She'd earned greater and greater responsibility and, along with Isaac, had become entrusted with executing some of the rebels' most critical missions. He respected her abilities and her dedication intensely, and there was no one he trusted more.

Though their friendship was rooted in their shared grief over Joe, it had blossomed into something much richer and much more profound than Isaac had anticipated. Over time he'd realized that the complicated feelings he had for Alessa were love. And along with that love came a deep, consuming desire that he had worked tirelessly to suppress.

As much as he cared for Alessa, Isaac still couldn't shake his old notions of Alessa as Joe's sweetheart. He remembered what Joe had said on that fateful day – "If I'm captured, I need you here to take care of Less," – and Isaac had taken his brother's last request seriously.

He was determined to do right by the memory of his brother, to be strong and brave and to protect Alessa, whatever the cost. But he was fairly sure that his brother wouldn't have been happy about Isaac becoming romantically involved with Alessa, and that guilt had thus far prevented Isaac from acting on his feelings.

But on this sweltering summer night with the heat of Alessa's smooth, soft body pressing into his side, strands of her glossy hair clinging to the droplets on her neck, and her striking emerald eyes sparkling in the night, he was starting to reconsider his position.

If Joe *truly* wanted Isaac to take care of Alessa, he reasoned, he would want him to be there for her completely, in any way she might need him. Right? The only question was whether Alessa *did* need him in that way, or if she still only saw Joe's kid brother when she looked at him.

Alessa turned suddenly to Isaac, disrupting his contemplation. She tucked her recently-cropped chin-length hair behind her ears, still adjusting to the new low-maintenance style she'd opted for in light of the colossal challenges they faced in the rebellion. "Wasn't the delivery supposed to happen by one o'clock? It's almost two now. I'm wondering if our intel was bad…"

Sweat glistened on her brow, her hair matted against her cheeks, and clumps of dirt clung under her chin. But as far as Isaac was concerned, she'd never looked more stunning. The mission be damned, it was now or never.

"Alessa, I… I have to tell you something."

She looked at him expectantly, her expression softening as she registered the emotion on his face. She searched his eyes, concerned. "Isaac, what's wrong?"

Isaac took a deep breath and rolled onto his side toward Alessa. She mimicked his movement unconsciously and they lie facing each other, close enough to feel each other's breath. He steeled himself for what came next. He needed to show Alessa how he felt, whatever the risk.

Tentatively he inched closer, watching her reaction. Her eyes widened as she realized what Isaac was about to do, but she didn't pull back. Encouraged, he plunged forward and gently touched his lips to hers.

At first Alessa froze, her eyes staring into his with alarm. But only for a moment. Then her body relaxed, her eyelids fluttered shut, and she wrapped her arms tightly around him as she returned his kiss with a passion he'd only dreamed of.

They clung to each other as everything around them – the sticky humid air, the scratching branches, all of their doubts and insecurities and fears – melted away under the intense blaze of their kiss.

And Isaac was certain he'd made the right choice.

31. TRUST

What was *going on*? Alessa's touch had unleashed a vivid flashback, but Isaac couldn't make sense of any of it. When had that memory occurred? What had he and Alessa been doing hiding under that bush in the middle of the night? And who was this brother, Joe, of whom he had no recollection?

All Isaac knew was that his body recognized the feel of this woman as *familiar*, and he didn't know how that could be possible. But whoever Alessa was, it was clear to him now that she was as vital to his existence as oxygen or water or food. Whatever she asked of him next, he would deliver. There was no turning back.

Looking down at the mysterious woman still wrapped in his arms, Isaac burned with anticipation. But before he could seal his lips to Alessa's, the lights flickered once again and finally went out. She pulled away quickly, the alarm exuding from her palpable.

With the sun still fading in the distance, there was enough light for Isaac to make out her face. She quickly glanced around the room, her wide eyes settling on his.

"Isaac, we only have a few seconds, so please listen carefully."

Her expression had changed. She was afraid now. And intense, alert. Her tension had triggered some sort of instinct in Isaac that told him to follow her lead – or else.

Letting their intimate moment pass was an almost physical ache, but he nodded to signal that he was listening, his eyes searching her face.

She continued. "Once the lights turn back on, they'll be watching us, so we'll need to be discreet."

Isaac was perplexed. He couldn't imagine who could be watching them – or how. "But why?"

Alessa warily skimmed the room again. Her words spilled out in a rapid tumble. "I can't now…" She took a deep breath. "You're in danger – we both are – and I need you to come with me. I'm here to help you escape."

"Escape?" But she'd already warned him of the fire – what other danger could there be? It didn't make any sense, and yet – given her behavior – he didn't doubt the sincerity of her words. But if there was danger, he couldn't possibly leave his family behind. "I can't leave without my family…"

Alessa hesitated before responding. "Isaac, they're not who you think they are…" Her expression softened. "They're not your real family. They're just prisoners here, like us."

Isaac shook his head in disbelief. This woman was clearly very confused.

Alessa's eyes bored into him, a pained expression on her face. "I know it's a lot to take in." The lights flickered once and a wave of panic swept over her expression. "Just please… trust me. I'll explain everything when there's time."

Isaac couldn't think of a single logical reason to trust Alessa. His family was his *family*. His parents and Josephine featured in all of his memories, back down to his earliest childhood. What did she mean that they weren't his real family? He didn't know what to think.

And wherever did she get the gall to make such wild assertions, anyway? If such a thing were true, how could she even know? To his knowledge, Alessa knew practically nothing about him; she was a stranger to him.

But somewhere deep inside, he knew that wasn't true. Just as his subconscious had known her name, he could feel in his bones that he knew this woman. Something drew him to her in a way that nothing else ever had.

Despite his better judgment, he decided to trust her. For now.

Isaac stood frozen, waiting for Alessa to act.

The lights flickered once again and she surveyed the room hastily, an animal look in her eyes. One of her hands released his and darted for the sheathed knife on the table. She snatched it up and deftly slid it into her waistband under her shirt, the motion smooth and automatic, as if she'd done it a million times before. Then she quickly retook his hand, resuming the same position they'd been in when the power first went out.

The lights flicked on once more and held, illuminating the room for a moment. Isaac looked Alessa in the eyes, unsure of what to do, and found a pure, almost feral determination staring back at him. With a twinge of fear, he wondered if he'd made the wrong decision.

32. PURSUIT

Isaac caught his breath as he waited for a cue from Alessa. She was unmistakably anxious. Isaac observed that she was nervously fingering the knife concealed at her waist while eyeing the room. He didn't know what to expect next, but he was ready to follow her lead.

When the lights flicked off once again, she wasted no time. She grabbed Isaac's hand and sprinted from the room, leading him out of the kitchen and down the hallway in the direction of the parlor.

Thousands of questions tumbled in Isaac's mind as he wondered about the circumstances that had led her here, but his thoughts were interrupted by Alessa yanking him violently into the foyer closet. She slammed the door shut behind him and pulled the string overhead to turn on the dim closet light.

"Isaac, quickly, we only have a few minutes before they get here. Help me barricade the door." An expression bordering on panic lined her face as she began frantically searching through the contents of the closet.

"*Who's* coming?"

Alessa snatched up a sturdy folded chair and wedged it under the doorknob. "The producers!" she replied with a grunt as she threw her weight at the chair to jam it in tighter.

The producers? "Who are 'the producers?'"

"Isaac, there's no time. I promise I will explain as soon as I can." She was unfolding a crumpled piece of paper from her pocket, her face scrunched with concentration. "According to the map, there should be a utility tunnel connected to this closet…"

She turned and started knocking lightly on the walls. Once she reached the back wall, he realized what she was doing – it sounded hollow. Gritting her teeth, Alessa turned and swung her elbow hard into the plaster. Isaac cringed, expecting a cry of pain, but when he looked up, he saw that Alessa had punched a large hole at the point of impact. As she withdrew, Isaac could see thousands of tiny blue and red lights blinking in the darkness beyond. What in the world…

She began tearing at the hole, ripping chunks of the wall away to reach the dark space behind it. "Isaac! Please, there's no time!"

Isaac put his confusion aside and complied. As his fingers wrapped around the edge of the hole, he was surprised to find that the wall was thin and light, a dusty composite material that broke readily in his hands. This was unlike any of the hard, thick plaster he'd ever seen.

Within seconds, they'd opened a hole large enough for Alessa to step through, and she beckoned Isaac to follow. Still reeling from the surprise of finding a hidden room in his hallway closet, he numbly obeyed.

Isaac stared in disbelief as he emerged from the wall and straightened himself. He was in a long, narrow corridor that dipped into the earth, with dark metal grating on every side. Behind the grating, hundreds of glowing blue wires wove together, running through the walls and ceiling with a panel of blinking red lights interjecting every few feet. The tunnel glowed eerily in a dim blue and red, Isaac and Alessa's shadows cast in all directions. Isaac scanned the room in wonder; he'd had no idea that this kind of technology even existed.

Noticing his confusion, Alessa grabbed his hand and drew him deeper into the tunnel. The passage was only wide enough for one, so Isaac followed behind, holding her tightly. In a hushed voice, she tried to explain as they felt their way through, shuffling quickly and quietly as they went. "There are all kinds of tunnels and shafts built into this replica of the house, more so than on my set, which is the original. If we follow the route on this map, we should eventually end up in a sewer that we can follow to the outside."

Isaac didn't understand. What did she mean that his house was a replica? Where did these tunnels come from? What were all these wires and lights and grates? Where were they going? "Set? What do you mean? How did this passageway get into my house?"

Alessa stopped and faced Isaac, setting her hands on his shoulders. "Isaac, do you remember anything from Paragon? Do you remember the compound or the rebellion or Joe?"

The strange dreams he'd been having popped to his mind, and his memory of kissing Alessa, but he still didn't know how they fit in with what he was seeing. "I… I'm not sure. Sometimes I have dreams about a man who looks like me but older… we're always sneaking about, and I feel afraid but excited."

Alessa smiled encouragingly. "That's Joe. Joe is your older brother."

"But I don't have a brother. Just my little sister, Josephine."

Alessa shook her head. "Josephine's not really your sister, Isaac. You're confused, but it's not your fault – that's exactly what they want. It's really 2114, almost two hundred years later than you've been led to believe, and this house and this farm are all part of an elaborate set for a show. You and I – and Joe – were rebels fighting against a secret government that was exploiting everyone we knew. We were captured and imprisoned, and they used some kind of mind control to erase our memories and give us new ones."

Isaac took a step back and just shook his head. No, this couldn't be true…

Alessa grasped his hands before he could move out of reach and gripped them tightly. "Listen to me, Isaac. You know all of this already. You just have to remember." She stepped closer to him and spoke softly, never dropping his eyes. "I know what you're going through. The same thing happened to me. I thought I was a college student in the 21st century until my best friend revealed that it was all fake. She was my *sister*, Isaac, and I didn't even realize it." She paused. "But Janie managed to infiltrate the show and now she's working with the rebels to help us escape."

Isaac stopped backing away, but he still couldn't process all of this. It sounded familiar, like the plot of a story he'd read a long time ago and forgotten about, but he just couldn't seem to remember what had happened.

"Isaac, we have to keep moving. Just try your best to remember."

Alessa continued to guide him through the tunnels, checking the map every so often. Isaac's head was spinning, but somehow he knew that Alessa was telling the truth. He willed himself to remember, but to no avail. It just wasn't coming back to him.

After a few minutes of trailing Alessa through the corridor, he could hear a commotion back by the entrance. It sounded like someone was trying to bang down the door, but he and Alessa were too far away to see if they'd been successful yet. Alessa threw one hurried glance over her shoulder and pressed forward ever faster.

A moment later she stopped abruptly, peering from the map to the wall on her left. She reached up and began pulling at the grate above her head. With a ping, it pulled loose and Isaac could see a small chute stretching away from the hole in the wall, barely big enough to crawl through.

Alessa folded the map and shoved it deep into her pocket. "It's a ventilation shaft. We'll need to follow it to a nearby surveillance room where we can switch to another route that will bring us to the sewer." She reached up and shimmied into the hole, bracing her legs against the wall for support. Isaac followed her lead and climbed in after her.

Once in the shaft, she passed the grate she'd removed from the wall to Isaac and he fit it back in place with a pop. Then Alessa led the way through a few turns and out through another grate into a small room with hundreds of illuminated panels lining the walls.

She checked the lock on the door and pulled out her map once more. Glancing at the glowing screens, Isaac saw images of his house – the barn, the kitchen, his study. At first he thought they were well-lit photographs, until he saw a group of men in dark heavy armor beating down the door to the foyer closet. Isaac realized they were tiny motion picture screens, somehow showing the current state of the various rooms of his house. In the parlor, he saw his parents and Josephine lying motionless on the floor. He peered closer at the screen to confirm what he'd seen and gasped. "No!"

Alessa dropped the map and jumped to his side. "Isaac, it's okay! I'm sure they're all right – for some reason the producers have seemed reluctant to kill anyone, so they just use gas to make the actors pass out. That's why those guards are wearing masks."

Isaac's chest was pounding, but he tried to calm down. Breathing heavily, he demanded, "Who are those people? And why did you say my family were actors?"

Alessa sighed wearily. "Well, they're not actors by choice. They're like us – rebels, or maybe just people who were unlucky enough to come across something they weren't supposed to see. Either way, they were taken prisoner and their memories wiped, then they were assigned to this show as your family."

"This show?"

"It's all a TV drama, Isaac. The producers did their best to wipe our minds clean, then whatever they couldn't get rid of – our feelings for each other, for example – they worked into the plot."

"I don't understand…"

"It's because they needed to keep everyone subdued. They use the shows and the drugs in our food to keep us oblivious and content so we'll keep working, thinking that we're all doing our part to rebuild society together. But someone else is running the show, and they're using us without our knowledge. That's why we joined the rebellion. To fight, for ourselves and for everyone in Paragon. Is any of this ringing a bell?"

As Alessa filled in the blanks, Isaac could feel something shifting within him. A rush of images exploded into his vision and a searing burst of pain zapped from one end of his brain to the other. He collapsed to the ground in agony as his neurons re-stitched themselves and a flood of memories came rushing back all at once.

He could hear Alessa calling his name, but she sounded distant, her voice merely an echo beyond the cacophony raging in his mind. Suddenly, everything she'd said made sense.

He remembered the war and the outbreak, sheltering with his brother in the government quarantine zone after their mother and father had succumbed to the virus. A wave of guilt flooded over him – their deaths had been his fault. As an unplanned child born to a working class family, Isaac had always carried the burden of taking from the rest of his family, of knowing he was just one more mouth to feed. And then during the outbreak, he had been their undoing. Isaac's father had gone out to find food after their stores ran out, and came back with the virus. His mother caught it, and within days they were gone. Then it was just Isaac and Joe.

He and his brother had somehow resisted the virus and made it to the quarantine zone, and after years without contact from the outside world, they'd joined their fellow refugees in deciding to start fresh. They'd christened their new society Paragon, a name to embody the spirit of equality that would underscore the sharing and mutual commitment that would define their community. Isaac and Joe had received their daily work assignments, ate their rations, watched the nightly dramas, and finally they had begun to settle in to their new lives.

And then Joe had come home one day babbling about drugs, and everything had changed. After Joe had restricted Isaac's diet, Isaac realized that he hadn't been thinking clearly for months. Together he and his brother had joined the secret rebellion. And then a mission had gone wrong – Isaac's mistake, for which he would never forgive himself – and Joe was gone.

After that, Isaac had resolved that Joe's loss would not be in vain. That conviction, and Alessa, were all he'd had left. As the only person who had loved Joe as much as he had, Alessa had become his rock, his constant companion and an ally in the war against whatever sinister forces were guiding Paragon's rule. And then they'd been captured during a crucial mission, separated in jail, subjected to endless torture, and Isaac had prepared himself to leave this life altogether, alone.

But then he'd woken up as a different person, a teenager again, on a pastoral farm in a simpler, more peaceful time. As Isaac Mason of 1917, he'd never quite felt like he belonged. He'd always known that something was missing from his life, and had carried a deep sense of guilt that he was, or would be, somehow responsible for his family's ruin. At the time, he had thought it was because he'd always yearned to leave the farm, abandoning the family business and leaving his sister behind. But he now understood that those feelings were a part of him, etched into his bones, and nothing that anyone or any technology could ever erase.

In the real world, a sinking depression had threatened to overtake Isaac as he struggled to accept his family's fate and his own entrapment in Paragon. But just as Alessa's specter had been the only catalyst to help the Isaac of 1917 focus on the present, her supportive presence in Paragon had provided the *real* Isaac with a reason to exist. And now she'd come back for him, to save him from the awful fate of living a life that was not his own, under the control of the exploitive Ruling Class who saw him and everyone else only as pawns for their manipulation.

Isaac Mason of 1917 was gone now, and in 2114, Isaac was a child no more. He may only have been a boy of 16 when he passed through what would become Paragon's gates, but he was a man of 24 now, a soldier. And with Alessa by his side, he would do everything in his power to avenge his brother, and finally prove his worth to his parents.

Isaac shivered remembering how readily his mind had slipped into 1917 without a single look back. It must have been months since then; Isaac's stomach tensed at the thought of all the time they'd lost. It was time now to finish their mission.

Isaac groaned as the rush of memories subsided. He reached out to Alessa, who was kneeling beside him, and croaked a weary, "I remember."

Alessa flung herself over his chest, breathing a sob of joy as she circled her arms tightly around him. "Oh, Isaac." After a long embrace, she sat up and cupped his face gently in her hands. With a bright smile, Alessa stared deeply into Isaac's eyes, her words infused with relief. "You're back."

33. BETRAYAL

Despite Isaac's irresistible sapphire eyes, Alessa was having trouble training her vision on his face. Still woozy from whatever the producers had used to knock her out for transport to Isaac's set, she was struggling to focus her mind on anything at all. It was a miracle she'd even made it this far.

But now Isaac – *her* Isaac – was finally back.

Alessa's body buzzed as she leaned in, hastening the moment when their lips would finally meet after so many months apart. They pressed together, their kiss releasing a dizzy burning that radiated throughout Alessa's being, taking her breath away.

For the first time in over a year, Alessa felt whole once again. She clutched the wall behind her for support as lightheadedness descended over her, born from the intensity of the turmoil Isaac's touch had induced. She ran her fingers roughly through his thick hair and concentrated on pouring every ounce of her longing into the kiss.

As they broke apart from their embrace, Alessa struggled to steady herself. She could see from Isaac's dazed expression that the kiss had shaken him as well. He closed his eyes and leaned back against the wall, a contented smile on his face.

Alessa gathered up the map from the floor and caught her breath as she allowed Isaac to rest for a few more moments. Having just regained his memories, Alessa knew from experience that it would be some time before Isaac could really process everything he'd been through. In the meantime, she would have to take responsibility for leading them to safety.

As the sound of the guards' voices drew nearer, she was forced to interrupt his repose. Shaking Isaac's shoulder gently, she whispered an urgent plea. "Isaac. I know you're exhausted, but we have to get going. They're getting closer."

Isaac moaned and nodded, rubbing his temples with his fingertips. Alessa crawled to a second ventilation shaft on the floor opposite the one they'd entered through and dug her nails under the edge to pop it from the wall. With a quick glance behind her to make sure that Isaac was following, she slid on her stomach into the narrow chute.

Shimmying on her belly, Alessa felt her way in the darkness through the path that the map had laid out. She and Isaac moved as quietly as they could, keeping their hushed discussion to a minimum. Finally they arrived at a vent that opened onto a large room. It was marked on the map as the most direct route for crossing into another series of tunnels which would lead to the sewer.

Alessa carefully peered through the grate to check that the room was clear. It was fairly well lit, and all Alessa could see from her position at the base of the wall were some empty desks and chairs a few yards away. For a moment she thought she'd seen a quick movement – a shadow maybe – but when nothing else stirred after two minutes of waiting, she decided she must have imagined it.

Using her elbow, she swung through the cramped space into the grate. It popped out of the wall and clattered across the tile floor. Alessa paused, listening for any signs that the disturbance had been heard, but there were none. She reached through the hole and started drawing herself out into the room.

It was only when she was halfway through the opening that she realized her mistake.

Alessa heard a soft click to her left and her heart dropped to her stomach. She wasn't alone. Slowly looking over her shoulder, Alessa was horrified to find four guards in heavy black armor with guns pointed in her direction.

The nearest one snarled a quiet, "Freeze."

Adrenaline surging through her body, Alessa knew her only chance was escape. "Isaac, run!" she screamed, simultaneously shoving herself back into the shaft.

But the guards were too quick. The nearest one swiftly reached into the shaft and snatched up the end of the long ponytail that trailed behind her. He pulled hard to drag her out of the tunnel.

Alessa flipped onto her back and clutched for the knife hidden at her waist, withdrawing it from its sheath and jabbing at the guard's wrist. The blade glanced off his armor uselessly. She aimed again for his hand, but the sharp blade was unable to penetrate his tightly-woven protective glove.

Alessa fought the urge to panic as she felt her body inching out of the chute. Isaac had grabbed on to her ankles, but in his shaken state, he was unable to do much more than slow the guard's progress. Alessa could feel her skin starting to lift away from her skull, strands of hair ripping from her scalp and dropping to the floor beside her as the guard tugged with all his might. Then suddenly, she knew what to do.

Alessa positioned her knife at the base of her scalp, swinging skyward as the razor-sharp blade sheared through her hair in one swift motion. And just like that, she was free.

As she slid back into the shaft, she saw the guard stagger backward, knocking into the three behind him as they all lost their footing like toppling dominos.

"Go, go, go!" she shouted to Isaac as they retreated into the depths of the tunnel.

Once they were safely away from the opening and hidden beyond an erratic set of turns in the dark chute, Isaac gasped for air as he looked to Alessa for a report. "What *happened* back there?"

Alessa tried to catch her breath as she replied. "They… were waiting for us. I don't know… it was like… they *knew*."

All of a sudden it dawned on Alessa. They *did* know, and there was only one way they could have. Someone had leaked their escape route to the producers; there was a traitor within the rebels. "No…" she whispered, her eyes wide with fear.

Alessa felt sick as she considered what her realization meant. First of all, she and Isaac obviously could no longer follow their planned route to the exit, that much was for sure. But that problem wasn't insurmountable – assuming that their map was accurate, they should be able to find another path.

More concerning was the fact that Janie was in the middle of executing her own escape, and Alessa had planned to meet up with her at the exit to the sewer. If the guards knew where Alessa was headed, would they set up an ambush there as well? Alessa shuddered. There was no way to send a warning to her sister.

Isaac sensed her trepidation. "What is it, Alessa?"

"There's a traitor… Someone told the producers where to expect us. And now Janie…" she couldn't bring herself to say it. She closed her eyes and shook her head.

Isaac's eyes grew wide and his breathing quickened. He whispered urgently. "Alessa, *what*?"

Alessa opened her eyes and stared ahead blankly, a numb look on her face. "She was supposed to meet us at the exit."

Isaac grasped the implications immediately. "Oh, no. She's going to walk right into their trap."

Alessa broke down as she nodded, tears streaming down her cheeks.

After all this, all they had survived together – the war, the outbreak, life in Paragon, the drama – she was finally going to lose her sister. Alessa couldn't move, couldn't think. Anything she did would be futile. She was powerless.

The hope drained from Alessa, left her empty and hollow. She would lose them all, one by one, everyone she cared about. It was only a matter of time before they got Isaac, too. And then what would she have left? What would be the point of any of it? Why should she even bother?

Alessa was no hero, she knew that now. It had been fun, for a time, to put on the rebel's shoes, to play at subterfuge and revolt, to feel for a moment that she could make a difference. But when it came down to it, she was only just a girl. How could she ever have thought that she could change things?

Isaac clutched Alessa's hand. "Alessa. Alessa, look at me."

Alessa sighed heavily, her head slumping towards her chest, her entire body collapsing inward. There was nothing to do now but wait, wait to be caught and put back on another show in another place. This time, she would stay there. Anything was better than here. Maybe they might even kill her, just end it all.

"Alessa!" Isaac shook her violently.

Begrudgingly, Alessa peeked up at him.

In a hushed voice, Isaac continued. "Less, come on, don't give up on me yet. Maybe we can beat them to the exit, get a warning to Janie."

Alessa only sighed in response. Now was no time for false hope – it was time to face the truth.

But Isaac was persistent. "Come, we have to keep moving. Where's the map?"

Without lifting her eyes from the ground, Alessa listlessly withdrew the map from her pocket and held it in Isaac's direction. She couldn't even bear to look at it, couldn't muster the will to hand it to him. Her sister was all but lost, and they would be next.

As Isaac pored over the page, Alessa distractedly ran her hand through her newly cropped hair. It fell to her chin in soft layers that framed her face, the strands at the nape of her neck – only an inch long at most – ending abruptly in her fingers.

Isaac looked up from the map and noticed Alessa nervously toying with the ends of her hair. He ran his fingers through a lock and let it fall back into place, smiling. "I love your hair like this. Do you remember the last time you cut it?"

Alessa thought about how she had felt the last time her hair was this short, a few months after Joe had died when she began working for the rebels in earnest.

At the time, she had told herself it was for convenience – with her late night missions and the constant stress of staying undercover, the last thing she had time to pay attention to was her appearance. But the moment she'd made the first cut, Alessa had realized that it was much more.

She'd been at the precipice of a new stage in her life, and she'd realized in that moment that her new style was symbolic of her transition. The frightened long-haired girl who had stepped through Paragon's gates clutching her little sister – and the world that girl had come from – was no more. Alessa had decided that she was done being afraid. With each strand that had fallen to the floor around her, Alessa's resolve had been strengthened. She wasn't going to be a victim anymore. She was going to fight.

And as Alessa remembered that feeling, her tears subsided and her heart filled with rage. Paragon could take everyone she loved – Joe, Janie, even Isaac – but she would *never* back down. As long as she had an ounce of life left in her, she would fight them every step of the way.

And Janie wasn't gone yet. Isaac was right – they needed to find a way to beat the guards there and warn her.

Fortified, her voice rang with tenacity. "Do you have a plan?"

Isaac beamed. He nodded, turning the paper in her direction. "Look – if we go back out and follow the first tunnel, it should lead to a maintenance room that has sewer access. There's another drain opening not far from where we were supposed to meet Janie. If we hurry, we might be able to make it there in time. But first –" a mischievous grin crept onto his face "– let's slow them down a bit."

34. DIVERSION

Isaac led the way through the shaft back to the utility tunnel they had first entered through. Carefully, he and Alessa worked their way through the long, narrow hall, listening closely for any sign that they'd been followed. Alessa was not about to walk into another ambush.

After a few tense minutes, Isaac looked up from the map. "If I'm reading this correctly, there should be a maintenance closet up ahead with sewer access." He pointed toward a door 10 yards away where the tunnel ended. "That's our path to the outside. But before we go, I want to create a diversion to distract the guards while we make our way to Janie."

Alessa nodded. She wasn't sure if Janie would even make it that far – after all, they may try to intercept her along her route as well – but she pushed the thought aside. If Janie could make it out, Alessa would be there to receive her.

Isaac reached up and ran his fingers along a set of gray pipes that ran against the ceiling. He knocked against the pipes a bit, testing for something.

"Some of these are carrying water and some are carrying gas, but I'm not exactly sure how to tell which is which… Do you have that knife still?"

"Here." Alessa drew the knife from her jeans and pointed the handle towards Isaac.

Isaac grasped the knife and looked up at the pipes once more. "Well, one way to find out."

With a swift swing of his arm, Isaac jabbed the tip of the knife into one of the pipes. Alessa could hear a quiet hiss coming from the hole, and a moment later she smelled the distinct aroma of gas.

"Got it," Isaac said. "Okay, let's move."

Alessa followed Isaac towards the closet, but she still wasn't entirely sure what he was planning. "Isaac, wait. What's the plan here?"

Opening the maintenance room door, Isaac headed straight for the manhole cover in the middle of the concrete floor. Grunting as he shifted the heavy round plate to the side, he explained, "I'm going to blow up the shaft."

"What?!" Alessa fired off questions. "How? Won't that kill us? What about Janie? She could still be inside!"

Withdrawing his head from the sewer hole, he replied, "These are 12-inch concrete floors, and we're going to be on the other side of them when the explosion happens."

"And what about everyone else, the other actors on your set and Janie?"

"If these gas lines were built correctly, there should be safety mechanisms that will keep the explosion relatively isolated, and we're far enough away from the set now that nothing but smoke should reach the house. As for Janie, we can only assume that she's still headed toward the original sewer drain, so this area of the tunnel shouldn't be in her path."

Alessa was still a little wary, but without any better options, she decided to go along. Even a small explosion would still cause quite a mess for the guards to deal with. Hopefully the diversion would buy enough time for Janie to make it to the meeting point unscathed. "Okay, and how are you planning to ignite the blast?"

"Simple – all we need is a spark."

Isaac propped the door to the maintenance closet open, giving him a direct line of sight to the pierced pipe. The scent of gas was overwhelming now.

He directed Alessa to descend through the manhole to the safety of the sewer below. She climbed down the ladder and scurried a few yards deeper into the tunnel away from the manhole, bracing herself under one of the overhead supports.

Isaac mounted the ladder and took a few steps down until he was mostly through the hole. Holding the knife gently in his hand, he took aim and whipped the knife toward the section of the wall directly below the open gas pipe.

The end of the handle glanced off the wall and the knife skittered across the floor. Isaac cursed.

Dipping his head into the sewer, he took a deep breath and scrambled up the ladder. A moment later he returned, gasping through the manhole, knife in hand once more.

This time his aim was true. With a skillful flick of the wrist, Isaac's blade hit its mark, glinting off the wall's metal grating in a shower of sparks. The gas ignited in a tidal wave of flame.

Isaac dropped through the hole and hit the floor hard, covering his head with his arms as debris and smoke raced behind him. Alessa grasped the sewer wall for support as the fiery gas raced through the pipes with a loud boom that shook everything around them.

"Isaac!" she called. "Are you okay?" The sewer was quickly filling with a thick black smoke – she could only barely make out his form.

Isaac coughed and stretched in the direction of her voice. "Alessa? Yeah, I'm all right."

He coughed more and began crawling towards her. Alessa dropped to her knees where the visibility was better and scrambled over to meet him. She knew he was drained to begin with after the shock of regaining his memory, and she was worried that he might be injured now on top of it.

Reaching him, Alessa was relieved to see that he had suffered no worse than bumps and scratches from the falling debris. He sat up and slumped against the wall.

"I just need a minute, Less. To catch my breath."

Alessa kneeled next to him, waiting. But every moment they delayed, the tunnel got darker, and the air more difficult to breathe. Finally, she took his hand.

"Isaac, we've got to go."

He nodded and followed her to his feet, but as he put pressure on his right ankle, he let out a small yelp.

"Are you hurt?" Alessa demanded, concerned.

Isaac gingerly put more weight onto the affected foot. He grimaced. "I think it's just a sprain. Let's keep moving."

Limping, he trailed behind Alessa as she made her way through the sewer, ducking to stay below the thick smoke that had filled the upper part of the tunnel. Luckily, there was enough light from the opening up ahead that they managed to avoid the stream of fetid muck that trickled down the center of the tube.

Hand in hand, Isaac and Alessa made their way towards the outside, praying they had given Janie the opportunity she needed to escape.

35. DELIVERANCE

Alessa and Isaac emerged coughing and panting from the sewer drain, a cloud of smoke leaking from the tunnel behind them. In the distance, they could see a thick column of black bellowing into the sky from the direction of the set.

Alessa laughed and flashed an appreciative smile at Isaac. "Well, I think your plan worked."

Isaac coupled his wide grin with a modest shrug of the shoulders. "I picked up a thing or two in my time with the rebels."

"No kidding."

The sewer had ended in a shallow ditch which dumped Isaac and Alessa in the middle of a dark wood. By now the sun had set completely, and a bright full moon had replaced it, illuminating the forest in an eerie crystal blue. Upon climbing from the ditch, Alessa could see that the old growth trees thinned out not far to the west, the orange lights of Paragon glowing in the distance, casting long shadows from the compound's walls on the snow covered ground. A veil of smoke hovered above the northern section of the complex, blotting out the lights below.

Gazing at the chaos in the distance, Alessa still couldn't believe they'd pulled it off. But there wasn't much time for celebration – they still needed to make it to the original meeting place in hopes of finding Janie before the guards did. "Let's move on."

Alessa and Isaac carefully picked their way north through the gnarled trees and thick undergrowth of the dark forest in the direction of the drainage pipe where they expected Janie to emerge. The frozen ground was littered with bare shrubs and a smattering of snow leftover from the recent storm.

Alessa shivered. She was still in the same jeans and sweater she'd been wearing when she and Janie had used the wormhole device. She'd at least had the foresight to throw on a couple extra layers, but anything heavier than that risked raising suspicion amongst the producers. And Isaac, who'd had no warning of what was to come, was wearing only his usual light cotton shirt. Alessa prayed that the rebels had left some equipment for them at the rendezvous point – otherwise, they may not even survive the night, let alone the oncoming winter.

As they reached the location of the other sewer drain, Isaac and Alessa slowed their pace and approached quietly, alert for any sign of the guards. All was quiet. Unfortunately, Janie was nowhere in sight.

Searching the area, Alessa spotted two heavy packs stashed among the bushes lining the sewer opening. She exhaled with relief, thankful that the rebels had found an opportunity to equip them for the mission.

They grabbed the packs and settled down in a thicket not far from the sewer to wait. From their vantage point slightly up a hill, they'd have a clear view of any movement from Janie but were still hidden behind enough cover to escape without notice if the guards decided to make an appearance. Alessa unloaded two heavy coats from her backpack. Slipping one over her shoulders, she was pleased to find a set of warm gloves and a winter hat stashed in the pockets.

Isaac, who had donned the second coat, scooted closer to Alessa and put his arm around her shoulders. "So, do you have any idea when Janie's supposed to show up?"

Alessa shook her head. "She was pretty vague – we didn't get a chance to talk in detail with the cameras always rolling. All she said was, 'Be careful,' and 'I'll see you on the other side.'"

Alessa dug into the backpack once more looking for Janie's coat, thinking she would warm it up against her chest before Janie arrived. When she didn't find a third coat in the first bag she tried the other one, but was dismayed to find that there was no coat stored there either. She wondered how Regina could have overlooked such a basic piece of gear… and then she understood.

Alessa gasped loudly, an expression of horror on her face. "Oh my God. She's not coming."

"What do you mean she's not coming?"

Alessa buried her head in her hands, muttering quietly to herself. "How could I have been so *dense*?"

"What? What happened?" Isaac urged.

Alessa dropped her arms in defeat and turned to face Isaac. "I don't know how I could have forgotten… 'See you on the other side,' were my mother's last words to us as we were separated at the gate. I don't think Janie ever intended to come with us."

Alessa couldn't believe her sister had lied to her. She closed her eyes and shook her head once more, disappointed and disbelieving.

Isaac nodded, his face grim, and took Alessa's hand. "Well, at least that means the guards aren't looking for her, right? As long as she stayed in character, she should be safe…"

"Safe from the guards, maybe, but what's next? Now that they don't need her for the show anymore, who knows what they might do to her?" Alessa couldn't bear the thought of leaving her sister behind. With the show over, they were no doubt going to toss her back in one of the cold, lonely cells in Paragon's prison to await her next assignment, subjecting her to who knows what ghastly tortures in the meantime. And what if the producers figured out who had helped her and Isaac escape? Alessa would never have agreed to this if she'd known.

Still holding Alessa's hand, Isaac brought her fingers to his lips and kissed them gently through the thick fabric of her gloves. With kindness in his eyes, he tried to reassure her in a soft voice. "It will be okay, Alessa. Regina will keep her safe, and we'll find her as soon as we get back."

Alessa wasn't as optimistic, but she knew there was nothing she could do. She just dropped her eyes to the ground with a heavy sigh.

Isaac released Alessa's hand and clasped his own together, blowing a long breath onto his numb fingers. "Where did you get those gloves, anyway?"

"They were in my jacket."

As Isaac withdrew the gloves from his own pockets, a small piece of paper fell into his lap.

Watching as he unfolded it, Alessa saw that it was a letter.

"It's from Regina."

"What does it say?"

Isaac held the paper out and adjusted the angle until he caught the moonlight just right. Then he cleared his throat and read aloud:

Dear Isaac and Alessa,

I'm sure you've been through quite the ordeal today, and I hope you are both doing well, at least as well as could be expected under the circumstances. Unfortunately, it's unlikely that what lies ahead for you is going to offer much in the way of respite. We don't know what to expect beyond Paragon's walls, but hopefully the supplies we've gathered for you will help in some small way to ease your journey.

I doubt I need to remind either of you of the gravity of your mission. The rebel movement will not survive much longer under Paragon's iron grip; we need a place of our own to regroup and build up the resistance. These past months have been difficult on us all, and we're counting on you to bring us back some good news.

By now you must have figured out that Janie won't be joining you. I apologize for our deception, but we knew that Alessa would never willingly leave her sister behind. Janie has become a critical component of our operation in your absence, and she can do more good for the cause here than she could have out there. I'm sure you understand. She sends her love and hopes you will find it in your hearts to forgive her.

As you scour the surrounding area for what I hope will become our next home, please remember that our situation here is dire. If you find anything encouraging to report, do not tarry. Every day that we delay puts the resistance more at risk. Once your plan is ready, return to the place where you found these packs and you will find instructions to contact me. I will expect to hear from you by the end of May, if not sooner.

I wish you a safe and speedy mission. Stay strong and remember your training. The people of Paragon need you.

--R

36. DUTY

Alessa awoke at dawn wrapped tightly in the warm cocoon of Isaac's arms. She lay still, listening to the silence of the forest and watching as the tendrils of her and Isaac's breath mingled in the cold air above them. For a few moments at least, she savored the tranquil morning, allowing the trials ahead of them to slip quietly away.

But a few moments was all they could safely spare. Having been hesitant to turn on a flashlight for fear of attracting notice, they hadn't been able to travel far in the night's blanketing darkness. They had settled in for the night on a high hillside not more than a mile from the sewer drain, and it was there they still laid now, limbs entangled as the sun's first rays crept over the barren ground. There was no doubt that Paragon's guards would be looking for them at first light; it was time to go.

Alessa nudged Isaac awake and he let out a groan as he stretched his stiff muscles. "Argh. What time is it?"

"Time to get moving." She brushed her lips softly against his cheek.

Isaac grinned and tucked a strand of Alessa's hair behind her ear. "I could think of something better to do…"

Alessa smirked. "At least let me do something about this hair before we go there," she teased. She couldn't imagine what her one-stroke restyling must look like in the light of day.

Isaac cupped her face in his hands and kissed her firmly on the lips. Pulling back only an inch, he looked deep into her eyes and smiled genuinely. "Don't do a thing. You've never looked more beautiful."

Alessa glowed as she and Isaac quickly folded the blankets they'd found in their backpacks. They took a quick inventory of the other supplies the rebels had left for them, now that it was light enough to see the contents of their packs.

"Fire starter, blades, flashlight, socks, a few days' rations, a bottle of water," Isaac listed the contents of his pack as Alessa dug through hers as well.

"Same here. Oh, and a compass."

"Good. Well, we should be okay for a few days at least."

"True," Alessa agreed. "How's your ankle feeling?"

Isaac rolled it tentatively. "I'll be all right. It's a little swollen, but I can walk on it without too much pain."

Alessa was relieved about that, but she was still worried about him in general. "And how are you otherwise?"

Isaac sighed. "Okay. I mean, physically I'm fine. I was tired after yesterday, after I remembered – it hurt, my memories coming back. It really took it out of me. But I'm feeling better now." He paused then and looked at Alessa, inquiring. "How do they do it? How do they just replace all my memories with whatever they want? It was the oddest sensation, like my brain was being –"

"Stitched?"

"Yeah, exactly."

"I know. I experienced the same thing." She sighed. "I don't understand it, either. All Janie told me was that the producers have some kind of technology that rewires your neural pathways, hiding your memories and sewing new ones in their place. The rebels are calling it the 'stitch.'"

Isaac contemplated for a moment, then shook his head. "I just can't believe we lost so much time. How long were we captured for?"

"A year? Maybe a little more than that."

Isaac thought that over for a moment, then set his jaw in fury. "Who *are* these people? Why are they doing this to us?"

Alessa just shook her head. "I wish I could tell you, Isaac. All I know is that the rebels are flailing, and they're depending on us to finish our mission. And as we learned yesterday, there's apparently a traitor within our ranks."

Isaac rubbed his temples, his anger displaced by dismay. "Ugh, I'd forgotten about that. I wonder if they know."

"I don't see how we could warn them if they don't. I guess we'll just have to trust in Regina to stay as on top of things as she always does."

"I guess so." His anger deflated, Isaac took a deep breath. "We should probably get going."

Alessa nodded. "So which direction do you think we should head?"

Crunching snow between his fingers, Isaac replied, "How about south?"

Alessa smiled. "South works for me."

They repacked their supplies and shared a small chunk sliced off a block of hard cheese from their rations. It was a meager breakfast, but it was heartening nonetheless.

Swallowing, Isaac commented, "We're going to have to be careful about how much we eat until we can resupply."

Alessa nodded. "There's not going to be much in these woods at this time of year. We should probably look for a route towards the city – maybe we can scavenge some canned goods."

"We'll be more likely to find shelter there too, maybe even the base that Regina is hoping for."

Alessa nodded, but she still held some reservations about venturing toward what had once been more populated areas. Though she knew that heading to the suburbs and city was the right plan, she also knew that the virus had no less than decimated the world population, and Alessa just wasn't sure if she was ready to face that. It'd been… not effortless, but *easier*, to put the total destruction of everything she'd ever known aside while safely hidden behind Paragon's walls. But there was no hiding from the truth anymore.

"Isaac… what do you think it will be like out there?"

Isaac set his mouth in a line and shook his head. "I really don't know. We headed for the quarantine zone relatively early, so I wasn't there to witness the worst of it. But the few people I saw who had caught the virus… it was horrible." He shook away the memory of his parents.

Alessa nodded. "I know… But it's been eight years since they closed the gates. I just keep telling myself that with no one left to infect, the virus must have died out too. Right?"

"Let's hope."

Alessa knew that her rationalization was speculative at best – after all, who knew how long the disease could lay dormant? – but she did her best to put her fears aside. At this rate, exposure to the elements or starvation were more likely to get them first, so she decided instead to focus on the immediate task of survival.

Regina had made sure that Isaac and Alessa were well prepared for this mission, and Alessa was fairly certain that she remembered most of her training. She knew where to look for food and water, how to build shelter and start a fire, the basics of first aid and navigation. But nothing had quite prepared her for the enormity of the task laid out before her.

The world beyond Paragon's gates felt *big*. Even the simple question of which direction to head held potentially life-altering consequences. In one direction, they might find sustenance, or the defensible facility that Regina was hoping for. In the other, maybe death. The problem was that they didn't know which way was which, and one small misstep could get them lost, sick, hurt… or worse. It was imperative that they remain always alert, vigilant. They couldn't let their guard down even for a second.

And the hardest part was that the rebels were counting on them. As far as Alessa knew, the survivors living within Paragon's walls may be the only people on the planet who had managed to escape the scourge of the outbreak. Given that mind control and drug-enabled coercion were what Paragon had come up with in the first eight years of its existence, Alessa didn't even want to think about what else might be in store. And she knew that if she and Isaac didn't return with a viable plan – or didn't return at all – they could be condemning everyone here to life behind the walls of the thinly-veiled prison camp that was Paragon.

Isaac seemed to be thinking the same thing. He took Alessa's hand with an earnest look. "Alessa, promise me that we're going to pull this off. For Joe's sake." He took a deep breath and brushed away the tears that had begun to well in his eyes. "He gave up his life for me, and I need to know that that was worth something. I need to do this to make his sacrifice count."

Alessa nodded solemnly. "He knew you'd make it count, Isaac. And so do I. We'll find a way to do this." And for the first time in months, Alessa truly believed it.

She'd spent so long feeling trapped, alone, lost. She remembered her long march to Paragon's gates, her family by her side. The quarantine center was supposed to be their salvation, but even then, Alessa had sensed that all was already lost. With each step, she remembered feeling like all of her hopes and dreams for the future were crumbling to the ground around her, disintegrating in a cloud of dust. And when she'd passed through the gates with only Janie to hold, she'd known her premonitions had been right. Nothing would ever be the same.

Her life in Paragon had felt like one big pause, even after she'd discovered the drugs. Every day was monotonous, one day bleeding into the next, and for five long years, she had simply survived, nothing more and nothing less.

But after Joe's loss had spurred Alessa to join forces with the rebels, things had begun to change. Alessa's missions had given her a sense of satisfaction that nothing else in Paragon ever had. As she progressed, she began to feel in control again, like she finally had some power over her own life. The feeling was intoxicating, addictive even, and she'd begun to crave it.

But then overconfidence had landed her in Paragon's clutches, and during her months in lockup, Alessa's old feelings of hopelessness had come back to her in force. For a time, Alessa had truly believed that she was capable of anything, that she was destined for greatness despite everything that had befallen her. And losing that conviction had been crippling. Even on the drama, these bitter feelings of powerlessness had overshadowed her every thought.

But that was behind her now. She and Isaac had an opportunity to make a difference in the sorry world that they'd inherited, and they would do everything in their power to achieve that goal.

From their position on the top of the hill, Alessa and Isaac had a clear view of the landscape around them in the bright, cloudless morning. The forest stretched out to the east and south, as far as the eye could see. And to the west, where the trees petered out into rolling plains, Paragon's thick gray walls rose abruptly like a scar.

Slinging her pack over her shoulders, Alessa took one last look in the direction of Paragon's walls, wondering when she would see them next. Not before she had a plan to bring them down, she vowed.

She turned her back and sidled up alongside Isaac, the crisp scent of pine needles and the soft, stroking rustle of the wind fusing with the taste of hope on her tongue. She knew this was a moment she would never forget.

Isaac held out his hand to her, his deep blue eyes sparkling in the morning sun. He motioned at the vast expanse laid out before them, beckoning. "Shall we?"

Grasping Isaac's fingers in her own, Alessa smiled gently, certain that with Isaac by her side, she could overcome whatever life may throw at them. "Let's."

And they took their first tentative steps away from Paragon together.

A NOTE TO READERS

Dear Reader,

Thank you, thank you, thank you for making time in your busy schedule to read Stitch. It is an absolute honor to share Alessa and Isaac's story with you, and I'm thrilled that you chose this book out of the millions of incredible books at your disposal. Truly, I cannot thank you enough. *You are a dream come true.*

If you enjoyed Stitch and are interested in reading the rest of the series, I encourage you to join the Stitch community at www.samanthadurante.com to sign up for notifications of future Stitch Trilogy releases and to keep up with the tons of exciting extra content that's published on my blog, Facebook pages, Twitter account, and Goodreads page almost every day.

I also wanted to take a moment to express my sincere gratitude to all of the fans who have so graciously spread the word about Stitch on their blogs and social media. This book could never have succeeded without your help, and I am utterly in your debt. You guys are amazing – I really can't say it enough.

I've been reading books since I can remember, but until I began writing professionally, I never understood how truly dependent authors are on their fans. As a reader, I always assumed that a good author would get picked up by an agent and publisher, and that those allies would use their arsenals of marketing and PR tools to ensure that the author's books would reach their rightful audience. And perhaps things *used* to be like this, once upon a time, but the publishing industry is changing, and unfortunately this is no longer the case.

The traditional publishing model just isn't working anymore, and as a result, up-and-coming authors are often passed over altogether in favor of proven sellers. And even those authors lucky enough to find a publisher are not afforded the same amount of support in the marketing department that they once could expect. That means authors now have to know not only how to *write* but also how to *market* their work effectively.

As an author, I've since learned that my *number one ally* in the challenging endeavor of finding an audience for my books is not the marketers and PR people I once thought, but the *readers* themselves. Every review on Amazon and Goodreads, every recommendation to a friend, every mention on a blog or Facebook post or tweet has been absolutely *invaluable* towards Stitch's success. So thank you a million times over to everyone who has done this for Stitch, or for any book – you have no idea how important (and appreciated!) you truly are.

As a reader, you hold *so* much power to aid the authors you love. If you enjoyed this book – or any book – I encourage you to write a review, tell someone about it, post about it online, and reach out to the author to let them know. Take whatever steps you can to share your love with the world, because your words *really do* matter.

Thank you *so much* for all of your support!
Samantha

ACKNOWLEDGMENTS

First and foremost, I must acknowledge my fiancé, Sudeep, for all of your dedication and assistance. Though your hypersensitivity to plot holes has ruined many enjoyable movies for me over the years, that critical eye was truly invaluable in strengthening my own work. You really made this project as much a priority as I did, and I am so grateful for all of your help and encouragement and love. This would have been a very different book without you.

To Mom, Dad, Mahe, Mikey, Nicky, Sam, Levin, Diane, Joan, Mel, Mayuree, Laura, Morgan, Carmen, Selina, Tina, Uncle Tom, and Anne Marie – thank you for bearing with me through the early drafts and for all of your feedback and support. Your enthusiasm was all the motivation I needed to make this dream a reality, and I very much appreciate how much time all of you have dedicated to making this a better book.

To those listed above and all of my extended family and friends, thank you for your boundless support in everything that I do. Your unconditional love has always given me the strength to follow my dreams, and I am truly blessed to have you all in my life.

To all the great teachers I've had over the years, especially Mr. Scanlon and Ms. Meehan, thank you for pushing me to hone my craft and to believe in my abilities as a writer. I would never have had the confidence to pursue writing as a career without your training and praise, and I am forever in your debt.

To the authors of my favorite stories – J. K. Rowling, Stephenie Meyer, Suzanne Collins, Christopher Paolini, Sharon Shinn, C. S. Lewis, Jane Austen, and many others – thank you for sharing your creativity with the world. I was a reader of novels long before becoming a writer of them, and the enchantment that your tales have brought to my life is what inspired me to compose my own.

And last, but certainly not least, endless love and affection for my Gio, for being my faithful assistant and for always keeping my lap warm.

ABOUT THE AUTHOR

Samantha Durante lives in New York City with her fiancé, Sudeep, and her cat, Gio. Formerly an engineer at Microsoft, Samantha left the world of software in 2010 to pursue her entrepreneurial dreams and a lifelong love of writing. A graduate of the University of Pennsylvania's Jerome Fisher Program in Management & Technology, Samantha is currently working full time for her company Medley Media Associates as a freelance business writer and communications consultant. This is her first novel.

Visit www.samanthadurante.com to join the Stitch community and sign up for updates about upcoming Stitch trilogy releases.

Read on for a Sneak Preview of Shudder

The riveting sequel to Stitch…

EPILOGUE: FURY

The General slammed his fist on the table, the noise reverberating through the large room. "This is completely unacceptable."

The Developer rested his elbows on the table, one lanky arm bending as he closed his eyes and pinched the bridge of his nose between his fingers. He let out a long sigh before leaning back in his chair, tossing his shaggy, unkempt hair back in an awkward motion. He waited for the grumbling to subside before he spoke – as the youngest billionaire on the planet, he'd grown used to having a captive audience.

"This rebellion has become more than a headache; it's putting our plans for Paragon at risk, and it's time we take more drastic measures to resolve the problem. We should never have let it get this far." His whiny voice and slouching shoulders didn't command much in the way of esteem, but the four other men in the room – the Engineers, as they liked to call themselves – sat rapt nevertheless. They had quickly learned that what the Developer lacked in presence and age, he made up for with brilliance and guile.

"If I may…" The Economist cleared his throat. Though this was technically a group of equals, he often found himself deferring to the others, being more comfortable with books than he ever was with people. But if their plans for Paragon were ever to succeed, this group above all else needed to keep their focus on the end game, instead of allowing themselves to be sidetracked by minor setbacks.

He continued. "It's only two people, and given the weather forecast, it's unlikely that they'll even make it through the week. How much trouble could they cause? I vote that we let them go and focus our efforts instead on reaching our goals for the collective. It's been years since the deliberations have made any real progress and –"

The Doctor cut off his remarks with one biting look. "Only two people? And what *traits* might those two people be carrying that are essential to our race? Do you *presume* to know why they were chosen for Paragon? Presume to *decide* who here is expendable?"

"N-n-no… I just…" He took a moment to compose himself. "We're supposed to be working toward a true communist society, and every day that the Ruling Class remains in power, we are one more step away from achieving that goal. The only reason the rebellion thrives today is due to the continued existence of the Ruling Class, so to me it seems that recapturing a couple of rebels is treating the symptom, not the cause. Let them go, and instead let's put our energies towards facilitating the deliberation process, thereby hastening the birth of the ideal society that was the entire *reason* for this whole undertaking."

The Doctor's silver hair glinted in the sharp artificial light as he devoted his entire head to the effort of rolling his eyes. "Save your pretty rhetoric, Ben. There won't *be* any society if we don't have the genes to support one."

The Developer nodded vigorously in agreement. "He's right. The algorithm was very specific in who was selected, and we need to trust that everyone here deserved to be chosen. Otherwise, what was the point of everything we did?"

Everyone took a moment to digest his last comment. They had agreed from the beginning that sacrifices would be needed to make this work, and indeed those sacrifices had been huge – the biggest the world had ever seen. But they had only agreed to the plan knowing that it was the only way to do this right, and that everyone would benefit in the end. Everyone who was left, anyway.

"So what are you suggesting?" The Draftsman – the oldest and most levelheaded of the group – spoke, as always, in a steady, reasoned tone, absentmindedly stroking his paunch.

Before the Developer could respond, the General chimed in with a suggestion of his own, his raspy voice filled with retribution. "We have the girl, the one that helped them escape. I say we make an example of her, send a message to the rebels that we won't tolerate their insubordination any longer." As he rubbed the scar across his lips, he muttered, "Stupid bitch."

The Draftsman wondered if he was referring to the girl or to the rebel leader, but either way, he dismissed his comments as bluster. Over the years he'd come to despise the General's deep insecurities, and his resulting tendency to overcompensate. It was a shame, really – the man had a magnificent reserve of military knowledge, but his personal flaws marred his usefulness considerably. And at least the rest of them had actually *achieved* the titles they'd chosen for themselves – the General had never earned that rank at all, he'd just christened himself upon finding that he had the power to do so. To say that the Draftsman found the General trying was an understatement indeed. But much to the Draftsman's chagrin, the others had not yet come to the same conclusion.

The Developer, in fact, seemed to be seriously considering a show of force. Shaking his head, he reflected, "If only we knew where Regina Green were hiding… we could drop the girl's head right at her front door."

"That's sick!" the Economist blurted, appalled.

The Doctor once again shot him down. "Oh, please. Like you haven't agreed to worse."

As barbaric as it was, the Draftsman had to admit that the Doctor spoke the truth. "Eugene has a point there – we've *all* agreed to worse. 'The ends justify the means' has been a de facto tenet of our philosophy…"

"Thank you, Pascal." The withering glare subsided from the Doctor's face. "Now, as I said before, I don't like the idea of tinkering with the algorithm's selections, but in this one case, I suppose we could make an exception. After all, she wasn't part of the original results set to begin with."

Chastised, the Economist held his tongue while the others nodded in agreement.

The Developer stood, signaling that the meeting had come to a close. "Then it's decided. We'll use the girl to send a message. Given that we *don't* know Regina's location, everyone think about what might be our most effective strategy and we'll reconvene in the morning to finalize the plan. And remember, as distasteful as this might be, the rebels haven't left us much choice."

He held his right fist at his shoulder in the customary gesture, and the others stood and followed suit. "For Paragon," he stated, accompanying the sentiment with an almost imperceptible nod of the head.

The room echoed in unison as the men added their response, each earnestly believing the mantra in his own way. "For Paragon, always."

30226962R00183

Made in the USA
Lexington, KY
23 February 2014